DIONYSUS

First published in 2023 by PRESS DIONYSUS LTD in the UK, 167, Portland Road, N15 4SZ, London.

www.pressdionysus.com

Paperback

ISBN: 978-1-913961-30-5

ASYLUM

WELL MET ISTANBUL
WELL MET LONDON

"A story of migration from Poland to İstanbul and from Istanbul to London"

Gülsüm Öz

Translated by H. Yiğit Değirmenci

PRESS DIONYSUS

Press Dionysus •

ISBN- 978-1-913961-30-5

© 2023 Press Dionysus

First Edition, July 2023, London

Translated by H. Yiğit Değirmenci

English Editing by Mesut Şenol

Cover art: Gulsum Oz

Cover design: S.Deniz Akıncı

Press Dionysus LTD, 167, Portland Road, N15 4SZ, London

• e-mail: info@pressdionysus.com

• web: www.pressdionysus.com

GÜLSÜM ÖZ

Literary Works

"Mübadele Aşkları – Loves of the Population Exchange" 2016, SOLA Publishing.

"Anneler Kızları ve Esrar – Mothers, Their Daughters, and Drug", novel, 2012, Astrea Publishing.

"İltica - Asylum" her first novel, October 2009, GOA Publishing.

Novels she co-authored: "Tanıklarla 12 Eylül – September 12th Through Witnesses", "Söz Kesmek Kına Yakmak – Betrothal and Applying Henna", and "Konan Göçen Kadınlar – Nomadic Women."

Awarded with of Yahya Konbolat Prize for short story worthy of publication with her story called "Bülbülün Çilesi – The Ordeal of the Nightingale" in 2010.

Motion Pictures – Television Series

She was one of the writers of the television series such as "Dullar Pansiyonu – Hostel for the Widowed", "Mahallenin Muhtarları – Headmen of the Neighborhood", "Çiçek Taksi – Flower Taxi", "Zoraki Koca – Unwilling Husband."

She authored the story of the television film called "Her Şey Oğlum İçin – Everthing for my Son" as well as the story and the script of the motion picture entitled "Yengeç Oyunu – Crab Game." Her motion picture script called "Bana Söz Ver Baba – Promise Me Dad" received the motion picture grant from the Turkish Ministry of Culture and Tourism.

Social Projects

Gülsüm Öz, received her first poetry award for her poem called "Vatan - Motherland" from the TRT (Turkish Radio and Television Corporation) at the age of 13. She worked as a proofreader at the Gelişim Publishing House for Grand Larousse - Büyük Larousse.

Gülsüm Öz who made a name for herself with her social projects alongside her artistic and cultural professions, enabled thousands of students to have education in sports and culture by establishing Turkiye's first "All Day Free Summer School" (Her Gün Ücretsiz Yaz Okulu) in Şişli and at İstanbul Metropolitan Municipality. Furthermore, she opened "Küçükçekmece Street Children's House of Hope" and had the authorities make us of it for the street children. By collaborating ÇEVKO, an environmentalist organization, she started projects of "Solid Waste Treatment". Gülsüm Öz inaugurated "Küçükçekmece Women's Shelter" in Istanbul.

Gülsüm Öz, at present keeps on writing novels and short stories beside teaching courses for writing at Marmara Arts Academy.

Memberships

(P.E.N) PEN Writers Association, (KYD) Kadın Yazarlar Derneği – Women's Writers Association, (FİLMSAN) Film Sanatçıları Vakfı – Foundation for Movie Artists, (SENARİST-BİR) Senaryo Yazarları Birliği – Union for Script Writers, (BESAM) Bilim ve Edebiyat Eseri Sahipleri Meslek Birliği - Union of Authors of Scientific and Literary Works, (THSD) Türkiye Halk Sağlığı Derneği – Turkish Association for Public Health.

ASYLUM
"WELL MET ISTANBUL, WELL MET LONDON"

My novel is based on the memories of my Jewish neighbour in London's Sloane Square district. Knowing him inspired me to examine the social and emotional consequences around a love story between two young people from different ethnic backgrounds.

The story I have woven starts in Istanbul, takes the reader on a trip to London and back again.

In it, the daughters of a wealthy Jewish family of Bourgeois origin, go out on a picnic and never return to Pera Palace Hotel where they lodged. Rosa and Lizet, best friends of these two young girls, look for them everywhere to no avail. Their family presumed they were killed by SS officers.

When Rosa's painful life ends, she entrusts her only son and a diary full of secrets to her sister, Lizet.

Rosa's son Cem Michel and Aysegul are in love. While conservative Lizet puts up a fierce opposition, Cem Michel struggles to maintain his relationship with Aysegul.

Love and endless suffering of war and genocide will continue to occupy writers and the film industry forever more.

Prelude

My heroes in this book live in various countries in Europe where they are tossed around like birds with broken wings. Inspired, I authored their stories as a film script. On my return to Türkiye, I felt the need to share these, often tragic, tumultuous lives with you, as a novel.

Before I started writing 'Well Met Istanbul, Well Met London' the moving memories of my Jewish neighbour in London's Sloan Square district, urged me to go to the Netherlands. There, in Anne Frank's shelter nesting in the attic room of a warehouse, now turned into a museum, I felt close to her; so much so that it felt as if her spirit and mine were one and the same. I paid many visits and did some research. I then went to Poland to confront other horrors of the second world war. There, I listened to the moving stories of Polish Jews. When I visited the concentration camps, like the victims imprisoned there, I felt suffocated just like leaving a gas chamber a moment ago.

I feel sure that the tragic memories of those on the receiving end of genocide at its extreme will continue to occupy both writers and the film industry in years to come.

Migration is a by-product of modernity. While writing about a migrant from Anatolia who struck a conversation with our Jewish hero, with the opening line,' Where are you from, my fellow countryman?' I felt tearful. When their conversation deepened and he shared his ordeal as a migrant in a foreign land, my tears flooded the keyboard.

And so... In this novel...

Aysegul and Cem Michel are two intellectual young people who are aware of the need to find a balance between love and logic.

Cem Michel, the son of a Jewish family with a painful past, falls in love with Aysegul, who is Muslim and wants to marry her, despite fierce opposition from his aunt Lizet. He struggles to maintain his relationship with Aysegul without upsetting his aunt who lost her entire family in the holocaust during the Second World War. Their struggle proves that intelligence, empathy, tolerance, and love, can overcome obstacles that may get in the way of happiness.

The two young lovers oscillate between love and logic and try to strike a balance between religion and communism. Halfway through the book they are separated - one is in Istanbul and the other in London. Their story resonates because they acknowledge and respect the love and trust of their families and the values and judgements of the society in which they live.

Lovers from diverse cultures, in their own stories show how their traditions, social and cultural differences enrich their union and add colour to it. They repeatedly prove that the only language people in this world can understand, is love.

Gülsüm Öz

Dear Cem;

It was 1942, a cold November. It was those years when we spoke Hebrew in Poland. As a whole family, we sat at the dinner table that was almost invisible in the dim light. Our cheerful and happy state we had in the past was replaced by fear and uneasiness. My father, who was only 45 years old, looked as if he had been getting old very fast. My mum was busy serving the food quietly. The only one among us still being cheerful was Lizet. She approached the table and said that she couldn't find the hat of her rag doll which she wouldn't drop from her hands. My mum pointed at the suitcases. The hat was in there. My brother, who is a humoristic and crazy boy, was nervous and lost in thoughts.

It was our last night at home. I couldn't eat anything because of my sadness. My father, who was very fond of us, warned me using an affectionate voice.

"Rosa… my beautiful daughter… Please eat your fill. It's going to be a hard day for us all tomorrow."

I was very downhearted that I would be leaving dad and grandpa behind.

"Why aren't we all getting on the same ship, dad?"

We were shaken by the sound of an explosion just right before dad was able to give his reply. We heard gunshots one after another and screeches of brakes. It felt like our house was being bombarded.

Mum immediately extinguished the dim light. Dad was making a hush gesture in the light that leaked into the house from outside. Mum and Dad were going back and forth to the windowsill and looking outside over the edge of the curtain.

"Mum... What's going on?" I whispered.

"Nazis..." she said slowly.

"Once more?" I said. I could see my mother's lips trembling in the dark.

"Yes... The whole Moshe family was executed by firing squad down the wall of the synagogue."

"No way... All of them?"

"All of them. I think now you gather the reason why we should leave here. They were executed today, and we could be the next."

Once my father drew the curtain, our room was plunged into darkness. We were talking very quietly.

There were convertible German war cars outside. Dad told us that about 10 soldiers executed about 30 Jews by firing squad in front of the synagogue wall enlightened by the moonlight. Meanwhile, they shot and killed our elderly neighbour as she was looking out of the window of the next building. The lifeless body of the old woman rolled in the air and fell on the street.

The next morning, with her elegant coat and silk scarf flying around her neck, mum helped my sister put on her hat. It was time to say goodbye. Dad and my brother were carrying the suitcases to the horse carriage in front of the door. My sister and I clung to my father's skirt. Dad was trying to make us laugh by joking.

"Come on, don't pull a long face. We'll be in Istanbul in three days at the latest."

My sister Lizet too started crying.

"But Dad… I don't want to go on this journey without you."

Dad brushed my sister's hair with his hand.

"One day, our whole family and relatives will come together, my girl. Don't worry about it."

In the meantime, the sounds of gunshots were approaching. Dad hugged Lizet and settled her in the carriage.

Mum was trying to shush my already crying sister.

"My girl, you should get it… Just three of us are allowed on the boat."

My father, brother, grandfather and aunt, who were left standing in front of the door, were waving at us.

"Come on, hurry… Have a safe travel."

This was the day when our family was torn apart.

Our silent sobs were flowing out of the carriage that drove along the forested road. We were going to get to Istanbul.

"I hope Hitler can't find us there."

I want a country

let there be no pain in the head, no yearning in the heart

let there be an end to brothers' quarrels

…

if there must be a complaint, let it only be of death

Cahit Sıtkı Tarancı

WELL MET ISTANBUL, WELL MET LONDON

Cem Michel's aunt Lizet looked as if she was one of those women in the fashion magazines of the 1950s with an old-fashioned pleat dress of high quality made from organza fabric dangling waist down, a beanie on her red hair combed in Marlyn Monroe style and a red lipstick on her lips. She has always been so elegant, but she has never been so unhappy lately. Since she found it out, she was brooding over the fact that her one and only nephew Cem Michel's affair with Aysegul was heading for marriage. Clasping her hands under her hunchback with the craziest ideas in her mind, she was pacing in the middle of the living room just like an old insect who wants to

17

protect its offspring against predators. The old aunt, who had never had her own child, was trying to find a way to make him fall out of love with Aysegul as he was her one and only nephew whom her sister had entrusted to her. No one in the family had married a Muslim until then. For some reason, she had started to remember the fact more often that she didn't have her own child ever since the day Cem Michel came up with this nonsensical idea of marriage. Who else did she have in her life but Cem Michel? What would she do, God forbid, if Cem Michel married that Muslim girl and their bloodline came to an end? Even the idea of it was enough to scare her. Lizet was determined to take action before this marriage thing of her nephew had happened. This old lady was actually a graceful and kind-hearted person, were it not this adamance and obstinacy of hers. Honestly speaking, she had done everything to bring up her orphaned nephew decently.

Cem Michel was a well-educated, intellectual and wealthy man. If examined too closely, he was not that handsome, though. In fact, he could be considered even as an ugly man with his big ears and his thin lips which looked as if two lines had been drawn under his bony nose. But he would flip his thick hair as if flagging in the wind from one side to another in such a manner that it was impossible to see the big ears hidden under his hair. The sweet smile on his face, the profound look in his brown eyes that could make one shudder, the tasteful style in the way he dressed up and his simple lifestyle… In short, Cem Michel was a charming man all in all. He was honourable, proud and a bit stubborn. He had a magic in his standing tall all the time. He was loved and respected by the people around him. Brought up with the ideology of a religious mother and a socialist father, Cem Michel was different from his relatives on this issue, and he was in favour of socialism contrary to other prosperous people despite being raised in a wealthy family in this country without having to see what it was like to be poor. He had a secret nickname used by the people around him. "Red Michel!"

The old lady had long been in an effort to match Michel with Margarita and she even attempted to arrange a romantic dinner for them. She thought Michel could not sneak off this time since she set him up by inviting the young girl to the house behind his back and presented the event to him as a fait accompli. Nevertheless, by the time she sat at the table with Margarita that was covered with a wide range of foods and appetisers, her nephew had already met his friends in Tas Plak, one of those taverns in Nevizade. In such an evening with a warm autumn breeze, the disappointment of his aunt at home doubled while waiting for him to show up with her eyes fixed at the empty chair by the table. Although it was the high time her beloved nephew got married and started his family, she would rather have him remained single if he were to marry a Muslim girl. She left the table dolefully... She took the newspaper that lay on the coffee table. Shalom was a weekly published newspaper. She glanced at the very first page. Today marked the 500th anniversary of the day when Jews were banished from Portugal. It was also the 505th anniversary of the day they defected from Spain to the Ottoman Empire. She felt overwhelmed. She put the newspaper back on the coffee table. Her mind was still on her nephew.

The live concert hadn't started yet. When the veteran waiter went to the kitchen to bring the olive oil dishes, Cem Michel and his lover Aysegul, who was sitting next to him, and their mutual friend Cemil together with his fiancée Melek were sorrowfully sipping their ice-cold drinks – raki... Due to the lack of their usual cheerfulness, an unpleasant conversation was very likely to be brought up. In the tavern next door, a belly dancer was dancing around the tables with a sad expression on her face.

Aysegul looked at her best friend Cemil carefully. In no way could she sit comfortably with the fact that this friend of hers from Istanbul University was planning to embark on a dangerous journey. Whenever she plucked up enough courage to start talking to dissuade him from his decision, she would give up on this very idea upon catching Melek's eyes on hers. She had not thought much of her for some time, yet Cemil had just fallen in love with her after a long time of loneliness. The girl insisted on going to London and marrying him there and her dear friend accepted this offer for all the risks involved. Melek's immaturity despite her age was a big concern for Aysegul. Holding the idea that a person's name reflects his or her character, she thought Melek, which means 'angel' in Turkish, should have been named *Sheytan* meaning 'Satan'. With these thoughts, she sighed angrily and asked her friend Cemil:

"So... You are leaving for sure, right?" she said.

"Yes," he answered in a decisive way without raising his head.

Upon the immediate reply her friend had given, Aysegul understood that she would not be able to make her friend forgo his decision even if he wants it or not.

"When is the journey?" she asked slowly.

"In two weeks' time, we are departing from Sile."

"So you are sure that it is safe for sure?"

"Don't worry! I researched it quite well. We will be in France within one month. Besides, Ahmet will meet us there. London will be only a few miles away."

Cem stared at Cemil's eyes wanting to read his mind as he considered all the risks involved in such an illegal journey.

"Has Ahmet done all the official paperwork for you?"

"Yes…"

Wishing to say "Don't go!" to stop her friend, Aysegul added.

"Tell me… You think Ahmet is happy in London?" she said.

"I have no other choice. You know that. I go there because I have to…" Cemil said in a reluctant but decisive; desperate but strong manner.

Aysegul took her eyes off the leafless poplar tree with its roots buried in concrete, and looked up at the sky. The Sun was floating towards Tarlabasi and it was being followed by the flocks of swallows ready to leave the country and start migrating to warmer regions as the autumn was coming. She hoped to find solace in those birds whose snow white bellies were shining like the moon under their dark blue wings. Her friend was going away soon to build a nest just like those migrating storks.

The hors d'oeuvres had been served before the olive oil dishes were eaten up. Aysegul pecked at the fried calamari with her fork for a while. Having difficulty in swallowing the food, she turned her look away from the calamari with an expression that was disapproving of her friend's decision to get married and set out on such a journey.

"Take care of each other while on board! Promise?" she said.

"I am not going with him," Melek said while hungrily devouring the pastry and lending an ear to what was being said at the table. Hearing this, Aysegul almost choked to death out of astonishment with a sip of drink she was having. Cem passed a napkin hurriedly. Cleaning her mouth, she asked the girl:

"You are not going with him?"

"I'll go by plane one month later. We will meet in London." Cemil gave a look wanting to justify his lover and reached for the hands of his true friend, Aysegul, who had been feeling sorry for him.

"There is nothing wrong going on for her. Why should she accompany me on this hazardous journey? If I could travel normally, I would go with her," he said. Then, he went on talking gleefully to change the topic.

"Well, my main concern is that I will have to go before your wedding."

22

"Normally, we would have got married by now, but Aysegul insists that we get married after we've got my aunt's consent. It's not my fault but your friend's…" Cem said to clear the atmosphere in a half-joking way.

However, Aunt Lizet was utterly resolute. Upon laying her eyes on the dinner table and her nephew's empty chair for a while, she diverted her look to Margarita. Before she passed on to the great beyond, she wanted her beloved nephew to wed Margarita, whom she had known well ever since she was a baby. "He will see who the boss is," she said and sighed. She was all ears to hear the door if it was to be knocked at. It was Michel's footsteps, whom she expected to hear.

Despite being a short and thin lady, Sara, Lizet's serving girl, was taking away the food, which she had meticulously prepared, from the table left almost untouched. In the meantime, the old aunt was running out of hope.

Although Lizet had invited Margarita many times before, she couldn't get these two young people, who were a perfect match, to bond emotionally. More tragically, her nephew was able to outwit her despite the fact that she hadn't told him about the occasion this time. Margarita wouldn't listen to Lizet who was making up excuses and repeatedly saying that Michel was absent from the dinner due to his busy work. She got up from the table with a sad smile on her face and sat on the armchair. She found herself playing with the knot on the waistband of her elegant spotty dress. She was not thinking any more if Michel was in love with her or not.

Lizet asked Sara to call her nephew's phone again which he wouldn't answer. Knowing quite well that the old lady was struggling in vain and she had been waiting until so late for nothing, Margarita was now looking at the leather shoes, having no more hopes that Michel would show up. She sulked her face after a moment of an unpleasant silence and asked in a heartbroken way to be excused for leaving.

As if he had been waiting and watching Margarita leave the house, Cem Michel came home showing up from the corner after her departure. It was obvious that he was not in the mood. He evasively apologised to his aunt, who was remonstrating, for having missed the dinner and went to his room. The old lady could only stay looking desperately from behind with all the things she had wanted to say.

Lizet woke up to a nice and sunny day the next morning. It was the last Sunday of September. She could talk to her nephew seriously as he wouldn't go to work. Laid on an elliptic table made of walnut trees, the breakfast plates on the snow white tablecloth were burdened with the bitterness and sweetness of the past. Most of these dishes were those they hadn't cooked and tasted for a long time. Since its dough was not put aside for resting for long, Matzo[1] bread was placed in a flat position on the table as if to symbolize an escape from torture. Hard boiled eggs were lined side by side as if wanting to spite the bread. Their arduous dessert Marzipan made from almond,

---

1 **Matzo:** Unleavened bread eaten in Judaism on Passover for eight days each year to commemorate liberation from Egyptian Slavery.

lemon and sugar looked tempting. Placed on the lettuce and celery leaves, Boyoz[2] and the other pastries, just taken out of the oven and still piping hot, were adding extra beauty to the table. As Sara was going out of the hall after she served the tea, Cem Michel came in, towelling his hair dry and said "Good Morning!" to his young servant. He sympathetically kissed his aunt on her cheek and gently took her arm. He hungrily examined the breakfast table.

"Mmm! I was wondering where this nice scent came from."

"We haven't had such a nice breakfast together for a long time. Come on and take a seat..."

"But aunty! What is the occasion? Am I forgetting a special day? What are all these for?"

"You are never at home on special days. All you think is Aysegul." Michel gave a confirming look for what she said.

"She is the rose that has blossomed in my heart."

"Ah... if each heart were to bloom roses, our hearts would be a huge rose garden," Lizet said ironically to reveal her discontentment with the situation.

Cem Michel impishly dropped a kiss on his aunt's cheek.

"Is that really so, my red magnolia? You are talking as if it once had not been the president of a modern European country who pledged to eradicate Jews' bloodstream, aunty," he said.

---

2 **Boyoz:** A Jewish pastry. A pastry made by Jews of Sephardic origin who came to Izmir from Spain in 1492.

He said this, but still there was something he had to say, which was left waiting in his mind for a chance to be spoken out. It was tonight's dinner with Aysegul, at which they had planned to tell his aunt that they were getting married. As for his aunt, she was biding her time to bring up the subject of Margarita. The best thing to do was to invite the young beauty to the house before her nephew left. Standing up slowly, she went to the kitchen and told Sara to call in Margarita immediately.

After finishing his breakfast, Michel headed for his room to change his clothes. Lizet was proudly looking at him from behind as she walked towards the armchair by the window which had been almost inseparable from its owner and became as old as her in years. She sat on her old armchair standing upright with its sharp corners, the mahogany smell it spread and the elegant silk taffeta fabric as well, most importantly, its challenging and surviving nature just like hers. Each time Michel wanted to replace this furniture, Lizet opposed and said: "Where on earth do you think you can find the same model as this mahogany style?" Cem Michel had already given up the idea and would never offer, at least, to have their fabric replaced and maintained as he knew his aunt would list her reasons again and say: "There are no more such silk fabrics, handcrafting and tailoring to be found out there." Lizet looked out of the window. As she was watching the road for Margarita, she went over the details of her today's boat trip plan in her mind. In fact, she had tried every option before. She had enumerated all the good qualities of Margarita and her family, mentioned her good traits, her mother's as well as other relatives' and she had even threatened him with the fact that she would never look at his face again if he ever married Aysegul. But Michel was digging his heels in and insisting on no other women but Aysegul. However, he had no choice. He was supposed to forget her and agree to marry Margarita.

On the other hand, Cem Michel was putting on his sports outfit he took out of his closet and thinking about his lover, whom he was going to meet soon. He had fallen in love with Aysegul when they were at high school. For the sake of seeing his girlfriend, with whom he played chess in the school team at Saint Benoit French High School, or holding her hand a bit longer, there was no other craziness left he hadn't done or punishment he hadn't got. They couldn't see each other often enough despite studying at the same school. It was because boys and girls studied in different classes. Every weekend, he would hop onto his violet bicycle and go to his lover's house, which was a few blocks away. On his bike passing by the houses with his shoulders seen first, Cem Michel was followed by the eyes of the girls who had been standing behind their windows and those eyes were as usual fixed at the orange building across the road. Unlike the other girls, Aysegul would not hide behind the tulle curtains but rest her head on the windowpane and wait for Cem Michel to show up every weekend. Her love, sympathy, anger or resentment for this young boy could be noticed through her manners behind this window. If she was directly going out to the balcony and not drawing the curtain angrily after sticking her head out the window, this obviously would have meant that she was happy.

Going out from his room all dressed up, Cem Michel tweaked on his aunt's cheek with a sweet smile on his face.

"I am leaving, aunty. I will be back with Aysegul in the evening. We have good news for you," he said. Aunt Lizet was in shock. She looked her nephew in the eyes and said:

"No way! Margarita will be here soon." She was trembling and holding on to her nephew's arm. She got so upset that neither her head nor her hands were in her control. Cem Michel, who didn't let her talk any more, dropped a kiss on the wrinkled hand that was holding on to his arm:

"No, aunty. Please, don't!" he said and left home. Lizet could only stay looking from behind and said to herself:

"His eyes turned blind to his own aunt, let alone Margarita. Soon enough, he will realise the right thing to do and finally give up on this love." She said all these while grumbling and tapping her foot on the wooden floor to look resolute in her decision. In fact, when he told her years ago that he was in love with Aysegul, she was very sure that her nephew would break up with her soon after she gave his mother's diary and made him read it. How on earth did this notebook not work out? Michel's mother Rosa had fallen in love with a Muslim boy, too. Nonetheless, she had given upon her love even before her family had to meddle in. As a matter of fact, she didn't know what was written in Rosa's diary. She never read it either before or after she gave it to her nephew. Her sister had willed that no one but her son should read it. She must have certainly mentioned somewhere how troublesome it would be for his family if he ever married a Muslim girl. Michel had avoided reading his mother's memories for a while. He handled the diary that smelled fusty with its burned edges. Fearing that these pages would cause a fire between Aysegul and him, he asked:

"But why? Why are the edges of this notebook burned aunty?"

"Listen, my son. It seems that this diary was set on fire and put out. What was left behind? The soot… only the black soot" she said in a certain and decisive manner, showing the notebook with its blackened edges. Michel replied:

"Love in my heart would not die down my dear Aunt. Do not ever worry about that."

After a while, when Lizet asked her nephew if he had read the notebook yet, he said:

"I have read it. The burnt edges of that notebook are the ashes left behind after a massacre that flared up, Aunty." It was obvious that he had read the notebook. But well… If he read it already, why didn't he break up with Aysegul yet?" Lizet was filled with intense curiosity whenever the thought of her sister's diary occurred to her. The same feeling of curiosity, which she could in no way restrain, once again wrapped itself around her while she was lending an ear to the sound of the elevator that Michel took and watching him leave the house behind the tulle curtains. She was wondering what her sister had written in that notebook. What would happen if she could just read it?

Being in a dilemma for a moment, she got up from her armchair and stayed where she was for a couple of seconds with Rosa's will in her mind that only Michel should read the diary and then made her way to her nephew's room with a deep sigh. Entering the room, she hesitated for a while, but she opened the drawer of the bedside stand and took out the notebook. As if she had burned herself, she instantly put the notebook back that she could hardly handle with her wrinkled and trembling hand and pushed the drawer back. Oh Lord! What a sin she committed because of what she had just intended to do. She apprehensively stepped out of the room. She handled the Torah[3] on the tea table. She looked up to the ceiling before opening the book.

"My Lord! I am grateful for your help to let me wake up from my sound sleep, grow up and learn about life," she murmured. She sat on the armchair. Slightly bending over it, she got down to reading her holy book.

* * *

Istanbul, heading towards a modern future, was also losing its charm that had come along with the past. The mansions that lined up along the coast on both sides of the Bosporus

---

3 **Torah:** The first of the four great books. The Torah, which is the Arabicized form of the Hebrew word Tura, expresses the meanings such as law, alliance, unity, agreement, contract, naming. In the Jewish tradition, it is the name of the collection of books called the Old Testament (Old Testament).

were resentfully sulking at the grey buildings that rose high above as though they had been torn apart from a love story. It seemed like the greedy landowners of the city had unanimously agreed to cooperate to erase all the marks that the history left on Istanbul, which had always been the capital of civilizations. As for Cem Michel and his lover Aysegul, they were watching an old mansion, the fountain and the green lands stuck between concrete structures, gradually increasing in number, with a fear of not being able to see them again and in the meantime figuring out a way to tell Aunt Lizet tonight that they were getting married.

They had been together for years. To be honest, neither of them had any intention of officialising their relationship until a year ago, when they were together to celebrate their anniversary, during which Cem Michel noticed that Aysegul had her slightly envious eyes on a family enjoying their meal with their children at the next table. That same night, Cem Michel instantly asked her a question: "Will you be the mother of our children?" As she couldn't say a word out of astonishment for a moment, he continued:

"What a nonsense question, isn't it?" Right after that, he proposed. Every time they met in the following year, they talked about how they would get married, how many children they would have or even whom they would name their children after. And that exact day, Cem Michel was beggingly hoping his one and only aunt to start having sympathy for Aysegul sooner or later and dreaming that they would perhaps bake cookies together. Meanwhile, they were hearing the talks of the people cheerfully sitting at the next tables. How ironic it would be if these guys knew that this young couple who had both become adults and built their own careers were actually struggling to start the conversation about how they would persuade an elderly aunt into approving their marriage decision without hurting her feelings? How could they know that this old lady had lost most of the members in her family during the Jewish holocaust and how much she feared to lose her nephew, Michel, who happens to remain as her only family. Cem, not knowing how to start the conversation brought up an irrelevant subject all of a sudden.

"How horrible it is!" he said in a way that gave a hint of the fact that he was an orphan. Aysegul looked at her lover. His eyes were fixed on that day's newspaper on the next table. It had an article titled "LARA MADE EVERYONE CRY AGAIN", which read as follows: " Lara, having lost her mother in the Blue Market attack on March 13, 1999, had a bunch of black carnations in her hands…" Aysegul turned her gaze to the newspaper.

"It is for sure not easy to forget about such an incident. The image of that poor little girl's coffin crying at her mother's funeral is still vivid in my memory," she said and the following headline caught her attention.

"I can no longer bear reading anything from newspapers," she murmured and sat upright on her chair.

Cem Michel's eyes were fixed on the boat that had been

sailing away by leaving foamy traces behind resembling a lion's mane. He thought back on his aunt taking his arm with begging eyes before he left home and Margarita, who was the guest invited to his house. He looked at the woman he loved with his usual smile while carefully preparing sentences in his mind to tell her that it would be more appropriate if they informed his aunt about their marriage plans not tonight, but sometime later.

With her modesty and tolerant attitude, Aysegul was the apple of Nisantasi's eye. She had fallen in love with Cem Michel as far back as in those high school years although she was in fact critical of his snobbish attitudes while trying to keep away from him. The fact that he was Jewish had never mattered to her dad, who was a mechanical engineer as well as being a member of the executive board at a holding company and to her mum who never gave up painting pictures although her pictures would not sell a lot. They had never treated him in a different way from their own son as of the time they used to be a student. The young man happened to be a common visitor to their house and to be on good terms with his prospective parents in law and enjoyed the warmth and comfort they were providing.

Cem Michel's father David and his aunt Irvin as well as all his relatives from his father's side were intellectual and liberal people. They had a number of family friends who were socialist artists. His father, whom he would never see these days, had remarried another woman after his mother's death and settled down in the States. Cem Michel, who had lost his mother when he was only ten, was devastated by this decision of his father's, whom he had a chance to see even once a week till he turned seventeen. He went through a long lasting depression as he thought that he was abandoned by his own father and it was only when Aunt Lizet embraced him with her love and affection that he was able to leave all his mental sufferings behind.

Aunt Lizet was his only relative from his mother's side who was still alive. His family never felt like an Istanbulite although they were enjoying their time in Nisantasi in winters and in Buyukada in summers those days, when there was nowhere else they could return to. His mum and aunt, who had started their education at a Rabbinical school in Poland and later enrolled in Saint-Benoit French High School, learned Turkish at an advanced level and took part in social and cultural activities while they were still holding on to their own conservative values within the family. His uncle, his aunt's husband was also known to be in possession of a great deal of money, having saved it in one of the banks abroad.

Cem Michel turned his gaze to his lover from a sea boat cruising as gracefully as a swan while a dozens of seagulls flew after it competing with each other to catch a bit more of the pieces of bread that people had been scattering for them to catch. He put his arm around Aysegul's neck and made her head rest on his shoulder to let her know that they would be together forever. Nonetheless, Aysegul was aware that her lover was actually not murmuring nice things. She herself had also not been feeling well since Aunt Lizet highlighted the fact that they were worlds apart because of their religion and ethnicity. Cem Michel was frequently haunted by the thought that he might have problems in his marriage because of his aunt, whom he in fact loved and respected very much. Though she knew very well that he hated talks about his family, Cem's lover Aysegul, holding his hands in hers, urged him a bit more decisively and asked him:

" If your mum was alive, do you think she would oppose our marriage just as your aunt does?"

"No," Cem said without having second thoughts. Aysegul was surprised by this sudden answer.

"Really? So you are saying that your mum was not like your aunt," she said. The cheering expression on Cem's face turned into a mournful one, which was obvious from his trembling voice. He tried to answer the question unhurriedly.

"Yes, mum was a traditional woman, but she was still different from my aunt. There was Neve Shalom Synagogue which had been built in Kuledibi long before I was born. Every time my grandma and aunt went there to pray, mum always played hard to get there. She was more eager to allocate more time to social activities. Once, mum had written in her diary..." he said and became silent stammering as he knew that he wouldn't be able to finish his sentence. Despite seeing that Cem suffered as he was talking about his family's history full of pain and sorrow, Aysegul still went on asking in a manner as if she already knew the answer she would get while watching a cargo steamer cruising slowly towards the Bosphorus Bridge:

"I hope it is not only your being a socialist what makes you different from your aunt, is it?"

"I have told you this before, haven't I? I am a sort of man who has set his own rights and wrongs as a result of cultural conflicts between my mother's side who were religious and my father's side who were democratic."

Hugging him as tightly as she could, Aysegul said to the man of her life:

"To tell the truth, it seems that you led a comfortable life in a liberal environment with your family."

"You know that the previous generation was not as free and liberal as I am," Cem Michel said and looked at his lover with a sour smile on his face.

"I know, my love… For me, it was just the opposite. In my family, the previous generation led a far freer life thanks to all the sacrifices their own parents had both materially and spiritually made in the light of republican revolutions. And later… We have soon given upon all these rights that were handed over to us on a silver platter. In the end, I found myself at university fighting for quite a just cause," Aysegul said to sustain the conversation.

"Yes… Most of the countries, which were in tatters after World War II, have won their power back in no time. However, this country, despite keeping away from the troubles of the war, was dragged into never ending fights and political conflicts and this is exactly what it has become now. Anyway Aysegul! Let's get up." Cem Michel, who seemed determined to enjoy the happiness that came with being his lover instead of being lost in the sorrow of the past, grasped his lover's hand looking at her face admiringly and continued:

"We shall get going," he said and pulled his lover towards himself, who was looking at him with curious eyes.

"Where to go?"

"Instead of talking about the same things over and over again, let's go and tell my aunt that we are getting married. I want to put an end to this thing."

"We were going to do it in the evening."

"Does it matter? I don't want to wait for another minute anymore."

"I have started to feel anxious now."

"I am not going to give up on either you or that oldie sweet witch. You are the ones who should bring a solution to the problem between yourselves. At the beginning, you may get hurt or feel upset. God knows only, perhaps, you will love each other more than you can imagine." Cem Michel seemed to have taken his first steps to the felicity of his upcoming marriage when he wrapped his arm around his lover's neck and started humming a song.

Having finished his PhD at Harvard Business School and begun working as a senior manager in a bank, he bought a spacious apartment in Cihangir which overlooked the Bosphorus.

The apartment had a saloon with a high ceiling on which a gold-leaf ceiling rosette designed elaborately was attached. He had it maintained and illuminated by using spot lights without changing its original shape. Aysegul herself had designed the lighting system that they placed between the crown moulding and squinch as well as the stucco arch stretching from the kitchen to the hall.

His aunt had resented him as he was designing the interior of his apartment with his lover and even stopped talking to him for days. The old lady who had no one else in life other than her nephew said:

"So you are abandoning me here all alone and going to live in another house. I would rather die." She reproached and blamed so much that Cem Michel felt guilty about what he had done and couldn't stay in this flat even for a single night, which he had prepared and furnished with bells on his toes. In this flat, which he occasionally dropped in to read books and have some rest for a couple of hours, he would also host some of his friends for dinner. Yet, no matter how late the clock showed, he would return to his aunt's place, which was full of his mum's and grandma's memories.

When Aysegul and Cem Michel came to the house in Nisantasi, Aunt Lizet was not there. Aysegul had been there before and she was then nicely treated by Lizet, who didn't reveal her true feelings about her. According to what Cem told her the following day, Aysegul thought that Lizet was probably of the opinion that her nephew was playing the field and was not serious with her. In truth, he was serious this time. She was curious if the old lady would be able to display the same polite manners when she was told that they were getting married. Aysegul was examining the gilded mirrors and invaluable paintings on the wall, but she couldn't pay close attention as the thought of Lizet's reaction kept niggling at her mind. She came to herself with Cem's voice.

"Why don't you take a seat?"

Aysegul sat on the hand crafted couch made of solid wood after she, using her hand, flattened its fabric with wrinkles on it, showing that it had been quite recently used. Meticulously placed on the tea table, the gilded candy dishes with rose patterns on them, handcrafted vases, brass chanukiahs[4], the pictures of smiling children in the silver frames, who would stay in them as children forever, were reflecting, just like a magic mirror, the past of the man she was in love with. Aysegul turned her gaze from the family pictures to Cem's face and said in a half-joking manner:

"It seems that your aunt has abandoned the house in order not to come face to face with me."

"She didn't know that we were going to come here at this time of the day. Perhaps she went out to do shopping for you…" Cem replied in the same joking manner. As Aunt Lizet refused to use the so-called mobile phones which were becoming pop-

---

4 **Chanukiahs:** Nine-armed candelabra. The middle arm of this candlestick is called Samash and it is higher than the others. This candle is lit daily during Hanukkah.

ular day after day, Cem Michel reached out to his phone to call their serving girl Sara. In the meantime, Aysegul went on to examine the black and white photos in the silver frames on the dresser. Cem's voice was getting lower on the phone. The young lady turned and looked at him. Cem's cheer was gone.

"Sara said that they had gone to the house in the Prince's İsland to get some belongings of hers and they would return tomorrow," he said. Aysegul's excitement had been replaced with an uneasiness she could not define with words. The young man walked towards his lover and held her hands.

"Don't fret. We are going to go and apply for a date for our wedding."

But what Aysegul wanted was more than getting wed. As for Cem Michel, he would not let anything make himself upset as long as his lover was standing by his side.

"I will go and get you something to drink. Meanwhile, why don't you put up a nice CD," he said.

Aysegul nodded approvingly.

Hand in hand, they both walked towards Cem Michel's room. When the young man diverted to the kitchen to prepare the drinks, Aysegul headed to his lover's room, which was quite spacious, luminous and tastefully furnished with modern furniture. As always, she felt a sense of relaxation upon moving from the living room to this room on that day. Idly standing in the middle of this room which was in full contrast with the general style of the house where a big family once dwelled, she had been haunted with a known thought that Aunt Lizet had gone to the Island just to avoid her when Cem Michel appeared at the door with the glasses in his hand.

"My love…"

Aysegul pulled herself together and made a move towards the stereo. The CD case, in which there was a wide range of music CDs, had been arranged in such a way which would enable one to find anything he wanted easily. They were placed in one of the many special rows depending on the singer, the music genre and the year the song was released. When Cem Michel put the glasses on the tea table and went back to the kitchen to bring the nuts, Aysegul got down to looking for the CD by Julio Iglesias. For some reason best known to herself, she wanted to listen to the song *"Oh mammy, oh mammy, many blue"*. As she was searching the CD case to find decisively what she wanted, her lover came back in with a big tray in his hands. Placing the cheese and ham plates from the tray on the table near the glasses, he spoke with a sweet voice.

"You couldn't decide yet?"

"I did. But I couldn't find the CD by Julio Iglesias."

"Isn't it there?"

Cem Michel thought for a while as he was filling the glasses with drink.

"Maybe, it is in the drawers of the nightstand. I might have forgotten to put it back in its place as it is one of those I frequently listen to."

"Ok!"

Aysegul pulled and opened the drawer. As she was examining the CDs there, she found some photographs on the backside of which there were some handwritings in Hebrew.

"Such special things as to be kept in the drawer by your bed... Who might they belong to?" she murmured and looked at Cem Michel with curious eyes. They looked at each other's eyes. The young man came closer to his lover. With his eyes questioning what must have been bothering her, he turned his gaze to the drawer. The photographs were lying in there. Handling them as carefully as he could, he commenced introducing the people in them to Aysegul.

"This is my uncle, Marcus."

"You mean he was the brother of your mum and Aunt Lizet."

Cem Michel nodded approvingly. He became silent and Aysegul kept talking.

"How much you actually look like your uncle."

"Yeah! Everyone says so."

"Who is that?"

"It is Aunt Rebeka."

"Shame on you, Cem! Why haven't you told me about your relatives before?"

"They are not alive. I don't feel up to talking about them," he said. He said this so sighingly that Aysegul wished that she hadn't brought up this topic ever. Thinking that she had made a mistake, she regretfully made for the armchair by the window with the glass in her hand which her lover had passed to her. After he put up a cassette in the stereo, Cem sat on the armchair beside the one Aysegul was sitting on and toasted his glass with his lover's with a sad smile.

"I am sorry," he murmured.

"There is nothing you should be sorry about, my love."

The room had been filled with sorrowful air and melancholy that the velvety voice of Julio Iglesias was also contributing to. The cries of a child aged 11 reflecting the sad memories he had had could be heard in the lyrics of the song. *"Oh mammy! Oh mammy! If I could only hold your hand,"*.

With an expression on his face showing he got lost in the memories of the past, Cem Michel reached out to his lover's hand to hold it affectionately. And suddenly, he stood up and walked towards the bookcase. He took out a worn-out notebook from the cabinet and went back to sit in his place with a smile that was dipped in sadness.

"To be frank, I should have read this notebook to you long ago."

As Aysegul was curiously looking at Cem and the notebook with the burnt edges, Cem continued.

"This is my mum's diary... In our culture, each and every parent's will is to advise the posterity not to forget the genocide and not to let it be forgotten. Every Jew is born with the natural responsibility to pass down the pains and memories of all those dreadful events that were targeted in eradicating our ethnicity. Humanity should remember such a shame forever so that the world won't ever witness such a tragedy."

"Did your mum write about the genocide?"

"The genocide as well as how they came to Istanbul… In other words, her whole life that had been spent with so many unfortunate and tragic events."

Cem opened the burned cover of his mum's fusty diary which she had started keeping when she was 10 and completed writing in the years to come. Cem took a piece of paper out of it that had been folded into four pieces.

"Take it and read this first."

"No way. I can't. It is addressed to you."

"In fact, I sometimes think that mum wrote this notebook for both of us."

"For both of us?"

"Definitely! You will see what I mean once you have read it."

Aysegul was reaching out to it, but then changed her mind.

"Ok! I can read out the letter for you. But I will give the diary to you and you will read it yourself only if you want to."

Cem Michel, as he was reading out the lines of the letter stained with the tears having dropped on it, started hearing his mum, whom he had to prematurely bid farewell to, in his ears from the days she used to tell him fairy tales with her sweet voice.

Dear Cem,

I started writing my diary when we were bidding farewell to Poland.

While you're reading this notebook, I won't be alive, my son. I will entrust it to Aunt Lizet to pass it to you when she thinks it's the time.

When we were on a dangerous journey towards Istanbul, a big crime against humanity was being committed in most countries of Europe. I saved it like it was a diamond throughout the sorrowful but exciting months for us, the kids, during which we were welcoming a new life in Istanbul. My beloved, noble-looking son... I have always tried my best to tell you about who you descend and inherited your nobility from. I have written those things that I was not able to tell.

As the incidents revived in my memory blow-by-blow, this diary, which became even more valuable after I added my father's memories written in his pen, had been my leg to stand on. I wrote and wrote for 30 years with a fear deep in my heart that I would not be able to finish all the things I wanted to tell you...

I think I will die soon, my son... I don't even have the strength to lift the curl of your hair that falls upon your eyes, my baby. Your aunt Lizet, who never drops the smile on her face even in despair, is trying to cheer us up by playing the glad game. You are riding your bike in the garden again this morning and Aunt Lizet is with you... As you ride your bike, she is running after you. She is breaking her neck to save you from being hurt.

She must have her mind on me because she is frequently

turning her head to look at the window of my bedroom. Do not ever let your aunt down who has always put her heart and soul into our family, especially you, my son.

While I am watching you through the window near my bed, I am feeling sorry not because of the fear of death but because of the fact that I won't be able to see you grow up a bit more. Maybe I will not pass away with my worries about you. Aunt Lizet will look after you quite well. I know that she will even hesitate to smell you lest she should hurt you. However, she wants to keep you safe from one thing. If you ever fall in love with a Muslim girl one day, your aunt will be very angry. Should this happen, you can read the things I have written in this notebook to her as it is my will.

Whilst Cem was still reading the letter, Aysegul's eyes were filled with tears. The young man, being unable to remain indifferent to his lover's emotions, hugged her and said:

"If you are going to cry even while listening to the letter, it is better that you not read the notebook at all.

"Did that happen? I mean, yes, it happened but did you read this notebook to your aunt?"

Cem Michel remained silent for a few seconds. And then:

"No… My aunt's thought of my mum should remain the same in her mind as it was before," he said.

Aysegul pulled herself together after she wiped her tears with her sleeves. She grabbed the diary and looked at its first page.

The first lines were written by Cem Michel's grandfather in Hebrew and addressed to his mum. Despite not being able to understand Hebrew, Cem read these lines out loud as he had memorised their meanings.

"Dear Rosa, I hope you will write your good memories on these pages. I want them to be filled with happiness. A. Michel Joshua, Your Father…"

With the bitter expression that perched on his face soon after he finished reading these lines, he reached out to get his glass and walked to the windowside. Aysegul turned over the page. Then, she looked through all the pages. She saw that the first pages had been written in French and the rest in Turkish. As several pages written in French were burned from the edges, she was having difficulty in picking out some of the words there. She gently flattened the burned edges as if stroking a baby's cheek. As she was set to complete the sentences in the lines, she tried to visualise Cem Michel's mother as a child.

Mum, my sister and I are on board…

My name is Rosa… I am 10. Only my mother and Lizet are with me here. This is the first time I have embarked on a journey apart from my dad and my elder brother… In truth, we are running away from Nazi genocide. I hope Hitler won't be able to find us where we go.

We embarked on this ship in Romania. We transferred to two different carriages before we arrived at the port of Constanta where our ship had anchored. The second one was a carriage whose horses were very beautiful. One of them had a snow-white mane. The port was so crowded that everyone except for us was showing the paper in their hands to the attendants and later going into the line. We did not have any paper to show them. My mum didn't say anything, but I think we got on this ship secretly.

Everyone including mum was praying for this journey to finish without any trouble. Mum talked to a man about the rumour that the country we were heading to had stayed out of the war and was hospitable to the Jews who escaped from the war. Another man said that Turkey was willing to keep its borders open to Jewish refugees. So… The name of the country we were going to defect to is called Turkey, ha? The thought that the war had not penetrated into the country we would take shelter in gave me some relief. At least, I am not as scared as I was before.

My best friend on board is Rita. She is at the same age as me. Lizet, Rita and I are engaging in long talks. How nice! Rita's whole family, her mum, uncle, elder brothers are all with her. She says they are all going to Palestine by a Turkish ship. I got a bit surprised and sad:

"But why? Why are you going somewhere else?" I asked.

"They say only those who speak Hebrew and who have skilful men in their families to work in various jobs are welcome in this country. They don't want the elderly, either."

"We are not old, either," I said. Rita shrugged her shoulders and didn't reply. I thought that if our father and brothers, who were both speakers of Hebrew and skilful people, were with

48

us, we could go to Palestine together with Rita and her family. And then I asked mum:

"Is Palestine or Istanbul more beautiful?"

Mum: "I don't know. All I know is that we don't have the luxury to choose where we go. Being in a secure place would be enough for us.

Inside the ship it started smelling bad. I went on the deck this morning. Watching the giant waves the ship was breaking through, a couple of Jews there were talking about a ship having sunk last year with Jews on board. The ship's name was Salvador. She was caught by a storm. She disappeared in the depth of the sea off the coast of somewhere called Silivri. The people who lost their lives totalled two hundred and fifty, most of whom were women and children. I got so scared. I ran away from there and rushed to my mum to tell her about what I had heard. I could hear her heartbeats when she asked us not to be afraid and embraced Lizet and me putting our heads on her chest.

The steward is serving food. My dad spent so much for this journey that all we could afford for food was biscuits and half a glass full of milk. I never feel full.

I am hiding from Lizet and Rita. They cannot find me here and I can write here freely.

I will write why we got on this ship in the first place. I will never forget how hard it was for us to say goodbye to our beautiful cosy home and our neighbourhood with all our relatives in it. I will write how we were forced to leave my beloved father and my elder brother, who was my only true confidant. And everything else...

It was November, 1941. It was cold. Bitter cold. I had just turned 10. My father, who was a doctor, had stopped going to his work at the hospital. He asked us to go to our room on the night of a troublesome day. My elder brother Marcos whose Bar Mitzvah[5] had recently been celebrated, but still whose voice had not deepened yet, had taken his place among the adults and must have foreseen that his mind would soon be poisoned by insufferable talks and ideas.

Hopping on the same bed, my sister and I sat cross-legged looking at each other. We had no intention of sleeping, for we were restless. We were wondering why our elder brother had stayed with the adults. Lizet must have been thinking about the same thing as me because once we caught each other's eyes, we rushed to the door to eavesdrop. Mostly, it was my father who was doing all the talking and the others were listening. He was saying that no one had ever again heard from our family friends who were arrested by SS soldiers. They were whispering so that we would not hear them, yet Lizet and I had listened to everything being said.

My sister, brother and I were trying to continue our education in one of those shelter schools in the underground.

---

5 **Bar Mitzvah:** For Jews, it is the age when a person begins to be responsible for his own actions and reaches puberty. "Bar Mitzvah" means "son of command" and "Bat Mitzvah" means "daughter of command".

According to Germans, it was not necessary for the Polish to have a proper education. In their opinion, just learning to write their names as well as that they should abide by any command given by Germans under any circumstances would be more than enough. When we heard this, we felt upset. Our grandpa told us not to.

"On the contrary, this idea of theirs humiliating the Jews should spur you to do better in science and literature instead of intimidating you," he said. My father agreed with my grandpa, adding that the first thing to do to eradicate a nation is to confine them to illiteracy and ignorance.

It was going to be our Hanukkah[6] soon. I placed the candles in the hanukkah menorah to be lit later. Although we were in December already, there was no excitement of celebration in the house. In the evening of a very cold day, my grandpa came to the shelter discreetly with some pieces of food in his hand. Replacing his hat on his head with his kippah[7], he said that America, which had remained neutral till then, would also enter the war.

On Sunday morning, the planes taking off from Japanese aeroplane carrier ships attacked the American battleships at Pearl Harbour on Hawaii Island and sank 6 of 8 battleships. My dad was trying to adjust the radio after he removed the cover on it while mum was preparing the meal on the makeshift table.

---

6 **Hanukkah:** Jewish holiday that falls at the end of November or December and lasts for 8 days.

7 **Kippah:** A type of cap that covers the top of the head, usually worn by Jewish men in religious ceremonies and sometimes in normal times.

Nothing but a buzzy sound came from the radio. His hands on the buttons, he was alert at finding any sound he could hear. Yes… From what we could hear, the US declared war on Japan, Germany and Italy.

"You are late," my father said. With his continuing reproaches for the US, my grandpa sat on the armchair and said to my dad:

"The US had not entered the war, but it was supporting England, which was in the war." My father looked uneasy.

"Never mind, dad. This is not something they can do with only 50 destroyers," upon which my grandpa said: "This war is bound to come to an end soon."

I sat on the lap of my grandpa, who always seemed to be the person to restrain my father's impulsive actions and make the discussion end with only one sentence he would say. When Lizet, in her smarty manners, came with a sheet of writing in her hand, I understood that she would again start questioning such stuff as when her religious liabilities would be handed down to herself from our father and why boys had their adolescence ceremony at 13 while girls had theirs at 12. She would ask things over and over again and wouldn't be satisfied with the answers she would get, not to mention that she would take us captives to keep preaching. No sooner had I sighed with these thoughts in my mind than my sister chipped in with all her cuteness and her soothing voice to break the ice in the house:

"Do you want me to read the poem I have just written?"

When she said this, the faces looking at one another started cheering. There were two things that Lizet would keenly do at this age. One was to read the holy book and later preach to everyone at home and school about what she learned and the other was to write poems. In fact, as far as I was concerned, she could be a competent poet one day if she kept writing poems like this, but I wish! My sister, instead, had become a person who would keep reciting **shabbat prayers** under the influence of our classmate Moche in recent times. My grandpa called her out and said:

"Ok! Read it out loud." Lizet first showed the picture of three birds she drew as well as writing the names of her siblings on them and later started reading the poem she wrote with her sweet manners:

Two birds through the peephole, they landed on a bush
Days after mummy bird, she lay on three eggs
One morning three hairless chicks, their eyes were closed
Their names I gave; Rosa, Lizet and Marcos
Last morning, daddy bird threw up wheat on to his nest from grass
This morning, five birds beat wings and flew for their freedom

We all applauded and said our appreciation with some exaggeration as well. Lizet became so happy that she ran to her closet to get her poem notebook and read a few more. Dad, mum and grandpa looked behind her sighingly. My father got very emotional and he averted his gaze to hide the tears that gathered in his eyes.

"In a place which lacks freedom, these poems evoke freedom…" He was only able to say this. My grandpa completed the sentence of my father which he couldn't finish.

"They will be the leaders of a society which was once intended to be eradicated," he said.

My sister and I went to our beds without being reminded of our sleeping time approaching. We could hear the guns being fired outside. We waited in silence for a while with our lights off. Once the noise died down, I couldn't help wondering and went to look through the peephole closing one eye. It was dark outside. The dim light leaking out of the street lamps was exchanging glances with the icicles that were hanging down from the roofs like pieces of carrots turned upside down. Closing the peephole tightly, I stared at our family photos on the walnut veneered dresser. While she was putting on her pink flowered bed gown from cotton, Lizet asked:

"Why have you been blankly looking at the same photo for ten minutes?"

"I want our faces to smile forever just like us in these photos," I said.

Pulling up her dress from her legs, she came closer and looked at the photos with a smile on her face:

"Oh! We had this photo taken just when I started losing my milk teeth. Look at me! My two teeth are missing."

"You could have closed your mouth."

"How could I do that when smiling?" she said and looked at my face cutely.

"I hope we can always smile like that even if we have no teeth at all," I said and hugged my sister. I think she was aware of what was going on.

"Why does Hitler hate Jews, sister?" she asked.

I didn't know how to answer her question. I told her the story that my mother had told me years ago although I did not know if it was a true story or just a rumour.

"When Hitler was a student at the age of 15, he called out to one of his friends that he was pissed at "Dirty Jew!". In truth, that boy was a Jew, yet Hitler said this without knowing that he was a Jew. If he had known, he wouldn't have said less than that and God knows even more. The Jewish student was a clever boy who listened to classical music and was interested in philosophy. What's more, he could beat Hitler in any competition that they were involved in. Every time they came together, they would begin quarrelling. Hitler, who already hated Jews, had it in for Jews in those days and took an oath to eradicate Jews."

"So, what happened to the Jewish boy?"

"He became an important man and rescued many Jews."

"But, why are we hiding? Is Hitler going to kill us, too?"

"No way! Our father won't let such a thing happen. Don't fret."

As I was talking to my sister, Lizet, in bed, a sense of despair flooded over me. Hardly had I reached out to the pillow Lizet was holding to sleep when someone knocked at our room's door lightly. I rushed out of bed. Our room was so small that reaching forth was enough to open the door. My elder brother, Marcos, was standing in his pyjamas right before me. He couldn't take his eyes off Lizet and me for a while. It was the first time that he had looked so desperate and sad. I was puzzled. I was haunted by these bad feelings again. I was trying to find out why he must have come by examining his face carefully. He said:

"Do you mind if I sleep with you tonight?"

My astonishment was replaced by horror. I stayed where I was while Lizet was jumping on her two feet:

"Really! And does our father know about it?" she asked.

"Yes I got his permission," he said although he didn't appear happy.

My brother never mentioned what he had talked about with my dad the other night. We already heard something. Lizet came to my bed and my brother took Lizet's bed. We were constantly talking about the good old days. Jumping from his bed, he came and lay between Lizet and me. Without knowing that it was going to be the last night he spent with us, he, perhaps intuitively, wanted to enjoy every minute with our company. While we were telling each other all about our family trips as well as the mischiefs we made in the past such as my brother's stealing cookies that mum made from the basket and bringing them to us on the picnics we had all together, we remembered the swing in our garden.

"It was you who swung me the most, brother," Lizet said.

"What else would I do? You could never do it yourself."

"Yes, but why aren't we allowed to go out and play in the garden? Is the swing still where it was?"

Marcos embraced my sister so tightly… Despite all these good memories being told, I felt so sad that I wanted to cry.

Once we were told by our grandpa the following morning that we were going on a long journey, I realised how childish it was of me to feel upset about saying goodbye to these places where I spent beautiful days when compared with the real problem itself. They managed to find places only for the three of us: my sister, my mother and me. My whole world came crashing down around me. They were going to have us mingled with Romanian Jews. I wished we had gone to Istanbul over Spain years ago just as our relatives did. If nothing else, our family wouldn't have to split then.

"But dad…. I don't want to go on this journey without you, my brother and grandpa," I just said. Touching my hair with his hand, he said:

"In a week or two, we will come there, as well."

"What about our other relatives? My uncle, my aunt…."

"Your grandpa and uncle are going to France."

"But dad… Why?"

"One day at some place, all our family and relatives will come together. Don't fret," he said.

I started to cry. I couldn't stop my tears. My father was telling me not to lose my hope under any condition.

We were going to our relatives' place who, years ago, came to Istanbul from Spain. During the preparations for our journey to Istanbul, we packed the items that were worth money and easy to carry along. It was obvious that my father had been prepared long before. He had sold some of our goods in return for gold and we set out with this gold as well as the diamonds. As for me, I took this notebook, my father's birthday gift, which I would never change with my favourite clothes. It was very difficult for us to bid farewell to my father, brother, grandpa and uncle as well as to all the other beloved people we left behind. They were going to come and join us later, but I couldn't feel comfortable with this idea at all.

I have already started to miss my father, brother and my other relatives. Alas!

I can hear Rita and Lizet's voices. I think they have found my place. I don't want them to see the things I have written here.

Michon, Anna and Izak met us at the port. The port was called Haydarpasha... There were big ships. While looking around, I heard a train whistle. I don't know if it was because I had been on the sea for quite a long time or because it reminded me of the place I came from, but I wanted to cry once I heard this train whistle. All those people who disembarked from the ship hugged each other. We said goodbye to those that were going to head for Palestine and wished to see each other again. All of them were cheering but I was a bit sad that Rita and I would have to split. Their route was to go to Palestine by different ships. We took a small boat to Karakoy port, at which we took the tram to go to Michon's place. We are at home now. I was told that we would stay here for a while. Lizet is sleeping near me. How comfortable a bed is! It is as soft as cotton. And the food... It is so delicious. They are all treating us well. Lots of things have happened, but I won't be able to write them all. My eyes are closing for want of sleep.

This morning, I am fidgeting around just like birds chirping and flying off from one tree to another. I am impatiently writing here about all the good things we experienced yesterday. We have heard about our dad. He writes that both my brother and he himself were OK. He adds that they are going to depart to Istanbul in a week. All the documents and vehicles are ready. My grandpa and uncle ran away to France. MyMum wandered around the house cheerfully all day and didn't get angry forthe mischief Lizet and I did make.

While I was writing these in my diary, my- mum called out to our Jewish friend Anna:

"I will have a dress sewed from organza fabric for the girls. Do you know any tailors?" she asked.

As soon as I finished my breakfast, I got my notebook and took my place at the table by the bay window. I am looking forward to writing about Beyoglu, where we all went together yesterday. Beyoglu is such a nice place with a lot of stores. Watching the elegant women with bowler hats and the men with suits and ties as well as adorned shop windows, we walked until we got to a place called Tunel. We entered a really chic bazaar. Lizet and I stopped in front of a bookstore whose shelves were full with books with colourful covers and we started looking at them. There was everything one could imagine. All of a sudden, I saw the book of an author I know. I couldn't believe it. Yes! It was the novel 'Fire and Sword' by Henryk Sienkiewicz. I felt like I was in Poland. I called out to my mum and told her that I wanted to buy the book. She said: "We have a lot to do right now. We will buy it another day." So that we could find this place later easily, I looked at the sign board of the store and memorised its name. Koeh Brothers Bookstore. Going past Mondus Printing Press and watching the women at the Krishtish Beauty Salon having their hair done, I was called by my mother.

"Come on! Hurry up!" We entered the tailor's workplace called 'Tailor Mulieorio'. I chose one of the fashion plates that were brought from Paris. A flared dress with bindings on its round collars and sleeves. Lizet, who would never swerve from her imaginative personality, had the tailor draw a model she had conceived in her mind in a smarty manner. Subsequently, we sat at the Markiz Patisserie to have some rest. This Patisserie was formerly called Loebon. It has changed to Markiz quite recently. I was having half an eye on the chocolates, yet my mum told us to eat Markiz pastry first. After we ate it, Lizet and I drank chocolate milks as my mum and Anna were drinking wine. Before we left, we also bought a box of fruit candies. I wish my father and brother had been with us.

Today, as soon as the sun rose, Lizet and I sat on the brown velvet armchairs on the second floor of the house again. As we were waiting for the teacher who taught us Turkish, we waved at our Turkish neighbours from the window who went back and forth to the greengrocer's. Anna's serving girl who had gone to the greengrocer's came back with a bag of varied vegetables in her hands. My mum was prepared at any time as if the doorbell would be knocked at and my brother and dad would show up. Although she was not as cheerful as she used to be, it was obvious that she was still hopeful. She made zucchini pie. It is called Mujver in Istanbul. Once our lesson had finished, Lizet and I prepared peaches with almond cream, which is Marcos's favourite, but unfortunately, my brother and dad haven't turned up yet. Mum was always saying: "There must be a mishap. For sure!"

Today, we are in Florya. The weather is really nice. There is a nice house in the coppice forest. So nice. It is called Ataturk's mansion. Ataturk, about whom I have recently learned, is said to have been an important person. According to what they say, he comes here by his boat to swim in the sea with people. I got very excited when I thought that he might come here while we were here and thus I could have a chance to see an important person. Our relatives, who came here long ago, are saying very nice things about him. They say that he was a great hero. In those days, when this country was once occupied, he repelled the enemy and freed these lands. He hosted many kings and queens of different countries at this mansion. Just as I wished to find a way to look inside, Lizet and the other kids started playing dodgeball. I joined them right away. In the middle of the game, a noise of crying was heard from the adults. Mum couldn't help but cry sobbingly. We stopped playing and ran towards them. I came closer to her worriedly. An acquaintance of ours, who ran away from Poland and came to Istanbul, was saying that my brother and dad were brought to concentration camps by the SS soldiers. It seems impossible for me to withstand this. It is unbearable to imagine my father, brother and aunt being in the camps. I am now haunted by such horrible thoughts that...

Mum has been shedding tears since the day we learned that my brother and dad were in the annihilation camps. As for me, I was always dreaming about bad things in my sleep. I see the gas chambers which I have never seen in real life. The children are screaming. They are all dying. Their mums, dads and grandpas... Everyone there... Even babies. Last night, they cut my aunt's hair and pulled out her gold teeth. There are so many things that I didn't know and that I couldn't understand. My hands are trembling while writing these lines. Mum tries her chance by knocking at all the doors she knows. She is making requests from her friends like Sir Abraham, who are known to have close relationships with the government and trying to get information about my dad's and brother's conditions. She's also sent a letter to the Red Cross. She wrote that she hadn't heard about her husband and son. God knows when an answer will come, if ever.

My mum told Uncle Izak today that we needed to buy a house of our own and settle down. We were going to buy it once my father and brother came, but I think it will take time for them to come up. And mum also said: "It is about time that girls started school."

My mum has already started searching for the schools. Together with Lizet, I am going to enrol in a French school in Beyoglu which has a section for girls. Our Turkish, history and geography lessons will be taught by Turkish teachers in Turkish whereas the others will be in French. We will go and see the school on Monday. When he has come, Marcos will enrol in the boys' section of the same school, too. I am very excited. I missed going to school so much.

We moved into our new flat. It is such a lovely one. My brother and dad will like it as well when they come. It is cosy just like our house back in Poland. The rooms have their names. I am not sure, but I think its previous owners gave these names. I got the room with flowers. Our house is very close to the sea. This place is called Kuzguncuk. I asked Uncle Izak about this place' name and he told me that it is an animal's name in Turkish. He didn't know exactly why this place had got this name but he said that all the residents of this place were Jews. He said there was even a Jewish cemetery down the road. Kuzguncuk is even said to be the last stop one has to drop by before he or she has set out for the holy lands. Apart from Turks, there are Greeks and Armenians here as well. Our neighbours brought us food just on the day we moved in. Whenever Munevver bakes pastry or dessert, she sends some to us with her son as well. Climbing up the armchairs on the second floor, Lizet and

I are watching outside through the bay window. It is our greatest pleasure to wave at our neighbours going back and forth to the district bazaar and to call out to them saying "Well met Istanbul". If only Marcos were with us, too. When she puts us to sleep every night, mum is telling us that we are safe in Istanbul and we shouldn't be afraid, but I know that she is so scared, too. She is always crying. I heard her speaking to Greysi. She said a reply to her letter that she sent to the Red Cross seven months ago arrived. It writes that there is no information as to where they are. We even don't know in which camp they are, but mum says they must be in Auschwitz-Birkenau camps, which are the camps the majority of Jews are taken to.

"Germans are said to be killing all the Jews there. I won't feel relieved until after I hear that they are safe and sound," mum says and cries hiding from us in the corners of the flat. She is wasting away. She says she can't eat anything without her husband and son. Oh Lord, I'm begging! Put an end to this war.

What's happening? Everyone is so agitated. Mum is burning all the letters and papers she received by the pool in the garden while I am sitting under the sour cherry tree and keep writing. Although most of our Jewish friends said that they could not kill us here, we were told that we had to go to the shelters in Balat. We, as well as all other families like us, entrusted their valuable belongings to our Turkish neighbours. Mum is coming towards me worriedly. "Give me that notebook right now." She wants to burn it... Why does she want to burn a notebook with only childish memories in it?

When Aysegul came home with a crying face and red eyes, her parents became worried. Their only child, soon to be 40 years old, has not been able to start her family with the man she loves. In fact, what upsets them was not that she couldn't get married yet, but that she was not happy. At least, it was obvious that she was troubled that night. However much they wanted to sit and have a heart-to-heart talk with her, she locked herself in her room telling them that there was nothing to worry about. Lying on her bed, Aysegul reopened the notebook, some of which she had read at Cem's house, and found where she had left off.

Dear Cem Michel!... My only child,

By the time I was given this notebook as a gift by my father, I was 10 years old just as you are now. His wish that these pages would be filled with happy memories did not unfortunately come true. As you must have understood from what you have read so far, I started writing in an environment that is full of sorrow and sufferings. When I start writing again many, many years later, I am no different from how I was before. It seems that these lines, which were in Hebrew at first and in French later on, will continue in Turkish.

You have just asked why the edges of this notebook were burned. You will get it when you read it. These pages are the remaining ashes of a flaming genocide. You might be wondering "but, why did my mum wait for many years to start writing again?" The only lie I told my mother and the only secret I hid from her during my whole life was the existence of this notebook. When she attempted to destroy it on those days, I saved it from burning and hid it behind the broken closet in the attic. Then, I put it away in the chest together with my father's writings and tried to forget about it. I felt as if I could forget about the genocide, all the pains and the atrocity we had to face up to. Until today, the day when I learned that I have fallen into the clutches of a deadly disease... This notebook had become a shelter in my childhood and I hope for you it will become a torchlight.

I wrote what the conditions were like when we came to Istanbul and how my mother grabbed my notebook to burn it on the day we went to the shelter in Balat. It was my only personal belonging those days and I couldn't have let it be burned. Barely had she ignited the notebook when Lizet called out to her. She went away from there leaving the notebook, not having flamed yet, on the burned documents by the pool. Immediately, I got the water in the copper pannikin and spilled it on the notebook to save it from burning right away. It seems that I somehow knew that no harm would be given to us in this city, Istanbul, which I had been welcomed. A couple of days later, we learned that the Turkish government would let no Jews be killed.

Each passing day, the number of our Jewish friends in Istanbul was increasing. We were arranging picnics and trying to have a nice time with our relatives who were sharing the same destiny with us. We also had many Turkish friends, but

66

I don't know why, my mother's side wanted to remain aloof from them. I found it a bit odd that our Turkish neighbours were telling us about what had happened in their homes. We would never tell anyone about the things that happened within the family. My mother would listen to our neighbours' life stories, their problems or happiness, yet would not say a word about what we had been through. I think she still did not feel secure enough to trust the people around her.

Finally, the day came and we reunited with my father. I can't forget the day we met him and the moment I saw him. His cheeks were sunken and he had become quite weak. However, he must have been delighted by the fact that he reunited with us. But in truth, he was not. We felt a bit strange, too. The half-smile on my father's face was signalling that there was something that would cloud our happiness. He was not with Marcos. We were looking at my father with anxious eyes.

He first told us how he rescued my brother and aunt from the concentration camp.

We exclaimed: "Really! Really!" and felt proud of my father's valour, but towards the end of his speech, the fact that his expression had changed and an apprehensive look had fallen upon his eyes, as well as the perturbation my mum had, caught our attention. My father was saying that all the arrangements were made for my aunt and brother, and that a car would pick them up in Romania and bring them here across Bulgaria.

"Marcos will be here, too," he said. Although he was telling us not to worry, the uneasiness of my father led the wound I had been familiar with to bleed inside me. I was trying to chase off the negative thoughts from my mind. I did not even think that something awful might happen to him and I was always looking forward to the day we would meet Marcos.

According to our calculations, my brother was supposed to arrive in Istanbul the following day. One day before he was expected to arrive, a feeling of excitement had surrounded the house. Assuming that his clothes might have become smaller, my mother bought him two turtleneck jumpers, pyjamas and underwear as well as a pair of trousers. A wide range of meals including, Morcos' favourite food, our 'prasipuchi'- the pastry with leek is its name here - were made for the following day. One day had passed, but Marcos was nowhere. He didn't turn up. Days turned into weeks, but we still hadn't heard from my brother. I started to doubt that my father was hiding something from us.

My father, who played the glad game when he was with us, was sipping his coffee under the vine trellis with a sad expression. I ran there and sat in front of him. I asked him to tell me about the concentration camps. I was wondering what sort of a place my brother was in and what he was doing. I felt that he avoided answering every question I asked. I told him that I knew he was doing so in order not to upset me. He had told us how he rescued my brother and aunt from the concentration camps, but he didn't say the reason why he had to leave them behind on his way to Istanbul. I wanted to learn everything. He gave in to my insistence and mentioned that there were some writings:

"One day, I will give them to you and then you will know everything. You are just too young to shoulder such a big emotional burden," he said.

A couple of weeks later, we got the bad news about my brother Marcos. I was just 10 years old then and my hands were trembling while writing some of the lines. They are trembling now again. I think it is my ill fate that took my loved ones away and turned my life into a nightmare.

My dear son, My dear Cem Michel...

My mother gave me my father's writings in Hebrew long after his death after I had become a young girl, now conscious enough to understand the things that had occurred. Translating these writings of his into Turkish, word for word, just as they came out of his pen, I will write here how my father was able to escape from the concentration camps and come to Istanbul.

My father's writings:

There is no time... I am writing what we have been through. It was 1941. Two years ago, Poland was invaded by Germans and it surrendered to the enemy forces. Poland, whose borders changed too often, was shared by Germans and the Soviets.

First, France and England declared war on Germany, yet German armies were able to defeat France and repelled the English out of Europe. Nazis were arresting the Jews in every country they invaded and sending them to the camps.

A cold wind was blowing in the shelter of our two-story stone house in Poland, which was surrounded by apple and sour cherry trees that were left here and there. We hadn't been blacklisted and wanted yet, but we were alert. We had set up a shelter in our house just in case and slept there at night. We were deprived of our fundamental rights and dismissed from senior jobs. It had been two years since I had to quit my job as a doctor. The war, in which civilians died as well as soldiers, did not seem to come to an end soon. Jews, who were confined to living in Ghettos, were starving to death and dying from the cold and epidemics. Most of our relatives were blacklisted and summoned. The prisoners were held in Gross-Rosen and Sobibor, which were the concentration camps notorious for its atrocious persecutions in its quarries. It had become a worrying word of mouth among Nazi opponents that those people taken to Auschitwz[8], which was the worst camp of all, were never heard from again and that any kind of experiment could be carried out on these people. And we were the next to be sent to those death camps. I had no choice but to escape from these lands to save my family from that ring of fire, but nevertheless it was not going to be easy.

A friend of mine, who would go to Istanbul across Romania, told me that he could illicitly sneak two or three people on the ship. He promised to do this in return for a great amount

---

8 **Auschwitz Camp:** The largest concentration, forced labor and extermination camp established by the Nazis during the Second World War.

of money. I got my wife and daughters to embark on this ship. One and half a month after I sent them off, my sister and I as well as my son, who was still in his teenage years, swarmed into another ship that would take us to Istanbul as well. No sooner had we embarked on the ship than we were disillusioned by the fact that we got reported. As we were waiting for the ship to depart soon, we saw Nazi officers rushing in. Hundreds of Jews with their new clothes and one or two pieces of mementoes were stuffed into the carriages and were taken to a camp, which was, as far as I could guess, quite far away from the city. On the gate, it wrote "Arbeit macht frei." That translates as "Work sets you free." First we were questioned as to whom we did get help from and where we had been heading to. Then, our photos were taken and we were thus registered.

That day, the unmellow voice of SS officers ordering us to get undressed was blending with the dog howls outside and the outcries of the Jews screaming here and there were echoing in the deep silence of the night like a roaring waterfall.

On the basement floor of the concentration camp, all of us, men and women, started to take our clothes off with the SS officers kicking and whipping us. The elderly and children were set apart. I took my clothes off as calmly and slowly as possible. Meanwhile, I was thinking whether I could find a way to take my son, if possible, everyone, out of here. Then, I remembered my friend, Angel.

Whilst everyone standing naked was covering their private parts, I was watching my son, Marcos, from far away. He was shivering as he was scared, but more than that, because he was embarrassed. Once we caught each other's eyes a couple of times, I made him understand that there was hope for escape. I think it made him feel good to see that the tree branch he had been leaning his back on was not yet bent over, but on the contrary that it still stood upright. The fearing and embarrassing expression on my son's face fuelled the fire in my mind.

After we were numbered in the courtyard, Nazis who distributed the camp clothes we had to put on left the guardians to attend us. I looked around and tried to understand where I was while being spurred on as if we were a herd of animals and led to our wards by the guardians. The officers on duty were mocking us and telling each other that the following day would be tough on us. They first said that the prisoners would be branded according to their guilt and that all the female prisoners would be sent to Germany after their hair was shaved off. My sister's hair that she didn't have the heart to have it cut was swimming before my eyes. I was hurt so badly in my heart. I had made up my mind to fight off. I was going to either die or rescue them, being a useful man. The camp clothes that I was asked to put on were in my hands like everyone else. Before we arrived at the place where our chambers were, I realised that the stores of food brought in huge sacks and the chests coming along with the last group of Jewish prisoners had piled up at random places in the aisle. I quickly checked the guards who had been absorbed in chatting with each other and by making use of their inattentiveness, I crawled under the prisoners' legs going past

72

the aisle quietly and hid myself first behind and then inside a chest which would be loaded with food. I was very lucky until then. Although I felt quite sorry about it, it was to my advantage that there were more prisoners than there were guards.

While the food chests were being taken by the prisoners to a place I had no idea about, - probably to the food storage of the camp -, I realised from their loud talks that my son Marcos, who saw me hide in the chest, and my sister Rebeka, who must have learned what I did from him, were holding my chest to carry it along. Hesitating to breathe, I felt that all my body had stiffened inside the chest. Then, I heard that one officer kicked Rebeka and made her handle a sack. I couldn't see what was going on and I could just understand from the ongoing talks that I was being carried into the food storage. I heard another Jewish man lifting my chest whisper that this chest was far too heavy, upon which Marcos offered loudly that he could handle the heavier part himself. I waited inside with a fear that an officer would come and check the chest. Finally, all the chests including the one I was inside, were being carried into the storage.

I couldn't hear any soundin the storage room, yet I was not supposed to hurry and had to wait till everyone had slept. The hardest part would be after that. No sooner had I managed to open out the chest using my head and hands than I heard some footsteps approaching and closed it back. The noise became even louder and closer. I felt many people come inside and held my breath waiting to see what would happen. From their talking, I understood that they were a few Jewish prisoners as well as Nazi officers near them. Some of the food was going to be transported somewhere else, but I couldn't hear where exactly. Those prisoners to carry the food chests were not the ones who had brought them here with my son. I thought because of the safety concerns or because the others were tired, they brought another group of prisoners to get the chests carried. As far as I could guess, the empty chests were being opened and filled with the food that was to be transported to another place. While I was thinking that I, most probably, was going to be headshot, when the chest that I was hiding in was opened. As soon as the Jewish prisoner, whose cheeks were sunken, saw me, his eyes were out on stalks. We caught each other's eyes. He took a bag of rice and put it onto me and closed the chest immediately. I heaved a sigh of relief and listened to the chest being tied with a rope. After a while, the chest that I was in was carried somewhere else along with the other chests. This journey, which lasted about one and half an hour, was probably made in a carriage through places I had no idea about. I did not know where the food and the chest that I was in were travelling to. When everyone else had gone, the only thing I could hear was my own breath. I slowly pushed the upper part of the chest with my head. Everywhere was in complete darkness. I could not see anything. I planned to come out of the chest and look around. I saw a spindly beam of dim light that fell and spread upon the floorboard like an egg yolk. I looked up. This light was leaking from the ceiling. Through that opening in the ceiling that led to the street, I got out of there, closed the opening back and started running naked with the fear of the gunshots that were heard all along the street. Seeing that a troop of soldiers were marching there and shooting their guns randomly, I slowly crouched down under the eaves of a school and waited for them to leave. It made me feel so terribly sad to see an old couple and a Jewish youth be raked with gunfire that I even forgot the fear that I might also be caught and share the same destiny at any time. Shivering under the eaves of the school, I took the old man's clothes off and put them on me although I felt ashamed for doing that.

In the cold of morning, I ran out of the city like a bat out of hell. I tripped and fell over on to the bottom of the walls a couple of times.

It seemed like a miracle for me to arrive at Anjel's house within two or three hour's distance. He was my friend from high school who lived near the Oder River. Jewish though he was, he had some contacts among the German officers who were not supporters of Nazi regime, possibly because he was an artist. I went on running, hoping that he might be of some help to rescue my son and sister using these contacts of his.

The soles of my feet were drenched in blood. I was completely exhausted. I saw stone bricked walls of Anjel's palatial house from far away just when I thought I was about to freeze. Taking a deep breath out of relief, I said to myself: "This job is done!"

I came closer to the apple orchards located on the slope

below the chateau at the end of the coppice forest road that fell to the west of the creek illuminated by the Sun, which repeatedly showed itself and soon disappeared. With a vigorous explosion, I was pushed towards the rubble that was once the wall of the garden. Anjel's small chateau had been bombarded. It was a matter of time that I was caught and shot by the SS officers. Where I was had turned into hell. I had barely run out of energy in my struggle not to be captured when SS officers got into military vehicles and headed to the north. Then, it became heavily silent all around. For a moment, I thought that all my hope had died away with the house having been bombarded. Trying to be back on my two feet, I checked around with my eyes. The small cottages remained untouched in the garden that was surrounded by a stonewall. It was obvious that hiding in these cottages standing out like a sore thumb wouldn't be safe. By the effect of the bombardment, the trees, whose branches had recently been pruned, were darkened and the basins of two fountains placed side by side had broken off. Given that I had no other choice but to hide in the devoured house and think about what to do, I walked there through the rubbles of the veranda with a pergola that was all along green two hours ago. I looked around. Everywhere was filled with smokescreen and gunpowder smell burning my nasal cavity.

I thought I heard a moaning from the bathroom side of the rubble. As I was going towards the place where the tiles broke into pieces and brought about a small hill, I tripped over something and I soon looked down to see that it was my friend

Anjel lying in dead silence. I checked if he was still alive or not. Anjel's heart, which was thumping violently each previous day out of fear of being caught at any time, had stopped beating. There was nothing to do for him anymore. Patting him on the back, I ripped off a piece of cloth from my trousers to wipe the fresh blood leak that smeared his brown hair falling under his thin neck. I closed his eyelids to cover his blue eyes pointing at the sky. I walked towards the moaning.

A German officer was severely injured and lying unconscious. He must have hidden here to make love. I bent over to examine his wounds. The bullet in his hip posed no life threatening risk, yet he could still die unless the one in his chest wasn't taken out. After a while, he came to himself and started giving me orders, though with difficulty in moving his lips, to remind me of the fact that he was Hitler's officer rather than a man who was severely injured:

"Call for help! Right now!" he shouted.

"Why should I do that? To give you the opportunity to kill me as well as other Jews?" I asked. He looked at me for a while. Having understood that his threats would be of no use, he took steps back:

"Help me!"

"How did you get shot by your own soldiers?" I asked.

"They didn't see that I was hiding in the bathroom. I got injured during the bombardment. They let off a volley of machine gunfire to see if there was anyone else in the house."

"Why didn't you call out for help?"

"I think I was unconscious in the closet. When I came round, there was no one around here."

He could hardly speak while his head tilted down. He asked me to take him to the main road, as having trouble keeping his eyes open. He ensured my safety. He kept telling me that he would not turn me in on condition that I took him to the main road. I desperately wanted to strangle him there let alone help save his life. If I was to spare the life of this officer, he should in return assure me that he would save not only my life but my sister's and son's as well.

"I am a heart surgeon. I can operate on you here and save your life, or I can simply stay and watch you die from losing blood," I said.

The officer could only nod approvingly out of despair. I understood that I could make him do whatever I wanted.

"In return for this surgery, I will have some conditions as well," I said.

I missed my wife and daughters, whom I had sent to Istanbul. I thought a new sparkle of hope was born for me to rescue my son and sister from the camp and take them to Istanbul.

"If you promise to enable me to go to Istanbul with my son, I will operate on you," I said, being certain that the officer would readily accept the offer.

Repeatedly losing and winning back his consciousness, the officer was striving to keep his eyes open for dear life. He took a breath with difficulty. Probably because of his psychological condition at that moment, he couldn't conceal the ironic smile on his lips.

"For the sake of my survival, I would set free a hundred Jews let alone only two," he said, upon which I realised that I should have done a bigger bargain. But instead I only said:

"Deal. Any wrongdoing will cost you your life. We have got nothing else to lose any more, but you…"

"Ok! Ok!" the officer interrupted me in a decisive manner. He took a piece of paper from his pocket and wrote the address of the hospital where I could get the tools for surgery and the person's name I should see. He also added that I could wear his clothes temporarily and that he would solve the clothing problem later.

Once I put on the officer's clothes, I saw that the back side of the trousers on the hip pocket had been torn apart. I pull the jacket down to cover it up. I could cover the holes using the jacket, but I had no choice but to stay still without moving even my finger. What's more, the blood stain on it was big enough to draw attention. It was not safe for me to get around in this way. Besides, the injured officer was very likely to be spotted by the time I came back. I turned to the officer to say:

"Even if we find the tools and the medicine, I cannot operate on you under these conditions. We should transfer to another house where you think we will be safe. There should be no one apart from us in that house," I said.

I saw the injured officer's eyes shined half open as if he really wanted me to take him away from there, but was not brave enough to speak out his wish freely.

"Really? Take me away from here," he said and wrote an address of an empty house which seemed to be in the vicinity of Anjel's old mansion that had turned into a ruin. He said that it was his friend's house who had gone to Berlin for a month.

I hid myself somewhere and stood sentry to watch the house. Three hours later, I carried the officer to this house. Any kind of comfort was available there. I carried out the first aid using the materials I found in the first aid cupboard. To be able to blood-type the officer, I took two drops of blood from his finger. There were no visitors to the house, but I still stood watch for days on a small and narrow aisle that led to the fire-wood chimney in the attic. I cut off all the electric and water supplies as well as the telephone line. I had to hurry and make use of the situation to be able to rescue my son. I put on one of the officer uniforms that was neat and ironed. Reaching out for the paper stating that I was a true SS officer, I said to the injured officer:

"You will stay alive to slaughter thousands of Jews." I spat out the emotions that had been bugging me inside. The officer attempted to speak, but his eyes closed. Now that I had found a way to go to Istanbul, I wasn't supposed to let him die and I had to treat him. The sun was on the horizon to set when I took the man's identity card and went out with the German uniform on me which stood in stark contrast to the spirits and wish in my heart to get to meet my family soon.

Whilst waiting for the surgery instruments such as ether, blood, scalpel, syringe, gauze, scissors, IV bag, gloves as well as the medicine like antibiotics and painkillers in the hospital room, the news bulletin on the radio caught my attention. It was announced that the Wannsee Protocol would be implemented. Having heard it, I was shocked. With this convention having been signed in Berlin on 20 January 1942, the mass murdering of ten thousand Jews became officialised. According to the list made, fifty-five thousand Jews were living in Turkey. I heard two officers standing near me joyfully whisper to each other to say that all the Jews in Europe would utterly be put to death and their bloodstream would come to an end at last.

After I got the instruments, I proceeded on my way without responding to a few officers' saluting me respectfully as I was passing by.

I arrived at home to find the injured officer sleeping just as I had left him. I searched the entire house trying to acquire information about the officer who would return from Berlin one month later. The noise I had made awoke the officer.

Once I told him about the news I had heard on the radio, he did not seem to be surprised at all. It was because he was one of the intelligence officers who were appointed to go to Turkey and exterminate fifty-five Jews living there.

I was in a dilemma whether I should kill or save this officer who happened to be a Jew killer. Upon the latest news, the condition on which I was going to save his life had also changed. I had the opportunity to kill two birds with one stone. I thought he should spare the lives of fifty-five Jews in return for this surgery rather than only my son's and other relatives'. With his identity card, I was going to be among the officers who would be sent to Turkey. My son, sister and other relatives were going to be released from the camp.

I got down to carrying out the plan in no time. As soon as I put the officer out and cut him open, I saw the bullet sunk into the pericardium. I thought that the officer would not be alive if the bullet had gone two millimetres further. Perhaps, God had always been with me to rescue my sister, son and my family in Istanbul. However, it was quite a risky operation. Under these circumstances and with the instruments I had, it was going to be a miracle for this surgery to run smoothly. I decided that leaving the bullet there that had sunk into the officer's pericardium would be a better idea than taking it out and that he could maintain his life with this bullet. Therefore, I didn't take it out. I injected antibiotics and painkillers in his hip. This medicine was to alleviate the officer's pain and let him rest. I waited for the anaesthetics to wear off. I just stopped the haemorrhage and sutured the cut I made. I resolved to take out the bullet in his right hip later as it posed no life threatening danger. First, all the paperwork had to be done for my conditions to be met.

The injured officer opened his eyes eight hours later. It was apparent that he was relieved. I told him that I had taken out the bullet in his chest and the one in his hip could cause paralysis if left untreated. The officer who was fond of his life seemed to believe the lie I had told. I demanded that all the paperwork and the necessary protocols be done for the release of my son and relatives from the camp before the second surgery. On the paper I prepared, I wrote that he was on duty and gathering intelligence on an officer's headquarters, the exact location of which he could not reveal due to security concerns and that he needed to interrogate two Jews, namely a Jewish boy, whose father had broken out of the camp and whose mother and sisters had escaped to Turkey across Romania, as well as his aunt who was still with him at the camp. These two Jews were my son and sister. "I am sending one of my trusted officers with my identity to collect them. I command that these two Jews whose names are written on the paper be sent to me in the custody of the officer," I added. He put his signature under it. Additionally, I mended the phone cables and made him speak to the camp officials and say the things I had written on another paper. The next thing to do was to arrange my own documents. However, it was going to be rather a dangerous and serious thing to be among the team that would be assigned for the mission in Turkey. I was being extremely careful for my plan to run smoothly and I was paying particular attention so as not to miss any detail. I constantly asked the officer questions as to the strategy to be followed.

"Yes… According to the intelligence you received from the officers in Istanbul, not you but one of your trusted officers will be the team leader using your identity on your behalf. I suppose you got it right, didn't you?"

Smirking at me through his yellowish teeth, the officer gave me the once-over:

"They will figure out in two days that you are a Jew," he said.

In fact, he was the one who had told me that I physically resembled Germans and I was the one who opposed it. He knew that I could speak German and French like my mother tongue. What he wanted was to discourage me.

"Let it be my own concern… Besides, neither you nor Hitler look like a true German… Yes… Now, I will go to Turkey and work for the eradication of Jews. How does it sound? Good?"

In line with the agreement we had, he was supposed to send another trusted officer with his identity as the team leader. From then on, I was a trusted intelligence officer who he had appointed to go to Turkey on his behalf.

He enabled me to see the contact officer that would provide me with the documents I needed. He was doing everything exactly as I said. While taking out the bullet in his hip, I knew that it lay in my power to confine him to the bed he was lying on. As I sutured the skin on his calf that was ripped due to the tile pieces, every stitch I made urged me to reconsider if I should kill him or save his life. I no longer needed him. I had made him do everything I wanted. I looked at him in the face. He was so innocently sleeping… In case of any predicament, I arrived at the decision that he should remain alive for a bit longer.

Once the officer's pain was eased, the last thing to do was to talk about the details of a journey that can be considered dangerous and finally to kill him. Looking at the officer who fulfilled all the things I asked him to without causing any trouble, I said:

"You don't think that I will leave you here alive, do you?"

It was clear that he had considered this possibility. Still, he talked quite confidently.

"You would not kill someone you saved. You are a good doctor."

"You are wrong. I may have second thoughts any time."

"I kept my promise. I gave you a chance to prevent the mass murder of fifty-five thousand Jews."

"You are a cowardly officer. You are fond of your comfort. For your life..."

Looking me in the eye in a rather serious and decisive manner, he broke in without letting me finish.

"If you really want it, go ahead and kill me. I don't care. But do not forget one thing. When it was decreed that all the Jews in Europe must be slaughtered, I came here to talk to Anjel to use my authority in favour of Jews. I was supposed to be in Turkey now for the annihilation of the Jews there... Why am I here? I don't want people to die any more. I want this war to come to an end."

"How on earth do you think I will believe that?"

"If Anjel was alive, he would tell you how much I tried to avoid doing it."

"Now that he is not, it is difficult for you to prove it."

"Why? For what reason do you still think that I refused to go to Turkey?"

"It is not that easy. Most European countries wouldn't let it happen."

"Is there any country left that can challenge us?"

"You're wrong… It is a matter of a moment for the allies to take control of the power."

As a matter of fact, I felt that the officer was fed up with the war, too. He no longer wanted to see corpses. The conservation between us went on and on reaching a level that could be considered emotional. I remembered that I had taken measures considering that he would set me up in this empty house first and later saw that all these worries of mine were actually baseless. I presumed that he could be an anti-nazist officer. I thought it over in my mind that, whether accidentally or not, he had been shot by his own friends and I considered what he told me as well as all the effort he put into collecting the documents I needed… I was in a big dilemma whether I should kill the officer or not. No matter what the conditions were, he was right that a doctor cannot kill his patient.

Finally, I carried the officer and laid him on the mattress on the aisle near the bathroom, tying his hands and feet tightly. I adjusted the rope long enough for him to reach the toilet, binding his feet on the water pipe. I brought and put some food and water in the middle. I thought he was relieved by the fact that I did not kill him. He breathed a sigh of relief:

"I can't run off with these feet being tied. Don't worry! Undo my hands," he said.

"You can eat and drink with your face downwards. Not difficult. Look! Like that," I said and lay on the floor to drink a sip of water from the bowl that was wide enough.

Telling him that I would send a telegram and inform the authorities about your situation after I freed those in the camp and finished my job in Istanbul.

There was an irony in the way the man looked, yet I couldn't figure it out at that moment.

Dressed in SS officer uniform, I set out with my identification and all other documents. Thanks to my uniform and identity, I was respected, let alone being suspected. In the area he mentioned, there was a military vehicle waiting.

Marcos and Rebeka were in the car. Once I saw them, my heart started beating even faster. Although I was almost sure that they would pretend not to know me because of the uniform on me, I still feared that Marcos might call me "Dad!" If so, my plan would fall through and they would rake us all with gunfire.

"Show me those bastard Jews!" I shouted loudly enough for my son and sister to hear my voice. As two officers were taking them out of the car, I ragingly took two or three steps forward and held their arms, plonking them down. My son must have been hurt so badly by the stone ground they fell on that he was writhing in pain and holding his waist with his hand. I pulled my gun and kicked my son and sister who had fallen on their back. Hard as it was, I had to do it. I understood from the smile on my son's face at that very moment that he would certainly not call me 'Dad'.

"Get these bastards in my car." I pointed at my own vehicle.

Everything was prepared for Marcos and Rebeka to go to

Istanbul over Romania. However, the ship was going to depart in one week. I entrusted my son and sister to another Jewish passenger's home who was going to Istanbul by this ship, as well. I was worried. I had to bid a quick farewell and go back to my job. Marcos was looking forward to seeing his mum and sisters. After seeing my son so happy, I thought I wouldn't mind dying. Rebeka kept telling me that my situation was even riskier than theirs and trying to dissuade me from this dangerous journey, whose consequences did not seem to be predictable at all.

My sister was begging me to join them, yet I had made my decision. I was supposed to put my plans into practice. Considering that I had caught such an opportunity, I had to use it and keep German officials busy until I could inform Turkish officials that they were planning to slaughter fifty-five thousand Jews. I said goodbye to my son and sister, hoping to see them in Istanbul again.

Dear Cem Michel, the yellowish stains on these pages are your mother's tears that dried up. I couldn't prevent these pages from getting wet while transferring my father's writings into this diary. I am trying to remember the events with all the details that happened later on, and quite interestingly, although I have avoided thinking about them for years, those days revive in my mind easily as if they had happened yesterday.

Is it because I will die soon or perhaps because they were engraved in my memory as deep as to remain there forever when I was still a small kid at the age of 10?

In those days, when my father had been planning to come to Turkey, there was an unrest among Jews. As we were living peacefully in this country, we heard from the horse's mouth that German officers led by one of the chief SS officers called Officer Otto Schenbrener were going to come to Istanbul. The decree on the mass murder of all the Jews in Europe had been spreading by word of mouth to everyone in Istanbul, causing all the Jews to worry. And death knocked at our door as well. Our family started to feel the fresh smell of death around us when the Winter Family, with whom my mother had recently been acquainted, was never heard from again after they checked out from Hotel Pera Palace. Shortly after, we heard that the Winter Family was murdered in Istanbul. We felt wretched. I found out years later that a gas chamber had been built in the premises of German Embassy in Tarabya and some documents came out proving that the Winter Family was burned in this chamber and their ashes were scattered over the Bosphorus; that German Ambassador Von Papen was held responsible for this issue and put on Nuremberg Trials in 1945, but was released on lack of evidence.

It was going to be too late for my father, who was coming to Turkey as a spy to hinder the slaughter at the risk of his life with the intelligence officers who were to slaughter Jews in gas chambers, to figure out how bad a decision it was to leave the injured officer alive. As my father was carrying out his confidential job, the owner of the house where he had left the injured officer, returned home from Berlin and learned everything four days after my dad had left. However, the officer said that he would return one month later. My father, who spent two weeks with the officer there, thought that the other two weeks would be enough to put his plan into his practice. Yet, the fact that the house owner returned earlier spoiled everything.

Being alert to the arrival of the telegram informing the German Consulate about the truths as well as some suspicious eyes on him, my father heard the bad news soon and left the premises in no time before the officials read the telegram on the excuse that he could find a map showing where the Jewish shelters were. We rejoiced at the news that my father was alive, trying to reach us.

A silence of death wrapped itself around every corner of our house when we learned that the injured SS officer, whom my father left in the house in Poland, was rescued and the same officer sent a telegram to the German Consulate in Istanbul reporting that my father was a spy. We had been too naive to hope that the officer would keep his promise in return for his life being saved. The officer lost no time at all to go to the camp my father had escaped from, reported to the officials that his sister and son were also released on his permission, which he was compelled to give and told them everything else that had happened. After months of mourning and crying, we learned that my brother and aunt as well as other Jews watching the clock for being rescued had been caught on the Romanian border.

Dear Cem Michel, we found Joseph in France years later,

who was one of those people who managed to escape from the camp my father had escaped from. We asked him about what the Jews had been through in those camps and what the last days of my brother and aunt were like there. Joseph was not eager to talk about it. It was obvious that he did not want to upset us. Upon my mother's insistence, he agreed to tell us about those days without mentioning the soul-shattering details in order not to upset us.

* * *

The things Joseph told...

At first, it puzzled us that Michel was able to escape from the camp and that Marcos and Rebeka were taken out as well although they were both returned. Having seen Michel escape from the camp, we were talking among ourselves about the fact that there could be a way to break out of there. Soon, we were convinced that it was improbable for us to do that. After it was understood that Michel escaped using food chests, there were more officers on duty watching us than there were Jewish prisoners. Spreading over a large area, the camp was enclosed with electric fences with a high voltage. The condition we were in was not even good enough for us to wonder how Michel managed to escape or if Marcos and Rebeka were still alive or not. At the factories we were carried from camps to, we had to work under appalling conditions for 12 hours. Before they could make it to the camp after work, some of our friends had been dying one after another due to fatigue, hunger or beating.

We, who had not yet died, but were soon to die, would swing up the bodies of our friends and take them to the camp by the orders of Nazis. At the main entrance, we were counted with and without a brass band.

Those Jews who fell so sick and thus were unable to continue working were sent to underground rooms. We would never see them again. Whoever was asked to take clothes off knew that he or she was not going to take a shower, but be killed. As far as I found out later, there were shower heads on the ceiling of these rooms. As you can guess, these heads were not connected to the water pipes. Upon locking the Jews in the underground rooms and closing the doors tightly, Nazis would start the poisonous gas flow through the holes in the ceilings, wait for them to die in 20 minutes, take away the gold tooth, ring, earring as well as other jewelleries and carry the bodies to the basement.

We also learned that the ashes of these people whom they had burned in the basement were buried in the banks of rivers and in river beds as a fertiliser.

The number of the Jews brought to the camp had increased so much that they had to waive taking photos of the prisoners for registration and started to tattoo the number on the bodies of the newcomers. Besides, we all carried straps on the camp clothes in the shape of stars or triangles depending on the conviction.

The camp doctors cut off some limbs of our Jewish friends who had a genetic disorder or discrepancies to conduct experiments on them. They tried experimental drugs on these people, causing many Jews to die. Those who were exposed to these and somehow managed to survive had lost some of their limbs and become crippled.

That day, lots of military jeeps and tanks came one after another to the front of the door during the roll call. After being counted, we were sent to our rooms right away. Our rooms were pretty narrow and two people had to share every single bunk, which was not big enough for even one person. There was something fishy going on outside, but we couldn't figure out what. I had leaned over a friend of mine who was about to die from starvation. I was whispering to him that the war would come to an end soon and he was supposed to hold out. All of a sudden, a pair of polished boots banged under my very nose. As I raised my head to turn my eyes at the officer's eyes, and in my eyes there was not even a bit of fear of death any longer. With gastly eyes, we all looked at the SS officer coming inside. The officer was circling me just like a small planet circling the Sun. He stopped abruptly:

"Bring him!" he ordered.

They dropped Marcos in the middle of the room as if he were a sack of wood.

The following morning, Marcos and Rebeka were brought to the wall of death as well as the other Jews who had been caught on the ship. Their offence was unforgivable. Even those who worked slowly at this camp were brought to the wall of death. They had attempted to flee. It was obvious that they would face the consequences. All their screaming was audible even to us, who were getting ready to start working. Marcos, Rebeka and the others were shot and murdered.

* * *

The diary had been wet with the tears dripping down from Aysegul's cheeks. It was apparent that she could not keep reading until she got over the uneasiness that had come along with knowing all these. She put the notebook in the drawer and went off to take off her clothes.

Aysegul was sitting with her best friend Cemil at a cafe in the vicinity of Sile Feneri. While waiting for Cem Michel, who left the table to pay the check, they were both lost in absolute silence. Aysegul's mind was again haunted by the thought of Melek. The woman, for whom Cemil was risking his life on this journey, was not sitting with them at the table. Her friend was in fact content with his life. He would attach a big importance to his friends and the concept of friendship and would never turn his back on his roots, yet he was about to set out for a journey to London to get married to the woman he was in love with. It was not certain that he could arrive in London alive, but nevertheless Melek did not see it necessary to see him off. Aysegul thought that she would have definitely been there if she truly loved him. It would be of no use to say this to her friend, who had started thinking that he was in love with this girl without having touched the hand of another girl only after she showed him a bit of warmth and affection. After all, it was too late for everything. His best friend was due to leave them soon. Fortunately, she had put everything off for this weekend to be able to be with her friend here and had not left him alone. While other passengers to set out for this journey waited in the tents for the crime ship to arrive, Cemil had been staying here at a hotel with a nice view upon Aysegul's insistence. Three friends spent all the weekend together and took a stroll down memory lane, but the time for parting had come. They hugged tightly and bid farewell to each other.

Aysegul followed Cemil with her eyes until he disappeared in the crowd. He was waving goodbye back to his friends once in a few steps while walking along with other passengers towards the readily anchored boats that would take them to the ship ahead. She turned her face towards her lover who had wrapped his arm tightly around her shoulder, which made her feel stronger. This farewell had touched Cem Michel as well. He looked at the crowd of poor people coming out of the hidden places of the sea and running towards the boats. He recalled the ship his mother and Aunt Lizet as well as hundreds of other Jews had to embark on. Whatever their motives are, it must be so painful for them to be forced to live away from their homeland. Cem Michel:

"I hope we will meet again on the lands where we were born and brought up," he sighed and pulled Aysegul towards himself.

"Come on... Let's go without drawing any more attention," he said and they walked together to the hotel a few blocks away.

Aysegul and Cem Michel sat on the wooden couches at the hotel's balcony watching the illegal passengers be taken to the crime ship in the vicinity of Sile Feneri as if they were on a moonshine trip. These people who barely had any chance to return to their countries reminded the young lady of the diary of Cem Michel's mother. The reddish, orange and yellow light beams that the Sun left behind where it was vanishing were striking across the sea surface. Aysegul's eyes were on the mottled sea and her mind on the diary with burned edges which she could not dare to read although she really wanted to. Thinking what sorrows were left to read, she turned her gaze on the area around Sile Feneri. A ship in the distance was still waiting where it was as if hiding itself in the open sea and shivering out of fear. Upon watching the little boats sailing towards the ship for a while, Cem Michel went inside to take a shower. Aysegul remained seated at the veranda until after the ship departed and went out of sight. "They departed from Sile without any trouble. I hope they can realise their dreams with no trouble at all," she murmured and went to their room.

Cem Michel lay on the bed and fell asleep with his bathrobe on right after he got out of the shower. Aysegul took the dairy out of her bag and kept reading it from where she had left off.

* * *

It was difficult for us to get used to the fact that my brother, aunt as well as the other Jews were brutally killed. I have never forgotten my brother, but I got used to the sorrow that came along with his death. My mother could neither forget him nor get used to the sorrow. She was no longer as healthy as before. On the other hand, my dad... He was the worst of us all. He never forgave himself because of leaving the officer alive. Since my brother's death, all special days and occasions had been going by unnoticed. We all wanted it to be known what a horrible thing the war was and hoped that it would come to end soon. The allied countries had established superiority and the German troops surrendered one after another, but the war was still going on. Our life in Istanbul was running on with us being sad and doing our routine work silently to avoid trouble. We welcomed the new year 1945 sorrowfully with a part of us missing as my brother was dead. It was the second month of the year. We heard the news that British and American air forces had bombarded Dresden city. The city where innocent people lived was levelled with the ground. All the schools, hospitals and theatres were in flames for days as was the rest of the city. At first, no one made any comments in our family. Later on, the papers and radio channels spread the news and came up with various theories as to the destruction of this city a few months before the war finished. Officials reported that more than 35 thousand people had lost their lives while unofficial numbers amounted to more than 100 thousand due to the bombardment of the city which, in fact, had no military status, but accommodated culturally diverse innocent people and possessed a long history. Lizet:

"I hope Hitler is dead, too," she said suddenly. We all caught each other's eyes. It was obvious that my father felt sorry about the news. He did not know what to say for a moment. Later,

"It's a pity," and this was his short comment. I was not sure about my true feelings. I did not want to utter a word. I didn't know whether I should feel happy with the fact that plenty of Germans who had pledged to completely destroy the Jewish bloodstream died or feel sorry about the fact that a lot of innocent people just like us including babies, children, girls, mothers, grandmothers who had nothing to do with the war were killed as well. When I was deep in thought, Lizet;

"Why do you think it's a pity, dad? Aren't they the ones who murdered my brother? Aren't they the ones who wanted to kill all the Jews?" she said. My father calmly asked her to sit down near him:

"We should know quite well who starts the war and why they do it, my girl. It is true that we should always remember all these attempts to destroy our race, but it is wrong to compare the deceased people. It is inhumane even to compare our casualties with theirs," he said.

My beloved father... He hoped that I would write my beautiful days and happiest memories in this notebook he had bought me as a gift. Unfortunately, these pages have been filled with sadness rather than happiness. The war is over now. Hardly had I breathed a sigh of relief thinking that no one would ever be killed when I understood that the peace wouldn't last long. In the last month of that spring, we felt very sorry again upon hearing the bad news. The war was over but the destiny of war slaves and refugees was determined at the Yalta Conference. 7 thousand Caucasians most of whom were women and children taking shelter in the Italian town Paluzza to escape Russian torture were killed. How they were killed was another tragedy. No one would think that the English would return the Caucasians to Russians as it was obvious that they would be killed immediately if this happened. Nevertheless, the English preferred to return the Caucasians to Russians rather than go into conflict with them. The English witnessed such tragic events after they returned these people to Russians that they regretted it soon, yet it was too late for everything. They even ignored one or two Caucasian boys who escaped and went into the woods. The mothers, so that they wouldn't surrender to Russians, held their children's hands tightly and jumped into the roaring waters of the Drau River. The river was filled with the corpses of mothers and their children and there was no one among the North Caucasians having surrendered who were able to return to their homelands. These memories were the worst ones some of which I had personally witnessed and the rest of which I had read in the newspapers. Don't ever feel sorry when you read these my son. I have also had good days. The time went by... The wounds have stopped bleeding though they are not healed. My youth has been a happy and cheerful one.

I don't remember when it was that I fell in love with our neighbour's son Cem in Kuzguncuk. Perhaps, I was even a child back then. In the first days when I had become a young woman, we used to exchange glances from far away and meet secretly every time we could. His father was a doctor as my father was. He was a student at medical school. He lived in a house with a bay window with his mother and three sisters near our house. Making up an excuse, I went to the seaside and ran towards Cem through the trees. No one knew that we would meet in the coppice forest behind the Fethi Ahmet Pasha Mansion. Hiding among the plane, fir and pine trees, we would talk for hours without even holding hands.

He was the first man I loved. One day, after we finished school, he told me that he wanted to marry me. I felt very happy, but I was taken by fear. "Is it not illegal? I mean… A Turkish man marrying a Jewish girl by law…" I was saying when Cem covered my lips with his fingers, touching my hand with his hand for the first time, to stop me finishing my sentence. He was devastated by words. "Do you seriously think so? How nonsense! What law can prevent two people from loving each other?" he said. "Of course, it can. According to the Nuremberg Laws, it was not allowed for a German to marry a Jew," I said. For the first time in my life, a man had held me in his arms tightly when I was sixteen. "No one can stop us from getting married… Don't worry!" he said.

In those years when I finished high school, our families found out the reason why Cem and I met very often. Cem's family gave consent to our marriage on one condition. Cem, who was a resident doctor yet, had to finish his residency and carry on with his studies and job until he guaranteed his position at the university. However, my mother was strictly opposed to this relationship. Though my father was impartial, my mother never allowed me to marry a Muslim boy. Despite being the stubbornest and adamant person in the family, I always avoided upsetting my family. Finally, I made the hardest and saddest decision of my life and I broke up with Cem. I didn't bring up this topic ever again.

After a short while, I went to France with my parents and sister. My grandpa, who had managed to escape from Poland to France, died of natural causes. We prayed in the Jewish cemetery there. For the first time, my mother allowed me to go shopping as much as I wanted. In Paris, we listened to the memories of those friends who survived and the death of my brother that Joseph had told. I wrote above what he had said. I knew for sure that the reason why my mother talked about these issues especially when I was around, was that she still wanted to eliminate any chances of my starting over with the man I loved if there was any. As for me, I had already given upon my love never to meet again, fearing that she would die out of despair. She wanted to guarantee our lives in her wisdom and was planning to settle in Paris lest one of us should get married to a Muslim. No way! I would never abandon Istanbul, where I came at the age of 10 and I spent here the best years of my childhood and youth safely.

I was never going to give upon those cheerful and hospitable people who had welcomed us and never gone past our door without asking us if we would like to order anything whenever they went to the bazaar or the supermarket; and those people who always shared their food with us, and our neighbours,

101

whom we had entrusted our belongings to when we went to the shelters and who had welcomed us and turned the neighbourhood into a place of feast when we returned from shelters. Until God takes my life, I will never leave this place which embraced us all and I was welcomed here quite well as soon as we stepped on it.

Soon after we returned from France, we moved from Kuzguncuk to Nisantasi. Your aunt Lizet married a shoemaker called Victor. Victor was sick and he could not have any children. Although we lived in this country freely and peacefully, to my parents, this place was not our homeland. On the eighth anniversary of my brother's death, my father's health went bad. He couldn't bear this pain anymore and he passed. Cem attended the funeral with his family as well. Fixing his offended and resentful eyes on me, he stood at the corner all the time. After the ceremony was over and I went to my room in tears, I promised myself. If I ever got married in the future and I had a son, I was going to name him after two men I loved very much. The first one, Cem, was the man I was in love with and I would never forget and the other, Michel, my father who had passed away. After your aunt, I got married to your father, who turned out to be a very kind man. I never minded the fact that he was far older than me. He was quite a tolerant and intellectual man. I loved your father, too, but I have never forgotten Cem. Finally, you were born, my son... The most precious thing I have ever had. My son, whom I love more than my own life. I kept my promise and I named you Cem Michel. Your aunt has never known why I named you Cem. She was vigorously against it. I tried to persuade my beloved sister in my afterbirth bed. I told her that what attracted me was what this name meant: Cem, which means gathering or coming together. Wasn't it our father who told us that someday, we would gather somewhere and be together again. I said that this name was related to this meaning as much as it was related to my first love Cem. I don't know if she was convinced back then, but at least she saw how determined I was. Your father didn't ask even for once why I had given you this name. I am so grateful to him for this. You are ten years old now. You look more like your uncle Marcos each day you grow up. Your face, hands, your walking and even your thoughts. It feels as if my brother had never died and was still standing before me. You are asking me what I have been writing every time you see me write in this notebook. My child, who bears resemblance to all my beloved ones in your appearance, posture, personal trait and name... You are so young. I cannot tell you what I am writing at the moment. Only when you fall in love one day, can you understand that I always thought of Cem in my marriage, that I had maintained it by playing the glad game, that, before I die, I still want to see him even if I can only see him from far away, and how I miss him. Your mum who has fought for everything else regrets that she hadn't fought for her love. Even now, my heart is still burning with my longing for Cem and my brother. I had to break up with Cem as he was a Muslim. But Marcos!.. Yes, my baby, it was not a Muslim country, but a modern western country which murdered my aunt Rebeka, my relatives and my brother whose moustache had not even appeared yet.

* * *

Aysegul closed the notebook. She turned her gaze at Cem Michel who was standing by her watching his lover in his bathrobe. Cem caressed his lover's cheek. The waves were striking against the crying rocks by the seashore singing a song of captivity when five birds took wing from the branches of Judas tree and flew across the high sea.

Aysegul for sure knew what horrible things Jews had once been through, but she hadn't felt it so deep till today. A part of her was still concerned about Cemil who was on his way to uncertainty.

On their way to Uskudar in their car, Aysegul asked Cem with a sad voice:

"Is Cemil going for his freedom?"

Cem Michel answered the question with a familiar thought: "To be free at a place where he was not born and brought up?"

* * *

The taste of this breeze comes from somewhere you have never tasted as these passengers come from somewhere you have never known about. The language they speak is one you have never heard of. Hide your eyes. You are a stranger here. The raindrops are falling over the railways through the night.

Attila İlhan

Having departed from Sile, the crime ship was being steered towards the open sea.

Cavidan called out to her daughter.

"Kader…"

"Yes mum."

"Don't let go of your sister's hand, my daughter."

"I won't."

Breathing in the thyme smell of the islands for the last time they had left behind, the crowd of poor people including the mothers and children who were being transferred from the fishing boats were swarming onto the ship.

Having left the smiling lemon blossoms on land in this beautiful autumn morning and gathered on the deck of the ship faring slowly in the sunset, some of the baffled and scared passengers wanted to feast their gloomy eyes on their home-land for the last time. Dropping the cigarette which was never put out between his yellowish teeth, the member of the crime ring Selcuk hurriedly pushed the passengers and warned them to go downstairs. One crew member was shouting at the top of his voice and yanking them, showing no mercy for women or children as if he had been driving a herd of animals:

"Come on… Hurry up. Look at their comfort. They are acting like they were on a blue cruise. Chop chop!"

Despite being burdened with the trouble they have had,

the people gave an intimidating look on the vulgarly behaving crew, implying their dissatisfaction with the way they spoke. Being probably in their 20s, but looking over 30 years of age or above and resembling too much to each other as though they had all been born from the same mother, some dark men could hardly tolerate being yelled at and they were swaggering around in a manner resembling that of roosters. After all, weren't they the ones who embarked on this journey as they thought that they were being despised in their homelands? And it fell to the family elders to calm down the youngsters who could hardly stop themselves from clasping each other by their throats. They did not ask for trouble just when they finally managed to board the ship from the boats. As most of the passengers were proceeding to their chambers in full silence and submissiveness for a better future, the youngsters, who had intended to give a black eye to those people, choked down their menacing rage and made for the stairs leading downstairs in despair.

In fact, the ship they were travelling on was a big one, yet the illegal passengers were not allowed to stick their noses out of the basement floor. In the chambers upstairs, the staff and crime ring members stayed whereas in the first floor where no sunlight could leak through, the illegal passengers were squashed in like sardines. These passengers were from varied regions of Turkey, predominantly from the South-eastern Region. There were 56 middle aged women and their husbands; 19 kids aged between five and ten as well as nearly 10 young girls and the rest were adult men in their thirties, making up a total of 150 people. Most of them had a common purpose. Some of them aspired to leave their poverty behind in their country and became short breathed for the sake of a piece of welfare that they would find in the far lands, sticking together with a hope for a better future. There were also some draft-dodgers or wanted people because of various offences, who would choose freedom over prosperity.

Different from all the other illegal passengers on board, there was a man shining like a diamond in the dark basement of the ship faring in the endless sea at full speed. Among the peasants and illiterate people, Cemil looked like a humble professor with his proper posture, handsome looks and well-educated personality. Due to his clean outfit, well-groomed body, his careful speaking with appropriate sentences as well as kind manners to avoid hurting other people's feelings despite all the hardships they had been through, Cemil, who drew all the attention quickly, was shy Kader's favourite person on this ship. Similarly, he liked talking to the young girl and being shown warmth and intimacy by her family, in particular by her mother, too.

As for Kader's mother Cavidan, she fell pregnant, after having had three daughters already, months before she got on this ship. Although the fourth month of her pregnancy had just begun, no one but her husband knew that she was expecting a baby. It seemed as if there was an uneasiness that she could not describe in the tiny belly of the woman rather than a baby under the dress she was wearing, the skirt of which was pretty loose. Cavidan was different from other women on the ship. She had a bold and serious character. She wouldn't hesitate to talk to men and she managed to achieve anything that she had intended to. She wouldn't sit in a corner with her head tightly covered. She would put her head cover over her head in a slapdash manner and she wouldn't mind it when it fell off her shoulders and her blond thick hair under it became visible. She would never mince matters and discriminate between men and women, speaking about any matter to anyone. She was more honoured than any other woman who claimed to be the most honoured. She wouldn't place any definite judgement on anybody and take interest in others' personal issues. It was obvious from the glorious love in his shy glances that her husband Haci, still like the first day, loved this woman who was quite different from her counterparts. Despite the uneasiness she had, she looked at her husband with a sweet smile:

"I hope that we get there in the blinking of an eye because I am getting short of breath in this stuffy place."

"Hang in there my love. Within one month, we will see the sunlight and we will be in a country where the Sun never sets."

"Well, I don't know Haci, but I miss my hometown already now."

Looking around first, Haci slowly put his hand on his wife's belly:

"Our baby will be born in an affluent country of Europe. How soon you forgot the poverty we suffered from!"

"We were poor, but not hungry. We could have at least had the baby aborted. I have got morning sickness already."

"Don't be mad, Cavidan. This baby will be a boy. It will be a boy and you will see it. He will bring us good luck. Please, don't be sad."

"Easy to say. You want to carry it for me? You think it's easy to deal with that for a month, not to mention the sea."

"Let me call Kader and ask her to take you to your bed."

"I can go on my own," she said and walked to their chamber. In fact, her husband was not a man as rude as their fellows from the village. He would follow his wife around looking at her with affectionate eyes and would dance attendance on her. Perhaps, he was staying on the right side of his wife on this journey, which they had embarked on against her will.

Their elder daughter, who had recently turned eighteen, was very fond of her mother and sisters, and she would follow them around as if she were their mother. She had resigned to her fate as her name Kader, meaning fate in Turkish, implied it. She was a girl with an outstanding beauty who would unconditionally obey her elders. She would conceal her small breasts resembling buds recently grown out of a young thin tree under her cardigan as pink as her cheeks - it was obvious that it was bought right before they set out for this journey and she wore it over her patterned dress with a faded colour all the time. She had a thin waist, blue eyes, which she had inherited from her mother and hair as dark as her father's. At a time when she was supposed to cheer and have fun with the vibe that her age allowed her, she would rather listen to what her elders spoke in a manner which could be considered sorrowful and desperate. She was interested in any kind of topic, yet she would save her opinion for herself as if she were forbidden to speak. In any criticism addressed to them, she would stand up for her dark skinned feeble sisters who had taken after their father's side and she would wrap their beautiful sisters up in cotton wool. Probably because they were weak and in need of care, their father loved them more than her and he would provide them with the best of everything. Due mainly to the fact that Kader drew a lot of attention from any passer-by, she was not allowed to talk, laugh, sit or stand freely. If her mother had not been with her, her father's oppression would be far from being tolerable. Even so, she loved her family so much that she would observe his rules unconditionally, thinking that he had his reasons. There were also some relatives of hers from her father's side among the passengers on the ship. After they went to their chambers, Kader felt relieved, which seemed obvious from any attitudes of hers. Her only solace on this journey was the thought that she would be able to go to a school in the place they were heading for.

"Cemil, do you think I will be admitted to the school when we get to England?"

"There is no age for school, Kader. Of course, you will."

"Seriously?"

"You have never been to school, have you?"

"I have. My father had me enrolled in school by my mother's

force. Still, I'd like to study even more. I don't know. Don't get me wrong Cemil, but I want to be a lawyer or something like that."

"Why not? You can even become the queen of that country as long as you keep fighting for it."

"Seriously?"

Cemil was profoundly affected by the fact that the young girl was dreaming with glowing eyes in an excited manner about having a chance to study in a developed country. The young man, who had been to London before, was a high school student those years. During the summer holiday, he both worked and improved his English for three months. He knew a little about the schools there. As he was explaining to Kader and she was listening to him and smiling shyly, that there were schools in London corresponding to any age or profession, their conversation was cut off by the arrival of the crime ring member Selcuk. The man's eye was half closed due to a knife scar that might have occurred as a result of a fight, which added to his scary looks. He sometimes patted himself on the right lower belly and seemed as if he was suffering from kidney pain, but trying to hide it away. Once he said that it was dinner time, most of the passengers in the basement rushed to the kitchen section where there were the food cases. The fear and worry on Kader's face, who had been carefully examining the man with her eyes fixed at him, didn't escape from Cemil's attention. He looked first at Kader and later at Selcuk. When he turned his gaze to Kader in a manner to look for an answer to her behaviour he was unable to understand, she whispered by pointing to Selcuk:

"These guys won't throw us in the sea, will they?" Cemil answered the girl's question confidently soon after he threw off the astonishment that had come along with such a question:

"No. They make a lot of money on this business. Why should they? If they did, they couldn't do this job again. Please don't worry your pretty little head over these things."

"Remember, while waiting for this ship by the crying rocks..."

"So what?"

"Were you there Cemil?"

"No, I was waiting somewhere else. I mean... I waited in a hotel with a friend of mine from university and her fiancé, but I saw you. You had caught my attention. You talked and talked to the girls all the time while everyone else was chilling."

"Really!"

"Of course... What did they tell you about it? Is it private?"

"No, no..."

"Selcuk's eyes caught them."

"Hey you! Get a move on. I said it's dinner time."

"Kader and Cemil, without turning a hair, kept talking. Looking at Selcuk out of the corner of her eye, Kader whispered:

"Why are the crying rocks crying among them there is also such a man..."

"Why do they say the rocks are crying? Tell me then."

"Long story. If I skip the beginning, its ending will be meaningless. If I happen to tell you the whole story, it will take days to finish it."

"Do we have anything else here other than days which will apparently go by free?"

"Kader was in fear and worry. Still, she did not seem eager to tell Cemil what she had heard in Sile. In fact, she had already said what she was supposed to say and warned that they had to be cautious on this journey. In a timid manner, she said:

"OK. I will tell you about it sometime later."

"As Selcuk was walking towards the kitchen and smiling through his yellow teeth as if to imply something, Cemil tried to relieve the young girl's mind:

"Do not think of bad things, will you!"

"Thank you Cemil."

Having seen his daughter come to the dinner area with Cemil, Haci immediately turned his head to his elder brother's side to know if they had seen Kader with this man. As they had eyes only for food and didn't see it, he felt relieved. He turned to his wife slowly and said:

"Cavidan! Talk to this girl and tell her not to hang with men."

"What? She said as if she found what her husband said a bit odd. In truth, she wasn't surprised at all. On the contrary, what Cavidan was surprised at was that he hadn't gone and scolded Kader before everyone:

"Look Haci! At least don't make my blood boil when we are on the way. What is this girl supposed to do? Who can she be friends with? With your relatives, who badger you to death? Auchh!" she whined.

"She became so furious that she got sudden cramps as if she wanted to suppress her husband. Haci got scared. He worriedly reached out to his wife's belly to feel the baby whom he had been expecting to be a boy. Cavidan pushed her husband's hand back under the table and pulled herself together by placing a smile on her smooth face. Looking at Cemil and Kader with a matronly smile who were approaching the table, Cavidan offered the young man:

"Come and sit! Have your dinner with us," she said.

"Enjoy your meal. I will fetch mine and come here," Cemil said in a kind manner to accept the offer of this family whom he thought were friendly and to avoid any resentment. As Kader and Cemil went to get their meal, Haci, who was afraid to piss off his wife more whom he loved very much, went on spooning up his beans uncomplainingly.

These people had a lot in common. The way they were dressed, they shaped their hair and beard and even what they loved and fought for were alike. So, at tea time after dinner that day, they got down to get to know each other more closely. Their conversations, which started with the general question asking where they were originally from, went on and on to include all the life stories of each other. As the wide body of the ship was proceeding in the endless sea, they found themselves enjoying the spirited chats over a cup of blood-red tea and talking about what a trouble-free life was awaiting them in an affluent country where there were obviously no financial problems, which was their main issue back in their country.

They discussed among themselves if this ship, breaking through the giant waves of the open sea, could take them to France or not, yet they had never considered that any other problem might appear as well. However, all the passengers were soon announced that the ship had to change routes as it was being followed. Luckily, they were informed right before they entered the Aegean Sea and they were able to take precaution in no time.

The passengers were commanded that they be quiet and hide themselves until after they made sure that the pursuit was over. The fugitives, instead of doing what they were told to do, started making a big fuss by throwing things around and yelling as loudly as they could to ask "Who is following? Why didn't you take measures in advance? Where are we going now? What will happen now?" with their voices that were mingled with one another. The crew went around the passengers and told them that they were lucky and that they would be on their way back home if the crime ring member Stuart hadn't received the message warning them about the fact that they were being followed. They announced that it would be known soon that there were people being illegally transported on board as long as they kept making such a lot of noise. They finally added that they could return where they had departed and speak before the court if it was really what they wanted. Another option that they were offered was that they could sit silently until they got rid of the pursuit and that they could dream about France and England meanwhile. As a matter of fact, the passengers, the majority of whom were made up of young and strong draft-dodgers in their 20s, despite looking 30 years of age and above, were ready to rise against the authority in case of a predicament. Nonetheless, it was unbearable for them even to consider a possible return to their homeland.

Their relatives had already started the preparations in their destination for their bright futures. The government was going to be at hand to provide them with the necessary social support, but the heads of the households were not going to settle for that and start to work for two or three days of the week at their friends' workplaces as a second or third job. The draft-dodgers were going to take over the Kebab - Doner restaurants of their relatives who had settled down there long ago or find a girl with British citizenship and get married soon. After they achieved all these, they were going to be citizens and businessmen of that country and they were going to have the opportunity to go back to their countries as tourists and do their military service only for 20 days if they still had to. The fathers were going to buy properties for themselves and their children when they got their indefinite visas. With all these dreams in their minds, some of them had sold their house while the others sold their estates or whatever they owned and given their money to these guys to be able to immigrate to that prosperous country of freedom. To be fair, the money they had given was not a small amount. 7.500 pounds per person equalled approximately 20 billion liras of that time and they could have started their own business in their home country with 40 billion liras that they had spent on this journey for two people. Nevertheless, the news they had heard from their relatives was too good to turn a deaf ear to. On the first day they arrived, they were going to be landowners without having to work much for it, have access to healthcare, education along with many other services and earn salaries without working. And of course, there were also other opportunities they didn't know about yet. Talking to each other and considering all these, the passengers desperately obeyed whatever the crew commanded.

Cemil had no idea about whether their ship was being followed or not, which harbours it stopped by or at what location they were at that moment. In his chamber in the basement, where he could only guess when the daylight turned into the darkness or when the darkness turned into daylight, he clean-shaved his beard every other day, made interesting toys from pieces of wood and paper and taught Kader Maths and Turkish. Finally, Haci left Cemil and Kader in peace and didn't mind the friendship between them. In fact, he had even started seeing him as a decent guy and thought that he became an elder brother for his daughter. Perhaps, he was still worried about angering his wife and thus causing harm to their baby. All the same, his brother kept provoking him with his warnings and told him that he should watch Kader and not let go of her. Haci was sweating blood to be able to explain to his brothers that Kader was not doing anything wrong. As the ship was being followed, the food they had was consumed in little amounts and they drank water like tea instead of generously brewed strong tea. Even those who liked tea very much did not put their glasses away for about half an hour. Those who preferred their tea with nibbles of two sugar cubes had to drop the number to one cube. Due to the lack of food on board, Selcuk didn't care about the complaints of the passengers and proceeded to his well-illuminated chamber turning a deaf ear to all the quarrels among them. Kader, watching Cemil with worried eyes, was not able to tell him why those crying rocks were crying. Although Cemil was curious about what might be this story as terrible as to scare and touch the young girl so much, he did not push her to tell it, but rather waited until the friendship between them matured to an extent to become strong enough to encourage her to speak freely.

While some of the passengers were sitting idly, the others were engaged in gossip or playing card games and backgammon to kill time. For men, who could not do without having sex, time lay heavy on their hands. Especially for those men who had left their wives and children behind on the promise that they would take them there late, the sexual desires predominated their talks all the time and they were wondering about what nationalities the women would be that they were going to have sex with as soon as they arrived in London. As for the passengers with a bit more intellect, they tried to stay away from the talks of these narrow-minded, incapable and cruel men and condemned them if ignoring them was not possible.

Playing the baglama[9] and singing quite well with his touching voice, Haydar from Marash was a tall, big boy who looked older than his peers with dark eyes and eyebrows as well as a rough moustache growing out of his upper lip. He was knowledgeable enough to make most high school graduates envy his brains. He would proudly go around showing off his hairy breast with his shirt's buttons undone. Some of the passengers said that he resembled İbrahim Tatlıses whereas some others thought that he looked like Saddam Hossein. He acted as if he ignored these comments although it was pleasing that he was thought to resemble either of them. He looked very strong with his hands which seemed huge enough to crumble a rock.

He was sometimes on good terms and other times on bad terms with Mehmet from Ordu, laughing or fighting over small things depending on the time. Mehmet was a tall man with fair skin and light brown hair. Unlike the big bony nose type of the local people, he had a good looking small upturned nose going with the shape of his face. He had bought the new cassette by a local singer Davut Guloglu, who had made his debut quite recently. He was going to sing along with the song "no use of hugging" for his lover whom he could not meet. He spoke with an accent when he was angry and it would be impossible to understand what he was saying at those times. He had a poor family. They were eating grass as a meal three times a day in

---

9 **Baglama:** A guitar like Turkish instrument with seven strings

their village. He was able to finish only the primary school. He was not interested in politics as Haydar did. His issue was the money he needed to get by. He blew up when someone said a word against his country where he could not gracefully work and earn his life. When Haydar did not watch his words and spoke indecently, Mehmet, our guy who seemed a feeble boy, turned into a super power and knocked Haydar down with his punch he hit once only, in which case the responsibility of breaking up the fight fell to Cemil. Cemil:

"Mehmet, don't you think that you have political opinions that are too nationalistic?"

"Is that what nationalism is?"

"What else would it be?

"Then, I am a nationalist. One hundred percent nationalist I am. Is it a shame to be one?"

"Of course not."

Despite everything, those who got on well with each other on the ship were Mehmet, Haydar and Cemil. Despite being reluctant to do so, Haydar added Mehmet's favourite song "the creeks of Ordu" to his repertory for his friend's sake.

"Hey Mehmet! This song is generally not favoured by the people who share the same opinions as yours. How come you love it?"

"Why is that? Is there such a thing as a rightist or leftist song?"

"There was an atmosphere on the ship which seemed as

if the passengers from the eastern part were leftist and those from other regions were rightist people. In fact, regardless of the region, all of them were uneducated people who had no idea about what the left or right wings were. They were mostly indifferent to the world issues and the events around them, being abused both by the government and terror organizations and left to poverty and thus struggling for nothing else other than looking for ways of being rich in a short time without working. Nevertheless, Mehmet didn't have a clean conscience. He was feeling low due to the fact that he was taking refuge. He envisaged the sentences he was going to say to the British police when they destroyed their Turkish passports and demanded the right for asylum. In truth, they had planned what testimony they would give the police before they embarked on the ship. Some were going to say that they were in trouble with Turkish Administrative Offices due to their political opinion. Some were going to testify that the Turkish Government, Police and Army were after them and they were in conflict with the government out of ethnicity, religious differences and they were ready to exaggerate their statements if they failed to convince the authorities.

"In short, you are going to say that the government is after us." Haydar kept reminding Mehmet of what he was supposed to say every day, yet it was no comfort for him.

"How am I going to smear my own country and the innocent people there? How will I stand with all these before God when I die?" With these thoughts in his mind, Mehmet was far from being relieved. Nonetheless, he had no other choice.

He knew, along with others, that he would be deported in no time if he said the truth that his family was poor and he couldn't have a proper education and thus there was no job he could work in to earn his life. Each of them was going to demand asylum for similar reasons and discredit their government. There was no other possible way for being accepted as a refugee. As a matter of fact, out of 150 passengers on board, 140 of them had no political opinions let alone being in trouble about them. Among them were Saban, Ramazan, Gulfidan, Recep and Surmeli. They would vote for whoever their tribes and leaders voted for. Of all the 150 people, the only one to tell the police the truth was Cemil, who was a victim of the 12th September Military Takeover. He was the only one whose application for asylum would be accepted as soon as he got there, but he was still displeased with the situation. Most of the passengers were saying to each other that they wouldn't mind telling the police whatever they were required to tell and could exaggerate the situation if they had to, adding that being honest was of no help when you were hungry. "Is it a lie after all? Although we are not wanted by the police, our lives are still no better than that." The arguments went on and on for days.

The good times that everyone enjoyed in peace and solidarity coming along with the first days of the journey were over and only a small issue was big enough to trigger big fights or disputes, for the high tension overwhelmed everyone starting from the seventh week. There was no single day that went by on which they did not curse the people who had obliged them to start this journey as well as those who were involved in human trafficking. Especially those discussions that Haydar and Mehmet started tended to turn into Turkish - Kurdish disputes. Always trying to settle the conflicts peacefully, Cemil reminded them, using a language they could understand, of the fact that there were actually no problems between the people of two societies and it was some other powers who wanted to set these two ethnic groups against each other and advised that they should not fall into this trap. However, the passengers supporting Mehmet were the minority and did say that Cemil was a communist who shouldn't be listened to, showing their reaction in this way. As for the ones who supported Haydar, they argued that Cemil was a typical Turkish leftist and no good thing could be expected from people with this view, adding insults and swear words to their comments. Cemil, who was insulted by the two sides, could be favoured neither by the Kurdish nor Turkish people. In a manner that underlined the fact that he had no intention of being favoured by anyone, he said:

"This ship is a good model of our country." He was struggling to explain patiently the underlying reasons for the problems that remained unsolved.

The ship finally arrived in the vicinity of Bombay coast after a journey that was going on day and night dealing with huge waves some days. With the ship approaching the harbour, Selcuk announced that they probably got rid of the pursuit and the passengers could disembark to see the city while the ship was being maintained there. Later on, they were going to make for France. In order not to worry the passengers who were readily waiting to cause trouble, Cemil did not say anything, but he was also not satisfied with the situation. France and Bombay were two cities far from each other. There was something fishy going on, but what was that? He thought thoroughly. He remembered that in the past there were also other ships which were involved in human trafficking to Europe, but somehow diverted their routes to Asia. If it became known that they were trafficking humans, it, of course, would be too dangerous to enter the Aegean waters. But didn't the crime ring members think of that possibility before they set off? While Cemil's mind was being haunted with these questions, the other passengers were gathering around on the deck at the back of the ship, looking forward to the moment they would step on land. As for Saban, the cunning man, he had already mingled with the crew and hit the roads of Bombay.

Having left his wife and children behind, Saban, a sex addict, was an ugly and ferocious man smelling like a wet ashtray with his unshaven face. There was a cruel look in his eyes glowing desirously in the sockets which resembled two bottomless pits. Whenever he came together with two men, he would somehow bring up the topic of fair skinned English women and start talking about how he would get laid with them as if they had lined up in a queue waiting for him to arrive. When there were no men to hang with, he would make use of this free time hitting on the women on the ship. After having been lost for some time, he returned to the ship with plenty of full bags in his hands.

"I heard the crew talk among each other. They say the ship will weigh anchor soon," he said to give the bad news. As he was feverishly talking about how he jumped at the opportunity to get on the lifeboat with the crew, Selcuk came along with his cigarette that he as usual had put between his yellow teeth and a bottle of beer in his hand. He announced that they could not get rid of the pursuit whatever they did and they had to head towards Asia and that only when they arrived in Singapore, they could step on land.

The news had infuriated all the fugitives on board, but there was nothing they could do. They gave Selcuk money to get him to buy snacks such as biscuits, sweets and cigarettes and went to the basement floor, which they had called 'the chamber of suffering'.

On his way to his chamber, Cemil's eyes caught Kader, who was anxiously watching Selcuk drinking up his beer and going away from there. The young girl was trying to understand if this man had anything to do with the story of crying rocks. She doubted whether this ship was going to drop them off somewhere else other than wherever they were supposed to get.

Approaching her, Cemil asked as if he had read her mind:

"So tell me. Why are those rocks crying?"

Kader was not going to forget those couple of days when she, along with other illegal passengers, waited for the ship to arrive in Sile. Two days before they embarked on the ship, they had been transferred from Umraniye to Sile by a van and met by three men looking like gangsters. They had carried their belongings by the sea and loaded them onto the boats and they temporarily settled in one of the tents to wait for the ship, which was said to be arriving in two days. At the end of the first day, they sweltered in the tents and looked for a secluded place where they could get into the sea. Finally, they found a silent rocky place and went into the water. The women with their dresses and the men with their pedal pushers on jumped into the water, giggling at each other. Some of them enjoyed the sea lying on the water on their backs. Some others had fun splashing water at each other to joke around as if it was the first time they had seen the sea. On the other hand, Kader preferred not to get into the water, but instead stayed by the sea watching the strong waves strike against the rocks and recede more calmly by forming white foams. She suddenly realised that the water was leaking from the holes in the upper parts of the rocks although they were positioned far too high off the sea for the waves to be able to reach and touch. It was apparent that tears were dripping down these rocks.

"They even have sockets. Tears are leaking out drip by drip," she thought and went on watching them for a long time. "It is not possible for a rock to cry," she spoke to herself to reveal her astonishment. At that very moment, a young girl, who was obviously a poor peasant judging from her clothes, appeared near her. Petting her feeble scabby dog's head, she said:

126

"It is possible."

Kader came up to her timidly.

"How?" she asked. The young girl turned her back to the sea and called out to someone. "Nesliguuuul…" The girl, standing further in front of a car and looking at the rocks, turned her eyes to them and called: "Yes, Binnaz…" Having a beautiful face and outstanding hair flying in the wind, the young lady was wearing a mercerized cardigan and flip flops as well as a pair of jeans ripped on the knees. She had frail-looking callus-free hands. It was obvious that she was wealthy. While everyone else was chilling in the wavy sea, Nesligul and Binnaz told the story of why the crying rocks are shedding tears and Kader listened.

* * *

I don't know how I can say it
How! How! How can I tell you about my suffering?
Such a suffering that it is heart-rending
Such a suffering to be wished on my worst enemy
If I said it is my soul suffering, it'd be misleading.
If I said it is my struggle for bread and butter, it'd be misleading.
It's such a suffering that there is no way of coping.

Orhan Veli Kanık

The gloomy air of autumn was felt all along the Sile coast.

The beach was silent. The sea, in which rubbish accumulated through the summer, was in an effort to clean itself with the waves bringing the waste to the shore and receding to go and get the new ones. Those few people remaining there were packing their stuff while others were walking towards the steep staircase extending from the shore to the main road. On the left ahead, a group of fishermen were clinking their raki glasses on a boat as the oldest one among them was turning the bonitos and sardines on the barbecue upside down using a pair of tongs.

On the beach, there was no one else but Gulcem and Kemal. The young couple were cheerfully walking along the beach in a close embrace, splashing water at each other jokingly and listening to the birds chirping as well as sniffing the beautiful smell of the sea. They were both unaware that it had become late. The roaring waves of the sea, free of its rubbish before the sunset, had left its place to a soothing whish sound. In response to Gulcem and Kemal who lay on the sand slowly, the birds were also flirting with each other near them. The young lady closed her eyes to surrender to the fervent and sweet feeling that her heart was filled with. The birds took wing and flew away.

Kemal bent over Gulcem. It was obvious that he loved his fiancée and he had been waiting for this moment for a long time. He placed his lips on the young woman's leg and he didn't realise that the cheerful expression on her face was disappearing as he kept kissing her smoothly down her leg. No sooner had Kemal reached out for his short's zipper than his frail and well-groomed hand became an old person's wrinkled hand along with his white short changing colour into brown. At least, Gulcem saw them in this way. She leapt up with the feeling of panic. By the time she walked towards the crying rocks with an expression of a mad person on her face, she had lost her strength to live on with her dignity in this world and turned her back on the greatest bliss that life could possibly offer her. Upon Gulcem's sudden leaving, Kemal, who lay aghast there out of astonishment for a while, immediately pulled himself together and caught up with her. Approaching her slowly, he held her arm in a sad and thoughtful manner. Gulcem got her arm off him and started walking with even faster steps. The thunder was heard when Kemal stood where he was and looked from behind at her to find out what was going on.

With the lightning flashing, the crying rocks were changing colours from red to white or the other way around. The giant waves were striking against the rocks as if beating them. The rain drops falling first one by one and later in the form of a sheet were mixing with Gulcem's tears. She took her engagement ring off and as if setting a sparrow free, she left the ring of happiness in her palm on the crying rocks. For her, there was no place for love on the horizon any more. Kemal, who could not make heads or tails of it all, came up to her slowly and attempted to dry off the wet hair and cheeks of the young girl with his hands. Despite this affectionate touching of her fiancé, Gulcem withdrew herself immediately. She finally answered her fiancé's persistent questions with two short sentences and a hateful look: "I won't marry you. Do not call me ever again."

Having an ambivalent feeling of resentment and astonishment, Kemal looked at his love who had turned her back on him and then made for the steep stairs which had fig, blackberry and pomegranate trees on both its sides and extended from the beach to the street. As she could not hear the footsteps of a love story that had just finished any more, she got her eyes off the ground and turned her gaze to the crying rocks. Lying in the middle of two cavities of a huge rock that resembled the eyes of the rock, her engagement ring was looking at her accusingly. Climbing the stairs with a slight stoop out of the big disappointment he had, he paused and gave a look at the crying rocks. Gulcem was not there. He scanned the beach with his eyes. He espied the young girl walking towards the cemetery.

It was getting dark. The storm and the clouds had dispersed as fast as they accumulated. There was no thunder audible any more. Gulcem's blouse stuck to her skin and the raindrops were glowing on her soaked body. As she was stepping on the thorny chestnuts having fallen off the trees, she felt hurt and kept stepping on them as if she had been pleased with the pain she was suffering.

Being bent double, an old man was lying by one of the graves. The back of his jacket collar was worn out and ripped into fringes. His hair that had turned grey, covering his thin neck, resembled the mane of a lion over his shoulders. His long beard was covering his chest like a blanket. The grave of his daughter, near which he was lying, was the most outstanding grave in the cemetery in contrast with the man's tattered looks. It was comprehensible from the inscription on the gravestone that she had died at 13. In spite of such a small girl having been left unprotected when she was alive, colourful flowers had been surrounding the rectangular marble columns that kept the grave free of any unwanted visitors. The dog near the man felt the footsteps approaching from far away. He stretched his long, slim and slightly haired legs. He sniffed around. Standing upright on his slim legs, he ran towards the person approaching in a manner welcoming the guest. Gulcem petted the dog's head who was looking at her with mattery eyes and sweetly snarling. The young girl's hand was the only female hand that petted him. Just like his owner, he did not want to approach people who stoned, mocked him and pulled his tail. He would always look around hesitantly and wander around places where there was no one else. The old man sat up and bent forward to the direction from which the footsteps were heard. He saw Gulcem coming towards him. He tried to stand up. But all he could do was to sit on one of the edges of the grave by holding the gravestone. He reached out for his boots which he would take off only when he slept. He put on his mid-calf boots over his tattered and torn socks. In contrast with his seedy appearance, there was a noble looking in his blue eyes. Resembling a map of all the pain he had to suffer, the wrinkles on his suntanned skin made him look like a philosopher.

He and Gulcem came eye to eye. It was obvious from the expression on their faces which the moonlight illuminated that there was an intimate relationship between them. This man, whom everyone else thought was a freak, shifted his gaze from Gulcem's face down to her fingers. There was no ring. He stood aghast for a while. Two drops of tears flowed down his cheeks. Gulcem was cleaning the eye discharges of her dog using the hemline of her T-shirt. The old man lit the torch that was lying at the bottom of his daughter's grave stone. The young girl took the torch and went down the road, both sides of which were planted with fig and mulberry trees. The man and the dog started walking with her like guards.

Once they came in front of a three story house in a huge garden, Gulcem passed the torch to the old man. She looked at both them thankfully. They said goodbye quietly. The old man and the dog went back to the same road and Gulcem entered the garden and went into the house.

The moonlight was falling onto the bricks on the roof, making them glow. In the last days of the autumn, only a slight breeze was strong enough to make the leaves of the trees and flowers fall into the pool in the garden. The lights of the first floor were reflecting on the pool's water. Having helped the serving girl with a studied smile on her face, Gulcem left the plates and walked to the kitchen. Watching his daughter from behind, Yalcin turned to his son:

"Have you sent the invitations?" he asked. Engin answered in a tired but cheerful manner. "I have, father." It was obvious that he enjoyed the relief that came along with the fact that the burden on his shoulders became less. Gulcem's fair skinned and fleshy mother piped up.

"Yasemin and I also had some changes made in the ball-room of the hotel."

Being satisfied with the happiness of her sister-in-law, Yasemin joined the conversation with her gestures with great enthusiasm.

"Everything seems perfect. Gulcem will love them. The guest tables have been covered with pink sateen and white cloth over them. It matched perfectly with the white bow ties of the chairs."

Meanwhile, Gulcem came in with the salad bowl. She tried to look fine and sat comfortably at the table. However, her cheer faded when Nesligul stood up to get the bowl from her and asked:

"May I come with you for the wedding dress rehearsal tomorrow, auntie?" She did not know how to answer. Nihal stroked her granddaughter's hair:"

"Why not? Of course. Isn't it, Gulcem?" she answered for her, upon which everyone else at the table noticed how sad she actually was. Engin tried to sound out his sister:

"For your information, district governor insists on being your best man," he said.

"You both grew up in his arms," she boastfully said.

"Gulcem, what's wrong with you, my love?" her father asked.

Gulcem was ashamed of having disappointed her family once again. She spoke slowly:

"I.... I gave up on getting married."

Cold air was blowing at the table. The noise of the forks and knives was not heard any more, everyone being focused on Gulcem's explanation. After a short break, Nihal looked at her daughter's finger. There was no ring. Gulcem drank up her water quickly:

"Please, forgive me. I am not considering getting married anymore."

Yalcin spoke with a playful voice in an attempt to alleviate the tension:

"Alas! Kemal was a very good guy."

"We were all thinking that you were happy."

Gulcem put her hand on her mother's hand and turned her eyes to herself that were sadly fixed at her plate.

"I couldn't, mum. I am so sorry."

Engin, who could not help frowning, said:

"I wouldn't make such a decision quickly if I were you. You've still got one week for the wedding." He was trying to hide the fact that he was getting angry with his sister, whom he actually doted on. Gulcem spoke decisively in an effort to suppress her embarrassment.

"I made my decision, Engin," she said.

"But why? What happened to make you change your decision?"

Gulcem kept drinking water, finishing one glass after another.

"I understood that marriage is my thing."

"Auntie! But you promised to bring a sister to me."

Nesligul's question made Gulcem smile.

"You'd better give up hope on me. It's your mum's job to bring you a sister from now on." She put a spoonful of food into her niece's mouth to clear the tense atmosphere.

Engin left the table angrily. Gulcem went on drinking water quickly, looking at her brother from behind.

The beach was silent at dawn. The hot days were losing ground to cool weather. Gulcem was going for long walks every day either along the sandy beach or in the bubbly waters that stroke against the beach. That day, she was again walking with her sandals in one hand while she was holding her hair with her other hand against the blowing wind. Her eyes caught the Crying Rocks. The Freak of Sile was sitting on the mound near the rocks with his dog and watching the waves. He was bending back and shaking to the front with each wave striking against the rocks. Gulcem came closer to him with faster steps. Hearing the footsteps approaching, the old man turned his head to her. The freak expression on his face, for which everyone called him the Freak, changed to a friendly and affectionate one. Gulcem sat near him on a mound as well. For a while, she stroked the head of the dog reaching its neck forth. And then she started watching the women from the village pulling the rolls of Sile cloth out of the sea to the beach that had been spread on the blue waters. She knew that the clothes made from this fabric was a health provider for anyone who wore them as this fabric, after being woven, was washed in the salty water first and then dried on the burning sand in the sun. "Dried fruit roll-ups are good for anaemia and Sile fabric is good for rheumatism," her mum used to say. She considered the effort people have to make to be able to produce this fabric. Although the machinery had recently overwhelmed the production, there were still those who maintained the handcrafted versions of it here and there. The little girls from the village with their braided blond hair that had turned white in the sunlight were helping their mums pull the fabrics out of the sea and lay them over the sand as well as playing with each other. Newlywed women were embroidering colourful patterns on the Sile cloth that they had stretched into tambours.

And later, she watched for a while the fishermen cleaning off the fishing nets near their boats. Some acquaintances were just passing by after they exchanged their usual greetings. The man, ignored by everyone else as he was seen as a freak, was being respected when with Gulcem and at least he could be safe from being stoned by the kids. These mischievous kids were hiding behind the corners and waiting for Gulcem to leave so that they could go on stoning the freak man whereas there were also some other kind hearted kids who brought a bag of food every now and then.

Having been able to speak quite well before, the freak had not spoken to anyone in the past nine years like a dumb man. After all, the old man had met Gulcem at the end of that ominous day. That day, he uttered just two words and Gulcem was the only person who could understand the reason why this man would never speak. When it was time for her to leave, she turned her eyes to the freak to say goodbye. The old man also saw her off with his expression bidding farewell. The only voice to be heard between them was the dog's soft barking. After she walked along the foams of the waves striking against the beach, she went up the stairs, planted with trees on both sides, and disappeared.

Having gathered around the table by the pool in the garden the following breezy morning, the family members of the great mansion still looked sad and nervous.

"In my opinion, Gulcem has no intention of changing her mind," Engin said to break the silence.

"So what? If she doesn't want to get married, she won't get married," her mum said in a manner supporting her.

"Mum, this is the third time that she has broken off the engagement."

"It's better than breaking off a marriage."

"Maybe you think this is a child's play but all the invitations have already been delivered. We are disgracing ourselves."

Yalcin put his hand on his son's hand, trying to show his affection for all his children.

"What matters to us is not what others think, my son. What matters to us is you and your happiness. It seems that they couldn't get along well, so I think they are better off this way.

In the meantime, Gulcem entered the garden as cheerfully

as kids. She put the white mums she picked on the table and gave Binnaz, the housemaid, to place them in a vase filled with water.

"Good morning, everyone! The mums have bloomed early," she said and sat on the empty chair that had been reserved for her. While her mum was spreading butter on the toasted bread, Binnaz came back with the tea glasses in her hands. Yasemin was complaining about her daughter who was late for breakfast.

"Nesligül hasn't woken up yet."

Yalcin pushed his chair back and stood up. "I'll go and wake my granddaughter up."

Gulcem stood up in a rush. "Sit back, father. I will wake her up." Yalcin sat back. Gulcem walked fast with a worried expression on her face, which escaped everyone's notice. Yasemin turned to her husband:

"We had better go back to Istanbul as well. There is not much time left for the schools to be open."

Engin looked at his father's face nodding and approving of this thought of his wife's:

"I will look for a job for Gulcem when I go back."

On her last day in Sile, Gulcem was walking from the beach to the Crying Rocks when she saw the Freak, who was dumb later in life, talk to a young man. Her eyes were going to pop out of her head. In nine years, it was the first time she had seen him speak to someone. Thinking that the old man would not be pleased to meet her this way, she stayed where she was for a while and saw that the Freak took a plastic boot from the young man. Her curiosity got the better of her and she quickened her steps. The Freak, throwing pebbles into the sea, said to the young man:

"Next time you try to destroy the evidence; you go to prison... If so, bear in mind that you will have to stay there for your whole life." He was fiercely threatening the young man when he realised Gulcem's presence. He panicked and made eyes at him to make the young man get lost immediately. The young lady watched the young man from behind who had averted his gaze and moved away quickly. She questioningly fixed her eyes on the Freak.

"You were talking to him. You... You are talking."

The old man lowered his head guiltily. Gulcem went on questioning as her first question remained unanswered:

"Why are you not talking to me?" The Freak turned his gaze, fixed on the ground, to the Crying Rocks. The moment Gulcem looked at these rocks and saw the flowing water out of the holes that resembled eye sockets, she felt deep in her heart the reason why he had been avoiding speaking for nine years like a dumb person. Then she started to speak slowly, thinking that she would be able to get rid of all the pain of the past if she went far away:

"I am going to Istanbul. Don't worry about me," she said.

With a sad expression on his face, the old man looked at Gulcem. She kneeled down and kissed him on his hairy cheeks slowly and used her fingers to comb his beard towards his ears. Two drops of tears mixed with those of the Freak's. His old eyes met Gulcem's eyes for the very last time and the young girl left there in a rush. Following her from behind with his eyes, the Freak first raised his hand to wave and then attempted to run after her for a few steps. The familiar clatter that his walking stick had made became a call for the Gipsy kids who were mocking him. He only smiled at those kids following him around just like a grandpa caring for his own grandchildren affectionately. Once Gulcem had got out of his sight, he turned his head, which he could barely hold upright, towards the cemetery so that he would ignore the pitying and cynical gaze of the people on the beach. He slowly made for his daughter's grave, where he had made himself home.

* * *

Kader was talking about what the girl had told her in Sile to Cemil, who was curiously listening to her by sitting across the decayed wooden table in the humidity on a chair with a broken back which made it look like a stool. The voice of her father alerted her:

"Kader! Go and check on your mother, my love."

"OK dad. I will do it right away."

The pupils of her eyes grew bigger out of worry and hurry and she ran to their chamber with the feeling of guilt as she had left her alone.

Cavidan's belly began to reveal the pregnancy and her baby was moving inside. However, her cheeks were sunken and her legs got thinner. The passengers, all of whom were experiencing both physical and mental downturn, were dealing, on one side, with the diseases that had spread due to the malnutrition and on the other hand with the rats that had invaded the ship. They made bait from gypsum dust for the rats and some of those who ate the bait got thirsty and threw themselves out of the ship. Some others became stiff because of the gypsum they had eaten. What's more, there were roaches everywhere. The moment Cavidan hit the bug climbing up her bed using the back of her hand, Kader came in. She calmed her mother down and got down to roach hunting. Soon after, her uncle's son Recep came for help. Cavidan got furious as she saw that he was hitting on her daughter, staring at her admirably and touching her hands and arms on the pretext of passing the broom. Cavidan could no longer bear the boy's manners who was treating her daughter as if she were his fiancée.

"OK. That's fine. We can do the rest. You can leave. Kader and I have some stuff to do," she said and got rid of him. Her husband's brother and his son Recep were also with them on this journey. If Cavidan hadn't been against the marriage of her daughter and the son of her brother-in-law, her husband would have already married these two. It was only two days ago that Haci, her husband, brought up this topic. Cavidan said in a decisive manner:

"I am going to marry my daughter only with someone she

loves. Tell your brothers to look for another girl for their sons. I don't have a daughter old enough for marriage yet."

"This girl has already turned 18. In our land…"

Cavidan, who hated the sentences beginning with "in our land.", didn't let her husband finish:

"We are not in your land any more. We are heading to Europe."

"Wherever we are going, our culture, traditions and norms come with us. Do not speak as if you don't know it. They want this girl."

"I am not accepting any excuses. If our daughter were willing as well, I would give my consent. You know quite well that she doesn't even want to see his face. Don't mention the matter of your brother's Recep ever again! Got it?" she said and warned her husband strictly. However, Haci, who was brought up with the belief that rejecting an elder brother's wish is equal to rejecting God's wish, had already promised them without informing his wife and daughter as he could no longer resist their insistent demand. He was going to marry her with Recep when Kader turned 18.

Ramadan, the fasting month, arrived when their second month on the ship went by. All the passengers were fasting despite all the bad conditions. There was a shortage of food for a long time on the ship and some of those people who were fasting were angry about the dinner being served. There were also a group of five or six people who were against fasting. As the others kept condemning them, fights breaking out frequently became a common thing of the journey. Every day for some reason, another fight broke out on the ship and taking these fights under control was becoming more and more difficult. Cemil, Haydar and Mehmet interfered with the last fight. Nevertheless, it did not seem possible to handle these five or ten furious people. They demanded to get the extra plate of food which was only given to those people who fasted. Meanwhile, it was reported that a storm was approaching. Soon after, the ship was in the midst of a great storm. The voice of roaring waves became louder. All the passengers were given anti-nausea pills and the women and children were provided with life buoys. The rear mast of the ship which was dealing with giant waves made sounds of breaking and the cracking deck was flooded with water. The passengers were screaming and trying to hold the edges of the deck to stay alive while some others were praying in groups. The ship swaying just like a cradle made everyone dizzy. When the passengers got used to the swaying motion of the ship, Cemil, running here and there, risked his own life to help the crew and rushed to the rope ladder to climb up. On the way up there, the waves splashing on his back like a whip made him nearly jump out of his skin, but nevertheless he decisively climbed up the steps swinging from one side to another. Finally, he managed to get to the captain's place. The height of the waves reached 3 or 4 metres and it was no longer possible to control the ship which had begun to waft in the sea. It was only a matter of time for the ship to be capsized. Mehmet and Haydar rushed to help Cemil who was fighting with waves risking his life. After a while, the giant waves receded as if they were summoned by someone to come back. Cavidan passed out after vomiting again and again when the ship careened and got in water. With the help of Cemil as well as the other fugitives who managed to stand during the storm, the ship survived the storm and the engine room was prevented from being flooded, but they all asked the crew for an explanation about their negligence and lack of foresight.

"How on earth could you take the bear by the tooth and risk so many people's lives. Why didn't you take any precautions?"

Cemil was especially surprised by the answer the Captain gave who seemed the only reasonable person with his old and wise looks:

"Look young man! I am saving your life and not throwing you into the water just because you put great effort to help us survive. Do you think it is easy to predict when the wind will blow and when the sea will surge?"

"What!"

"Now, back off!"

"I will, captain. But don't forget that the sea wouldn't surge all of a sudden and no storm would come without any signals."

Cemil angrily threw his cigarette into the sea and left the captain alone who was deep in thoughts. He went downstairs while the crew were tidying up and fixing the damaged items.

The young man went into his room and started looking

at the photo of his lover longingly who he had left behind in Istanbul. He got down to writing about the storm in his diary. The sorrow that flared after the storm was preying on his mind, but he did not want to write all these as he did not want to upset her. To him, the information that the ship was being followed was a big lie. These people were probably planning to drop them off to Singapore instead of France. Putting all these aside, he wrote his lover other things on the ship, namely his excitement and the effort he made to be able to reunite with his lover without complaining at all. This notebook was his friend whom he could confide in for what he experienced during this journey.

The passengers welcomed Eid on the ship. They watched the crew offering sweets in a plastic bowl with glowing eyes as if they had never eaten sweets in their lives. They each took one from the bowl and joked with one another.

"The plan was that we would spend this Eid in London."

"The way things are, it seems that we will have the following Eid, the feast of sacrifice, here on the ship."

"I hear some goats bleating on the ship," one of them said to joke around.

Those of them who were cross with each other due to such issues as being Kurdish or Turkish and being Alevi or Sunni made up with each other this morning. They put all the pain they suffered aside and dreamed about the day they would step on land in England without being caught by another storm even if it was late. They played the saz, the Turkish musical instrument, sang songs and danced. Cavidan played the drum in such a way regardless of the critical gaze of her husband's relatives that even Kader was startled by her mother's bravery. The festival went on until one of the crew came and warned them to be quiet.

Kader and Cemil spent their free time studying a lot and chatting with each other, yet Cemil was still curious about the event. She was beating about the bush and couldn't say it.

"Shall we give a break?"

"OK."

"So, what happened then? Tell me."

"Gulcem, who said goodbye to the Freak at the Crying Rocks, went to Istanbul…"

"Why did she break up with her fiancé?"

"You are going too fast, Cemil. Let me tell you the story before that first."

"You're right, Kader. I just wondered how it ended. Forgive me."

"No problem. Gulcem started working and fell in love with another man there. But remember the Freak's story. What puzzles me is the man that the Freak talked to.

"I liked this freak man."

"So did I. But this Freak once saw Selcuk dump so many people into the sea."

"You believe that?"

"I swear it's true. They all drowned and died.

If it were so, he would have gone to prison."

"No one but the Freak saw what he had done. The other members of the crime ring drowned in the sea too. Selcuk swam towards the Crying Rocks and came face to face with the Freak of Sile. After that, lots of things happened. I can tell you about them later. But if there is a scar on Selcuk's belly on this ship, it means that this Selcuk is that Selcuk."

Cemil became even more nervous with these words. He should go and see the man's belly at all cost.

"OK. I'll figure it out. So... how did he get injured?"

Kader was about to start talking, but Haydar came near them with his curious look:

"But I am jealous. What are you talking about for hours?"

Right in the first week of their journey, Haydar fell in love with Kader who was a very beautiful girl and he was planning to declare his love to her once they got to London. Nevertheless, he could not wait for any longer as the journey got longer and he revealed his feelings for her. As soon as Kader saw that he was not just showing a friendly intimacy, she got away from him with her cheeks blushed and kept her distance. After all, she had neither the time nor the luxury of thinking of herself those days. She was looking after her siblings and feeling sorry for her mother who was starving to death. What's more, her father constantly called her aside and asked her what she was telling Cemil in whispers:

"I don't want to see you do this again!" he warned her. She never told Cemil or her mother that her father was threatening and oppressing her. However, she had so many things she desired to tell and ask Cemil. For what reason did her father forbid talking to him?

By the end of the third month on their journey, it was announced that they were going to have another stopover in Singapore. Cemil was sure that this ship was carrying something else other than passengers to Singapore and it was not actually being followed as well as that all the passengers would be dropped off in Singapore, not in France. He shared his concern with Haydar and Mehmet. There was no visa restriction in this country. These people could stay there only with their passports, which they had ready in their hands and the members of the crime ring would be able to buy their way out of the trouble. In this case, none of the promises of the crime ring men they met in the first place would not be kept and the intermediary men in France and the members in London would not have to move a muscle. They decided to put their plan into practice while the crew was evacuating the ship. Cemil explained how they could enter the wheelhouse in detail as he had explored all the ways on the ship during the storm.

The crew announced that the ship would undergo maintenance and this stopover would take longer than the others as well as that they could roam freely and kill as much time as anywhere they wish. In the meantime, Haydar was pointing a gun to the captain's forehead who was chained on his seat behind the wheel and sweating blood. Cemil grasped the walkie-talkie and the mobile phone which was as big as the walkie-talkie and spoke as if he was sure that this Selcuk was the same Selcuk who dumped people into the sea in Sile. He told them that they knew the tricks they were planning to do and they had every chance apart from this walkie-talkie to be able to contact the police as well. Stuart, who was a man near the captain, was stuck with consternation. He started to look in a way implying that these guys must know something and danced to their pipe. He knew that he should do so as they were the majority, namely they were 15 people themselves and they were 150. What's more, these bastards had managed to get on the ship with their guns.

While Haydar was keeping on guard by the captain they took hostage, Cemil, Mehmet and Stuart went into a huddle on the deck. Their talking lasted quite long. The last thing Cemil said was:

"We will have you arrested in no time. We have sent two guys to the police station. They are waiting for us to let them know. We have got nothing to lose." Stuart and a man nicknamed "the chief" swore that the ship was really being followed; that's why they had come here and they would take them to France as they had promised but they couldn't convince them the least. Stuart gave some detail about the deal between them and the intermediary people in France as well as the exact route that the lorry would follow, after which he said:

"OK! Here is the deal. If we don't continue our journey to France as soon as the maintenance of the ship has finished, then you can have us arrested."

The obedient manners of Stuart convinced Cemil that he was right to be suspicious. He called his friends aside:

"This Selcuk is that Selcuk." He went on with his speech in whispers:

"If so, they cannot stay in Singapore. But we had better not let our guard down."

Mehmet was trembling in a way that looked like dancing because of anger. The young man, who tended to speak with his accent when angry, was speaking with his accent again. His friends covered their mouths with their hands in order not to laugh even when there was such tension. What Mehmet wanted to do was go and strangle Selcuk's throat, but his friends who were busy laughing were not even listening to him. Mehmet kept talking his head off.

"So, this bastard dumped fifty people into the sea and sat watching them. What's more, he was carrying guns to terrorists. Don't stop me! I said do not ever touch to stop me!"

Upon calming down his friend, Cemil told all his friends that they should hold the captain hostage; the chief and Stuart should be detained and they should watch these guys, going out for a break in turns until the ship got underway again. Mehmet said that he would not leave the captain alone to go out. Meanwhile, after they evacuated the other passengers from the ship, some members of the crew showed up to find their captain chained to the chair. Having become worried, they attempted to hit the three friends. Stuart did not let this happen, ordering them to supervise the repairman fixing and maintaining the warehouse of the ship as well as other cracked and broken parts.

When the ship was taken under maintenance in Singapore, Cemil was examining the documents of the ship. There seemed to be no problem about the register licence of the dry cargo vessel, the ownership certificate, timber load visa, an old tonnage certificate and regional harbour administration document. The only thing that was not legal was the illegal passengers on it, but they had all got on this ship of their own free will. Cemil and his friends were commenting on this action of theirs on the ship, which they managed to put into practice quite easily, while the other passengers were scattered here and there. They had been on land for about 8 hours. Stepping on the land under the shining sun did good to all. Those who had money bought the things they needed at this break. Those who didn't, just went sightseeing without going too far.

Kader could not help admiringly looking at tropical fruit trees and orchids. When she felt tired of walking and sat with her sisters in the shade of the trees by the seashore, her eyes caught her father coming towards them shaking the little plastic bag in his hand. Haci took a packet wrapped in a paper cover and passed it to her daughters. Kader's eyes looked around for her mother. Cavidan was sitting on the concrete in the front and hung her feet down in the water. The young girl shared the three pieces of rolled pastry with her sisters. These small things weren't even enough for one person to be full, yet their father, despite not having enough money, had been nice and considerate enough to buy them some food. She learned from her father that its name was Chinese pastry. She was carefully chewing the pastry full of vegetables for minutes and watching Cemil, who was going inside and outside of a telephone box uneasily. Her brother, Cemil, who had been impatiently waiting to step on land for a long time, had just got off the ship for some reason. Haydar and Mehmet had not stepped out of the ship throughout this long day. There was something fishy going on, but what was that?

Cemil called the girl he loved using the captain's phone many times but he couldn't reach her. Thinking that there might be no reception, he rushed to the telephone box outside, yet he couldn't still hear the voice of his lover. He gave a smoking break and went back to the telephone box. He listened to the long rings of the phone call until they were cut off as if he had been listening to the voice of his lover. With a hope of hearing some news about her, he called his aunt Leman in the end. After he asked after his aunt, who could speak only with a trill in her voice out of curiosity and excitement, he said to her briefly, instead of having a long conversation that the ship had been watched and the journey lasted so long for this reason. His aunt wanted to tell him about Gokce and Bora, but Cemil was wondering about his lover as he was peeking at the ship.

"I am calling Melek, but she won't answer," he said. There were cut-offs in his aunt's voice:

"She hasn't called me for a long time, either. Do not worry. Perhaps, she is simply not at home. I'll drop by their house on my way back from school tomorrow."

"Thank you, aunty. I'll keep calling her for a bit more. I've still got some time."

His aunt showed no offence at all and just hung up the phone. Cemil wanted to dial his lover's number again and again, but for fear that the ship could flee away, he sadly walked back to the harbour without being able to talk to his lover.

After the ship had been filled with the illegal passengers and departed once again, Stuart gave the good news that they finally managed to elude the pursuit. Cemil smirked in agony. As he became suspicious due to what he had heard from Kader, they were able to foresee the plan of the crew and make the ship divert to the country they had wished to go to in the first place, yet most of the passengers were getting short of both food and money. Everyone seemed to settle for despair and became afraid of cherishing any hope or dream of anything.

In the eighth month of her pregnancy, when Cavidan had just lost the hope of giving birth to her baby in an affluent country, Cemil made a beautiful wooden cradle for her. In fact, Cemil was one year older than Cavidan, but he addressed her as if she were his elder sister out of respect to the fact that she was a mother. He tried to give some hope to the woman, who showed her gratitude with a sad smile on her face while accepting the cradle as a gift:

"You cannot find this kind of a cradle in London, Sister Cavidan. I have made it to remind you of us each time you lay your baby in it."

"We shall see if it is our destiny to see London, Cemil." The young man put his hand on her shoulder sincerely to try to give strength to her:

"We shall see, Cavidan. Everything will be alright. Even if your baby is born on the ship, it will grow up in London. He will be educated. He will be a free and happy person."

Since the moment she started this journey, the light had gone out of the eyes of this persevering mother, who had faced up to all the hardships with the Dunkirk spirit till then. Still, those words carrying sprinkles of hope to her heart made the woman feel relaxed to some extent.

"Hopefully, Cemil. I hope what you have just said comes true."

As the day Cavidan would deliver her baby approached, the other women started to unravel their satin outdoor clothes and sew baby mattresses and blankets. Some of them even unravelled their cardigans to make baby shoes and baby cardigans. The warmest and best spot of the ship had been reserved for the baby cradle. Not only the children but also the adults would come and visit the most amusing corner everyday which Cemil had adorned with wooden toys and ornaments made of carton boxes. This baby, even before being born, had brought hope, love and solidarity to the dark basement floor and made even the offended ones forgive each other with all these nice emotions, of which they would be mostly deprived in the country they were heading to.

Cemil, Mehmet and Haydar built a strong friendship and started a habit of talking about love affairs in their time left after their regular talks on politics. What was so special about these friends was that they could maintain their friendship as if nothing had happened although they argued very often. Just as they always did, they once came together again in a corner and started talking. Cemil unintentionally brought up the topic of his lover, Melek. As he was telling his story, Mehmet, who was, as he listened, suffering as if he were the one missing his lover, turned to Cemil, who wouldn't easily reveal his feelings and talk about his personal problems:

"Oh Bro… We weren't able to go to university. We have no profession. There is nothing we have inherited from our parents. Finding a job for ourselves is not easy at all. But your case is different. You have finished the best universities. Why do you have to leave home and go abroad?

Showing his despair, Cemil scuffed:

"It is because I was wanted in Turkey."

"You don't say so! Really! But why?

"What did you do?"

"Nothing."

"Are you a terrorist?"

Mehmet regretted so much that he had said such a thing. How could he ask such a question to his friend who had always stood up for peace, love and friendship since the very first time they got on this ship? While he was preparing an apology sentence, Cemil put his arm on his friend's shoulder:

"It's not a big deal Mehmet. No problem. I know that you

didn't ask it maliciously. We all have taken a run at something that we have good faith in. I did not know what imperialism and capitalism meant, but I loved humanity as much as to understand the fact that all human beings should have equal rights as well as that masters' and lords' becoming rich by enslaving others would do no good. I read books all the time and I started thinking that socialism was the solution, which is why I did my best to become a socialist person. I believed that it was the best way for our country to be fully independent and stand on its two feet. I also believe that we should all strive for this aim to make it a reality. In fact, neither my knowledge of politics nor my experience was enough. I kept reading, researching and struggling to acquire my friend's accumulation of knowledge to let the sun shine over our beautiful country. In August 1980, I was taken under custody by the police on our demonstration for our country's becoming fully independent.

"And..?"

"One month later, a military takeover happened. After I stayed at the political police custody for forty-three days, then I was sent to Hasdal Prison. Back then, I was a feeble boy at the age of only nineteen. My father had hired a lawyer, but the trials were getting longer and longer. My body, which underwent a series of torture, could no longer bear the humid air of the prison. I coughed all the time and could not breathe. Thanks to the efforts of my lawyer, I was taken to a hospital on suspicion of pneumonia. I escaped from prison with the help of my aunt, Leman. Since then, I have been around with someone else's ID."

"Such a bad situation!.."

"Absolutely, it is, but that was all before I fell in love with Melek. We met three years ago. We loved each other. We decided to get married in London. She had heard about this ship. I also did some research. It was being said that two hundred people were taken to England by this torture vessel. There were one or two losses, though. Still, I said "why not". Two people from the crime ring were British. Right after the coup, I called my friend Ahmet, who took refuge in London. I told him that I would embark on this journey. Although he was unable to find a proper job, he said he could be of some help. He was delighted with the fact that I decided to settle down in London. Ahmet was my mate from university. To be more exact, we were best friends. The plan was that Melek would take the first flight to London as soon as I got there. She thinks that I will be there in four months at the latest. Guess what happened. It has already been four months."

Haydar, who was touched by his friend's story, seemed to have got the answer of a question which was straining his mind:

"Now I get it. You were busy in that telephone box that day for this reason."

"True. But I couldn't reach her."

"Don't fret bro!" Most of it is over, the end is near. You can call her as soon as you get there."

The best and most memorable part of this journey for Haydar was the fact that he met the love of his life. The glow in his eyes was visible while he was mentioning what big storms blew up in his heart the first time he met Kader, how sweetly his heart beat every time he saw her, that he could actually bear this prolonged journey only thanks to her existence and that even Kader's dream was enough to illuminate his days and nights in his dark chamber just as the Sun could.

"When Kader falls into my mind, there are so many butterflies flying in my stomach that.... Then I just say to myself... This must be what they call love, said Haydar, upon which Mehmet's eyes were filled with sadness:

"There is nothing to be so happy about, Haydar. Being in love means suffering. In fact, one should close his heart for love affairs," he said. In contrast to the sadness in his eyes, he talked smiling Cemil spurred his friend by saying:

"Don't abandon yourself to despair, Mehmet. You will love someone again. Is there anything else better out there than loving someone and being loved by someone."

Upon Cemil's words, Mehmet told intermittently the story of how he fell in love for the first time with his usual sad smile on his face. When he was just a teenager, he met Emine at a wedding ceremony. He fell in love with her at first sight. Among all the girls serving Keshkek, the traditional wedding dish, to the men, she had immediately caught his attention with her linen shirt with silver buttons and her tie-on waist dress. She had tied a striped cloth belt around her thin waist tightly. Emine was so beautiful with her never fading smile and her hair flowing out of her head scarf embroidered with sequins on its edges. Mehmet soon happened to dream about her fascinating beauty all the time. But unfortunately, the girl he loved didn't requite his love. He heard that she had married someone else when he went into military service. When he was back, he neither looked at another girl nor joined his friend who would make love with foreign girls among nut trees in return for a jersey blouse. Everyone became quiet. They did not know what to say to their friend who was suffering from unrequited love. They tried to find a sentence to console him, yet they couldn't. After a short moment of silence, Mehmet smiled at his friends by nodding his head.

In a manner eager to change the topic, he turned his curious look to Cemil.

"I will ask you something bro. It's been in my mind for a long time.

"Sure. Go ahead."

"Do you remember that they kept us waiting in tents when we were in Sile?"

"I do."

"You were not seen around at all. It was like you flew and landed on the ship just like a bird."

"I was there, too. I stayed at a hotel with my friends for two days. My friend and her fiancé came to see me off." Having lost his attention for a moment, Cemil fixed his eyes at the stinky wall in the stuffy chamber. Already now, he misses his only love Melek, his family in Istanbul, his aunt Leman, Gokce and his friends, especially Aysegul. He murmured all those things he was considering in his mind:

"My dear Aysegul. She had never wanted me to embark on this journey."

* * *

Cem Michel's and Aysegul's wedding ceremony took place at the marriage office in Besiktas. Only their family and close friends attended the ceremony. All of Cem Michel's relatives in the US from his father's side came for the wedding. It was obvious from his father's sincere and caring manners that he liked his daughter in law so much and thought that Cemil Michel should not care much about Aunt Lizet's cold attitude. Aunt Irvin, who had become very old, did not let go of her hand with trembling fingers from Aysegul. The bride and the groom walked towards the exit door of the building where they were supposed to thank the guests attending their ceremony. Gokce, the daughter of Aysegul's friend who passed away years ago, handed out wedding candies from the basket that she had put on her arm. The newlywed couple had photos taken with their loved ones and accepted best wishes. While the guests, some of them rich and some others poor but generous, were leaving the ceremony one by one, the invited guests for the next wedding entered the building in hustle and bustle with their finest clothes on as if they were rushing for free food in a manner that was mostly associated with that of the poor. At the marriage hall, which is one of the few places where the rich and the poor share the same happiness, the guests who were seated on their chairs with outstanding outfits but soulless manners were waiting for the bride and the groom to show up when Cem Michel and Aysegul in her elegant wedding gown got in their car hand in hand and set out for their home.

When they got to the house in Nisantasi, Aunt Lizet was still nagging. This plain ceremony had made the old lady very upset. Would it have been bad if they had been wed at Cıragan Place with an elaborate ceremony? Though thrifty, but rich at the same time, Aunt Lizet had loosened her purse strings to be able to prepare wedding stuff for her beloved only nephew as if they were the bride's family. As though these were not enough, she wanted to organise a wedding ceremony that could match with Michel and her family's name and Cem and Aysegul had hard time talking the old lady out of this wish of hers. Lizet would not even look at the bride's face, but Aysegul didn't show offence at all and seemed to have already forgotten the fact that she was the one who tried everything to prevent this marriage from happening for years. She embraced the old lady with affectionate eyes who had a life full of sorrow and she was worrying about hurting her feelings. She held Lizet's wrinkled bony hands, who was still complaining:

"As there are lots of people suffering from poverty out there, we could not have the heart for being extravagant and making the money fly," she said. Lizet was, in fact, very pleased with what her niece in law had said, but in order not to reveal her true feelings, she just preferred remaining silent with a frown over her sagging eyelids. Smiling as if she found something pleasant about her being in a brown study, Aysegul held her husband's hand that was reached out to her. Thanks to the strong attachment to each other and their thoughts making this attachment even stronger, they were finally able to convince the old lady of this marriage without breaking her heart. The rest was not a big deal at all. It was true that the newlywed couple suffered a lot until today, for Lizet had done all the tricks she could to prevent this marriage. She had even done things that could put a shame on her in her community. She had found two smart and educated women, made them become friends with Michel and Aysegul separately, used them as spies to be around the couple, attempted to set them against each other, yet failed to do so in the end. Without being noticed, she had her nephew's phone calls wiretapped and got informed about every step her nephew took. Nevertheless, these efforts did not work either. The talks between this couple did not go beyond their commitment to a suffering member of a race intended to be eradicated. When her attempts also failed to divert her nephew's attention to someone else by inviting Margarita to the house and making rose-coloured promises to her, she arranged a job in England for her nephew using her powerful contacts, but the couple had already been married by the time this trap could take effect. Having been left with no other solution, the old lady had to accustom herself to the morals and lifestyles of her nephew and his wife, which she had found unacceptable before. Perhaps, she would manage to love her niece in law, who happened to be a Muslim girl. Cem Michel, who was once unaware of the tricks played against him, was now taking his time to enjoy seeing the two women side by side that he loved the most. He put one of his arms on his lover's shoulder who became his wife one hour ago and the other on his aunt's:

"So my ladies! Go and change your clothes. It's time to visit my mother now," he said.

Lizet got worried.

"Do we really have time for it? We have a flight to catch," she said, addressing only her nephew without looking at the newly wed bride's face.

"We've still got three hours. We will make it," Cem Michel said to calm his aunt down.

Although she had done it many times before, Lizet went to speak to Sara to remind her that she should clean this house once a week and the house on the island once a month as well as make sure that she timely paid the pills. In the meantime, Aysegul was reading the congratulating messages she had received from her loved ones in Cem Michel's room before she undressed her wedding gown and wore the clothes for the trip that she had made ready on the bed in advance. One of these messages was from her friend Ahmet, who had taken political refuge in London years ago. Her other friend Cemil, whom she hadn't heard from in five months, fell into her mind again. His last words had been about when the wedding would be held. Aysegul sighed sadly. "He must be in trouble for sure. Even if he had no money, he would have definitely found a computer and written to me," she thought. She took off her wedding dress with the intention of researching about the ship Cemil had got on months ago.

* * *

At the end of the fifth month, everyone on board was informed about what Cemil, Haydar and Mehmet had done
back in Singapore and why they did not step on land. If they
hadn't done it, the ship, God knows, might have left all the passengers there and got back on its journey without them. The
passengers started grumbling all together. They wished they
had known it in the first place and beaten this captain's brain
out. Cemil knew in advance that such a thing would happen
and wanted to keep it a secret to prevent the passengers from
blowing up. However, Haydar told it to Kader's father to keep
it a secret, but he told it to the other one and the other told it to
another one, which, in the end, resulted in everyone being informed about the situation and angered those passengers who
already tended to look for a reason to do so. It was impossible
to avoid an uprising when those many passengers who already
had a tendency to fight came together. Most of these people
who didn't even have enough strength to say a word spread
all across the ship with their guns hanging around their waist,
seized the diesel oil cans and took the crew hostage with all
their strength for dear life. They were like a group of freaks
having broken away from the madhouse. They announced to
the crew that they were determined to set the whole ship up
on fire unless they took them to France in no time. The crew
tried to talk to these furious people and calm them down, but
it was in vain. The crew talked to each other saying although

they had been in this business for years, they hadn't seen such violent, rebellious people in their life and they had to get rid of these fugitives safe and sound as soon as possible.

It seemed like all hell's breaking loose on the ship… Upon seeing that this rightful uprising would soon involve violence, Cemil proposed that the problem should be solved not by using violence, but using their words and finally managed to alleviate the tension to some extent and collared Selcuk.

"You said that the journey would come to an end in one month!"

Haydar, Mehmet and the others shouted as loudly as they could, too.

"You were totally fine and pleased while collecting our money, right?"

"Where are we now?"

"If this ship does not reach France in one week, we'll set it on fire, got it?

"We have nothing else to lose."

"We are ready to breathe our last…"

When the passengers started swearing and harassing the crew as well as the crime ring members, it was like the sign of bad news approaching that Selcuk fired his gun into the air and made all the people shut. All the crew talked in unison:

"We have had a predicament, guys. As we said before, the police were on our tail and we had to change our route. Our aim was to elude the police, which is why the journey lasted longer."

"We are not a big fan of living on board for months, either."

"We have a close brush with death."

"You should be thankful for your current situation. We have been able to keep the ship afloat, but we went bankrupt. We have got neither money nor food."

"We have been able to elude the police. We are about to be in Italian waters."

"We'll be there in less than two weeks."

"So now! Everyone! Please go downstairs."

Upon this word of Selcuk saying "In less than two weeks", the rioters cooled down a bit, but still went on making threats while going downstairs.

Most of the passengers got down to talking in their groups that they had formed depending on their worldview, kinship, city of origin or profession. It seemed as if strong and dark men in their thirties had dropped their guard on this long journey. Already now, nothing had gone as well as they dreamed. As their dreams faded away day by day, they also stopped caring about their appearance. Their faces could barely be made out under thick beard and hair. They all stank. Their glorious shoes on the first day of the journey had become worn-out, some turned into slippers and some had to walk barefoot. They all looked like something the cat dragged in. These guys, who had never been anywhere other than their own village, did not talk about how they would make love with foreign girls and they started to remember their lovers they had left behind in the village. How they missed their loved ones. Most of them had the intention of marrying a British woman as soon as they got there and once they were able to acquire the citizenship, they would divorce them and marry in big ceremonies those beautiful girls in their villages who could understand their needs better. As for the mothers, they were mentioning how they missed even the smell of the manure of their village which they had abandoned for a better future for their kids and how they were all suffering to be able to have a life in peace.

Haydar had planted himself in front of the people from his town and was telling about what opportunities a life in a prosperous country would offer them. He was also keeping half an eye on Cemil who was chatting with Kader. In fact, all the men on board had an eye on the young girl who wouldn't look at no one's face other than Cemil and they did not have the heart for eying her up, let alone speak to her because of the fear of her uncles following her around everywhere she goes, the sons of her uncles who were no less than their fathers and giving no chance for anyone as well as her mother who could run rings around men. Therefore, these boys had to settle for trapping dark skinned thin girls resembling old women in a corner, touching them and playing with themselves.

In the meantime, Haydar was still talking to the villagers, yet in contrast with the first days of the journey, when they were respectfully listening to him as if listening to a professor, they were turning a deaf ear to his words and answering him back.

"We wish that instead of trusting you, we had put our money in a bank and gone there legally with a tourist visa," they said.

"A tourist visa. What is it good for? What's more, do you really think that it is easy to get that tourist visa, which wouldn't be worth a shit? Those of you who haven't served in the military have no chance of getting one. Let's assume that you have got it either legally or by using a counterfeited passport. Do you think that the British police officers will let you all in easily? Or let's assume that they let you in with no trouble. How are you going to be an asylum seeker and ask for a right to refuge and thus a flat, salary and so on? When you tell the police that you are a member of an illegal organisation and thus wanted in Turkey, don't you think the police would not question how a wanted man could be given a visa? You have no money, no car. In this country, the police even know what brand of toilet paper you use. What are you going to do when your visa expires? On the contrary, everything has been arranged properly in this way. I have told you what opportunities you will have even on the border once you say that you are wanted in your own country."

Haydar noticed all of a sudden that Kader and Cemil were not there anymore. Having been bored of listening to the same conversations again and again, the man and girl went off to the side to be away from everyone. Besides, Kader was always alert as if something bad would happen in this journey.

"Please rest easy... We'll be in France in less than two weeks," said Cemil," Cemil said.

"I think this Selcuk is that Selcuk, Cemil," the young girl said timidly. Cemil was sure about it, too. Still, he kept asking to feel her out.

"Suppose that this Selcuk is that Selcuk. What is it really that scares you?"

"I am telling you that he dropped those people into the water, dear brother."

"Is that all?"

Upon Cemil's question, Kader's cheeks blushed and her head fell forward. Thinking that there were still some things she couldn't tell as she was shy, Cemil followed her timid eyes that she was hiding with his own eyes. In the end, he asked in a decisive and precise way, undermining the young girl's shyness.

"So, Were Gulcem and Selcuk in an affair?"

"Yes, they were."

"What kind of an affair was that?"

"The company sent Gulcem abroad for a week. Remember?"

"And?"

She was just about to start telling when they saw Kader's father was approaching them.

"Is it OK if I tell you the rest later on, Cemil?"

"Alright… I'll appreciate it if you tell me in your nearest availability. I have some questions to ask you as well."

"Sure. I should go and check out my mother," she said and turned her back to find her father under her nose, upon which

Cemil put his arm on Haci's shoulder and said to him: "Come with me brother Haci. Let's go and play backgammon for a round together." Having rushed to her mother, Kader could do nothing but feel sorry about the baby in her mother's stomach as she heard the rumbling sounds coming from her own empty stomach.

The following day, Cemil took the last handful of olives he had to Cavidan as if he had read Kader's fears like an open book. He was feeling sorry for her as she was pregnant and she had some other kids. That combatant, blunt talking and straight shooting woman had turned into a feeble and thin one and become a person with the baby in her stomach resembling a snake having swallowed a nut piece and been too weak to be able to stick her tongue out. As for Kader, she was watching her mother and pouring her tears into her heart while she was sharing a piece of dried bread with her sisters. Having stopped minding herself long ago, Cavidan was nagging her husband about the situation that he put her and their kids in. She stared at Haci, who was the only responsible person of their decision to go on this journey and said:

"Oh my blessing! He sold our shack in the slum for a song and made us all hit this road. I wish my legs had frozen and refused to go on this journey in the first place. Would all these have befallen us if I had stayed with my kids in our town? How on earth did I get tempted by you to agree to do such a thing?" she kept complaining. It was heard by Ramazan, her brother-in-law, Haci's brother, who added gasoline to the fire to protect his brother, triggering an argument between Kesanli Cavidan and Urfali Haci, which soon turned into a Turkish - Kurdish conflict with the involvement of other people around them. Mehmet, defending the Turkish side and Haydar defending the Kurdish side got engaged in a serious fight this time and started punching each other. It was again Cemil who intervened:

"What do you guys think you are doing?" Drop it for a moment!"

They went on punching each other by jumping over Cemil's head even harder let alone drop it. Having run out of his patience, Cemil was standing between them:

"You must be ashamed of yourselves," he said while pushing Haydar to one side and Mehmet to the other side with his arms. They seemed to come to themselves a bit when pushed and hit against the wall on one side and the table on the other side by a force which they would never expect Cemil to have. While his friends were looking at his face surprisedly, he spoke in a calm manner in contrast with his previous one:

"What is it that you cannot share? We are the people of the same country. Our ancestors lost their blood and lives for the same country. We must be able to bring peace and live peacefully on this piece of land that has been entrusted to us."

Haydar spoke in a decisive manner:

"How is it going to be possible?"

Cavidan:

"In the country we are heading to, there are people from seventy different nations who have managed to live in peace. So why not us?"

Before Cavidan was able to finish her words, her nine-year-old daughter Songul approached her father and asked:

"Am I Kurdish, daddy?"

"Yes, you are, my child," her father replied without hesitating.

Her mother remained silent for a while and then started speaking:

"No, you are Turkish, sweetheart." Her father insisted:

"No, you are Kurdish."

"No Turkish."

"No Kurdish."

Haydar looked at them curiously:

"I can't really get it, Cavidan. Where did you two meet each other? One of you is from the east and the other of you is from the west."

"Where else could it be? They had come from Urfa and settled in the house next door in Kucukcekmece as tenants."

Haci looked at his wife with an affectionate glow in his eyes and then spoke boastfully:

"She was watching me behind the curtains while I was carrying the furniture in the house. She fell in love with me at first sight," he said and completed his wife's sentence.

"Yeah right! I was not even looking at you. Yeah of course,

we saw each other later on. It's true that we loved each other. But how could I possibly know back then that you would change."

It was apparent from Cavidan's rising voice that there was something going on wrong in this marriage.

"What is it that has changed?" Haci snapped at his wife.

"Which one can I add to the list now?"

Being curious about the answer, Haydar broke in.

"Without chatting, time hangs heavy on this ship. Count the ones on the list. As many as you can, Cavidan."

"Before I got married, my family was poor, too. We did not know what it is to be Kurdish or Turkish. Regardless of his ethnicity or religion, what we knew was that a man is a man. Those days, that was the case for Haci, too. When they first moved into our neighbourhood those days, my parents rejoiced at the fact that they had well-mannered neighbours. "Our neighbours' son is such a gentleman," my parents would say for Haci. It all started after we got married. "This is not how it works in our family. We are not like your family," he said and said… I asked him: "Who do we happen to be? Who do you happen to be?" So it meant that this bloody man was hiding those things! As you see, the 'you' and 'us' issues grew bigger and bigger. Then, I got my daughters with me and went to my father's place. He came after me and apologised. He told me that I got him wrong. I also thought that I got him wrong. He was the father of my three daughters after all. We reunited. I wish I hadn't done it and weren't in this situation right now. I asked him to go first and said that I would come back later, but he wouldn't listen. He did not let go of me." Cavidan's voice became louder and louder, sounding almost like roaring. Kader gulped with a fear that this argument would again grow into another fight. This time, her father started speaking:

"Our traditions are pretty well. Are we really expected to put them aside and not follow them?"

It was obvious that Haydar liked this man whose daughter he had a crush on and whom he saw as his future father in law.

"Of course, we should follow them, Haci. It is us who own these beautiful traditions and culture!"

Cavidan became really furious.

"Oh, here is another traditional freak. May your traditions go to hell."

Haci turned to Haydar, whom he found more educated than himself.

"Oh how sweetly you talk, my boy, Haydar."

Cavidan raised her voice angrily.

"Listen to me, Haci. My kids won't know what it is to be Kurdish or Turkish. We won't teach them your traditions preaching how it works for 'us' or how it works for 'them'. Like it or not. My kids and I can stay in Turkey and you can go anywhere you find. If you really want it, you can get a visa and come to see us here every now and then."

As the husband and wife were in an argument, Cemil broke in:

"Stop quarrelling in vain. Aren't we going to England after all?"

It seemed that this couple had talked about this matter many times before, but couldn't reach an agreement.

"In our way of life, a woman goes with her husband wherever he goes. You get it?" Haci said, upon which Cavidan stood up in anger to shut her husband up:

"Not in 'our' way of life!" she said and left there quickly.

The bold and decisive manner of this Rumelian woman surprised all the men there. Ramazan, Haci's elder brother, frowned to express his discontentment of the situation. To him, women are expected to shut their mouth and not to speak. If he weren't after her daughter, he knew quite well what he would do to her, but he had to tolerate this behaviour for now.

"Enough is enough, Haci. Tell your wife to shut her mouth. She has been trying my patience since we got on this ship," he said to his brother to warn him in his own way. His brothers were saying that Haci had become as timid as a mouse since he married this woman. Cavidan, in the meantime, was already in her chamber and her husband was running out of patience to compromise with his relatives. Just like everyone else!...

Cemil was lying on the rug which had turned as black as the ace of spades in his chamber. God knows how many times he had dreamed of how he found a job for himself, how he would share a small flat with the woman of his life and go into a business, more specifically a commercial agency in cooperation with Ahmet. He was bursting with hope.

Nevertheless, his friend Ahmet, who defected to England many years ago, lived at a small rental flat in London's Stoke Newington district and had to work, just like most other foreigners in this country, at positions which were generally assigned to unqualified workers whose previous schooling was mostly neglected. Just like many other expats, they could not bring themselves to invent health or psychological issues to get an incapacity report and thus be granted unemployment benefits by the government such as being paid allowances and provided with housing that was generally given to the homeless and unemployed. It was not his thing to rent a room with one or two single friends of his at a shared flat, either. He did not want to wait for his turn to use the toilet or bathroom and watch the movies that his flatmates watched with puffs of weed smoke wrapping the air in the room after this age. He did not deem himself worthy of living a life in which everyone in the family including the wife and kids worked and earned money and they came around the table to be able to eat rice of wheat grains and potatoes both at breakfast and dinner, either. To Ahmet, who got away from it all and lived at a small house furnished with old stuff, what was the meaning of the life if he could not buy a newspaper and magazines or hold a girl's hand from time to time and take her to taverns to kill time by listening to music there with only 100 pounds he was left with after he got his wage and paid the rent? He was looking forward to

Cemil who was his friend both in high school and university years. He knew that his homesickness would be relieved a bit upon his arrival just as it was relieved to some extent every time he met someone from his country. When this person was to be a friend like Cemil whom he could share his youth memories with, there was nothing that could bring him down. He also knew that their friend Aysegul from the freshman year of the university had come to London after she got married, too, but he hadn't called her yet. He had read the news about them in the journals at the London Association of Universities in Istanbul. The reason why Aysegul came to London and her conditions here were not similar to theirs. She did not come here illegally. In the journal, it wrote that they would live at a small mansion among the coppicing trees and her company had rented this place for her. Even during the university years, it was obvious that Aysegul was different. Although she had much to lose, she joined and fought along with her friends for the sake of a better future for their country.

Ahmet was very excited that he would meet Aysegul at Fulham Broadway that night. In truth, Aysegul had called him many times as soon as she arrived, yet these calls were not answered on his mobile phone which was forgotten on the alcohol tables. Ahmet never thought that Aysegul did not call her because of the difference in their social status or her being arrogant. He knew that he was the one being faulty. He remembered that he had lost his mobile phone and changed his number a couple of times, upon which he reached Cem Michel's number through their association and got in touch with his friends. Walking with all these thoughts in his mind, he looked at his watch. There was still some more time for their reunion gathering. Aysegul's husband was going to join them later and they were going to have dinner together. Cem Michel had a good position at the Foreign Banks Union. They had come to this country for this job.

Ahmet bought his public transport card and walked to the station. He was excited to see Aysegul. He took the District Line, the green line, to get to Fulham Broadway where he was supposed to transfer to another line to be able to reach their meeting spot, Earls Court. There was the rumbling noise coming from the Chelsea Stadium right next to the station. The football match between Chelsea the hosting team and its arch-rival Arsenal was in progress with a high tension and excitement of the spectators. The huge crowd, too big to fit into the stadium, were overflowing into the streets, avenues, pubs and pub fronts. The pubs and bars here were not located only at centres as were those in Istanbul, but sprinkled at every corner of London, at least two of them almost at each footstep or neighbourhood, having mostly lined up one next to another. The locals would drop by one of those district pubs after work and go back home before it was late upon drinking one or two glasses of something. As seen from outside, they did not stay there till morning to have fun. Otherwise, they would be inefficient at work the following day and their institutions, whether it be a public or private one, would give their drowsing employees a sack soon unlike those back in Turkey being far more tolerant. Hanging out until late was possible for them only on the weekends at central places of entertainment. And also the match days were the times they could not get enough of drinking. Those days, even the air smelled of beer. The mounted police officers were lined up everywhere as if they were on parade. No sooner had Ahmet wished that his friend could show up before the crowd in the stadium overflowed after the match was over than he saw Aysegul walking towards him. He felt happy that his friend was still as elegant and cheerful as she used to be at university. Having been apart for years, the two friends longingly hugged each other. Ahmet was asking so many questions... Questions about Istanbul, his friends, especially Gokce... How he missed them all! Aysegul was cheerful, too. She had seen an old friend. She pulled Ahmet's hand and said to him: "Come on! We are going to the pub first. Aysegul had called Ahmet to let him know that they were going to the pub first before dinner, but couldn't reach him as he was on the tube.

Her husband was waiting for them at the restaurant below the Thames Bridge. In fact, Ahmet felt flattered as Cem Michel had left work earlier for this meeting and showed that he attached a big importance to it. On the other hand, he knew that his friend had married a rich socialist guy, for which he was relieved. It was possible that this man could have been one of those snobbish and arrogant guys. There was already no rich or poor distinction between his own friends with whom he shared the same struggle. No one would know who was rich and who was not. They all wore the same type of boots and coats and they all walked on the same path. Their lifestyles reflected quite well the democracy which the governments valuing people's freedom, independence and fair income distribution should be providing for their countries. He could not get enough of speaking hand in hand to his friend in the streets of London, who had set aside and grown out of the upper class culture. Being far too excited and happy to know what to do or say as he had been longing for a friend for a long time with whom he could share his past and struggle for the same values, Ahmet sympathetically talked and talked to tell his friend how he had been doing in this country without letting her answer back. On their way to the pub, they mentioned the names of the scientists, philosophers and artists who once lived and breathed the air of the city they were now in. As they cheerfully talked and waltzed around as if those people's souls had still been there and flying over their heads, they came near the piers of Thames Bridge. Before they went in and sat, Aysegul caught a chance to speak:

"Have you heard from Cemil?" she asked.

"They should have been here by now… I got worried and called his aunt in Istanbul as I couldn't hear from him."

"And?"

"She said that he called her from Singapore."

"From Singapore?"

"Yes, the ship was being followed. And they changed the route to trick the police."

Aysegul's cheerfulness was totally gone after she had heard this news. They met Cem Michel at the pub, drank something together and went to have dinner. During the dinner, they talked more about the past than the future. They also mentioned Cemil's name quite often.

Getting home half-drunk in the middle of the night, Ahmet sat on the edge of his bed. He was holding the photos of the wedding he got from Aysegul. At great length, he looked at the photo of Gokce, his first love Ayşe's daughter, who was standing between the bride and the groom. "She is going to university ha?" he murmured bitterly. The same feeling of doubt, which he hadn't shared with anyone, filled his heart again. His eyes were filled with tears due to the lack of a supporter for the words he said although he had been in this country for years. He sobbed, covering his face with Gokce's photo as if he had caught the smell of the past.

* * *

In the dead of the same night, Cemil went out to the deck and fell into the dream of the day Ahmet would pick him up from Dover. He envisaged the time when the endless dark blue waters would fall behind and he would meet the people he loved on a piece of land. He really wanted this journey to come to an end and was looking forward to hearing the voice of his lover, Melek's voice as soon as possible.

Next morning, Kader was trying to divide a half loaf of bread, as hard as stone, into shares when Cemil brought his last piece of cheese, dry and dark, to her. His heart sank as he watched the young lady sprinkle cheese particles into the bread pieces and the kids eat this rigid mixture as if they were enjoying pastries or desserts. Then, Kader went on telling the story of the Crying Rocks from where she had left off as she was brushing her sisters' hair.

* * *

Gulcem was abroad on a business trip for a couple of days. Yasemin, having spent her summer in Sile and returned to Istanbul, went shopping with her friends to buy the missing school supplies for her daughter, who had just started school. Bags in their hands, they all got off the escalator joyfully. Nesime, pointing her finger, showed Yasemin a scarf she saw at the shop window.

"How do you think this suits Yucel? Shall I buy it for him?"

Pointing at her mother, Doga called out to Nesligul.

"We are done with shopping. It seems that now it is the time to buy my father's orders." Nesligul looked at the shop window.

"I assume your father does not like shopping just like my father."

"That's right. He doesn't like it at all. I really don't understand why men find shopping boring."

"It's because they don't have a proper sense of taste."

Doga admirably looked at her mother, kissing her on the cheek in a cute manner: "But look! They have been very tasteful in choosing a mate for themselves," she said. Nefise hugged her daughter affectionately:

"Well, well! Just see who has grown up and knows about this stuff," she said. Yasemin looked at her watch and turned to her daughter as if she remembered something very important:

"Let's hurry my love, shall we? Your aunt's plane will be landing soon." Nesligul made for the door in a hurry.

The mothers and daughters said goodbye to each other. Doga and her mother went into the men's store while Nesligul and Yasemin took steps outside through the exit door.

In the meantime, Nihal, Yalcin and Engin were excitedly waiting at the airport. Gulcem's flight had only a ten-minute delay, but despite this, Gulcem's father:

"Where has this plane been?" he said, pacing restlessly. Both he and Nihal were nervous as if they had been waiting for hours. They were waiting such that their restless manners were due to something beyond their longing for their daughter. Wanting to relieve his parents to some extent, Engin put one of his hand on his mother's shoulder and took his mobile out of his pocket with his other hand:

"But, I am getting a bit jealous. I have been abroad many times before, and neither of you were so worried about me. Let me call Yasemin in this gap. They are late," he said and dialled the numbers.

Nesligul and Yasemin cheerfully put the bags in the car trunk at the centre. They were about to get in the car. Realising that her phone was ringing, Yasemin had no sooner put her hand into her bag than a very big explosion happened. The car moved so high that they thought it would turn upside down. The mother and daughter hugged each other in fear. The noise and screams were getting louder and louder. Everywhere one could see, there was dust and smoke. The huge shopping mall had been turned into a ruin with a bomb explosion. Almost all the windows had been shattered and a cloud of dust had covered everywhere. The timbers, gigantic doors and stones were falling down here and there. Most of the cars in the vicinity were smashed under the huge pieces of ruins. The shopping centre where Nesligul and Yasemin had just done shopping was razed to the ground. The mother and daughter looked at each other and burst out: "Nefise! Doga!" They ran in terror towards the rubbles and remaining columns of the ruined building which had nothing to do with being a shopping centre any more.

Yalcin tried to calm Engin down who was worried as he could not reach Yasemin on the phone:

"Perhaps they are still stuck in the traffic jam. Yasemin does not answer calls when in traffic, you know well."

Nihal excitedly said: "Look! A plane is landing," upon which they all looked outside the window. While they were watching the plane touch the ground and arrive at the parking position, Yalcin was repeatedly reminding his wife of not saying anything about the new flat they had bought for Gulcem and let it be a surprise for her. Meanwhile, the announcement for the plane that had just landed was in progress. Nihal expressed her disappointment, saying "Oh no! That's not hers, either," when Engin got his mobile and started to dial the numbers to call his wife again.

There was still dust and smoke around the shopping centre. The siren sound of the ambulances was screaming the place down. The noise of people crying and columns collapsing could be heard here and there. The sight of the people being taken out of the debris on stretchers was appalling. Nesligul was trembling in fear:

"Mum! Nothing has happened to Doga and her mother, has it? Mum! Tell me! Has it?" she was deliriously asking her mother. Being extremely terrified, both of them attempted to pass beyond the police barricades and see the stretchers carried into the ambulances to be able to find them. " Dogaaaa!.. Nefiseeee!.." they cried. Nesligul's teeth were chattering. Upon calming her daughter, a bit, Yasemin saw Doga walk sadly in despair near a stretcher coming closer. Her face, having fallen between her shoulders, looked pitiful. She was desperately looking at her mother who lay over there stock-still. Holding her daughter's hand tightly, Yasemin took faster steps towards them with an escalating worry. The people were going back and forth and looking for their loved ones among the rubbles of the debris in panic. Once they got to the ambulance the stretcher would be taken to, they saw that Nefise's green eyes were closed and her face was dead yellow. Crying constantly and murmuring things too quietly for others to hear what she was saying, Doga was not in a condition in which she could notice their presence.

"Let me in… Let me in… I am her relative… Please!" Yasemin said to beg the policemen as Doga was lending an ear to the sounds around her. Confirming that they are related, the police let them in. Once they passed beyond the barricade line, Yasemin and Nesligul rushed to Doga who was tightly holding on to her mother's stretcher. They approached the stretcher that the paramedics were pushing towards the ambulance. Nesligul called out to her friend who was preparing to get in the ambulance with her mother:

"Doga… Your mum will be just fine… Dogaaaa!" she was crying out as she was scratching her back with tears running down her cheeks. Doga fell flat over her mother and put her ear on her chest to hear her heartbeats. The doors of the vehicle were closed and it departed. Yasemin immediately stopped the official and asked him which hospital they were taking her to. Nesligul, who was left standing behind the ambulance having departed, started in despair to say a prayer she knew by heart for her friend's mother to be saved. Yasemin finally remembered to take her mobile which never stopped ringing out of her bag and answer the call. She mentioned the bomb explosion in the shopping centre and told him that her friend was taken to hospital, but they, themselves, were quite well. Checking her daughter with one eye to make sure that she was not listening, she spoke with a sad expression on her face:

"I think Nefise's condition is not OK. We are going to the hospital," she said.

"Ok! We are coming, too," said Engin. In the meantime,

Gulcem was smiling and running towards them with a small suitcase in her hand. The cheerful and smiling expression of the young girl changed once she had seen her family. She apprehensively took faster steps. The fact that her niece Nesligul was not among the welcoming team worried her even more.

Unfortunately, Nesligul was able to endure for only a couple of hours after she was injured in the shopping centre and had become a victim to the bomb attack at this age, leaving an orphan behind. The attack was carried out by someone she hadn't known or even she hadn't seen before, someone who was not directly her enemy. Doga was exhausted by her mother's coffin with a lump in her throat. Nesligul did not know what to do to alleviate her friend's pain. Scratching her coffin, Doga spoke to her mother silently:

"I am missing you already, mum. How am I supposed to endure your absence?" she whispered. Tears were running down Nesligul's cheeks as well while she was touching her friend's hair with her hand. As a result of crying so much, Doga's nose was reddish and her lips were swollen. She put her head on her mother's coffin as if she was putting it on her chest and remained so for a while.

* * *

"I can't take it anymore. I swear! What have you got so much to talk about for hours?"

Saying this, Haydar came near Cemil, Kader and her sister as Kader was telling them about the Crying Rocks. The young man in love looked at Kader out of the corner of his eye… They caught each other's eyes. Just as she always did, the young girl averted her eyes from him and lowered her head in a shy manner. Escaped unnoticed by everyone, this vibe had been exchanged between these two young people for months. As Kader walked towards the aisle to get to her mother, Haydar followed her. Crossing her path, he said to her at once that he liked her and he would ask for her father's permission as soon as they arrived in England. Kader was surprised. Was it OK for such an important intention to be revealed in this narrow and dark aisle as if asking for a slice of bread? Despite not having met what they called love before, Kader enjoyed the fact that she was desired by a young man in this horrible journey and left the aisle quickly in a shy manner. After her, her sisters followed into the chamber. She got down to combing out the lice in their hair when she noticed her stomach rumbling out of hunger. What about her mother? How on earth could she bear this hunger with a baby in her stomach? And her sisters… they must have been feeling dizzy because of being hungry. Fights were breaking out for no reason. Kader could do nothing other than writhe in pain. She looked at the expression on her father's face whom she loved so much. Haci was pacing in the small chamber only by taking one step forward and two steps back. He turned to his wife and daughters who were already thin and feeble girls and tried to cheer them up:

"We have got only one week ahead of us. If we can grit our teeth and bear it… Hopefully, we will step on land in one week's time. The prosperous country will give us food. They will give us a place to live. Our baby will be born as a citizen of a rich country. What else do we want from our God!" he said and went out of the chamber. Cavidan had no strength to wiggle her fingers let alone answer her husband. When she suddenly held her belly and started to writhe in pain, Kader got so worried.

"Mum! You're OK?"

"No worries, my child. I will be fine in a second," she said to try to hide the pain she had. Thinking that her mother was suffering from hunger, Kader's lips were curled in despair.

There was no rat poison left for the rats swarming on the ship. These feeble animals were wandering around every corner as though they had been making fun of the passengers there. The passengers were given only one meal a day, which was just a handful of rice or chickpea on a plate boiled in water. Except for three or four people, no one had any food left they had taken with them from home. Kader's attention turned to the food basket of Saban, the guy who was fond of his sexual life. He had done the most generous shopping at their stopover in Singapore. He must have had the biggest amount of food. She went to his side slowly. If she could get a pack of biscuits or a piece of skim-milk cheese, she could relieve her mother's pain. She gathered all her strength and said:

"Uncle Saban… Could you please give me some skim-milk cheese? My mother is not fine."

The man grasped the young girl's breasts and bent over her to whisper to her ear:

"Meet me in the aisle some time. Let me touch you a little bit. Then you will get two packs of biscuits," he said.

Kader was shocked… She must have stuck her fingernails so deep into the man when she pushed his head back that he took a few steps back in pain and ran off quickly.

Cavidan had been suffering for almost 24 hours. Her face was yellowish and she was holding her belly and moaning all the time. Kader was sobbing and looking for a place to hide her crying from her mother. She saw Saban sleeping at a corner on her way to the tea house. His food bag, which he never left unattended, was between his legs wrapped by loose baggy trousers. With her mother's moaning in her ear, Kader reached out to Saban's bag slowly and took it at a moment she thought she was free of any eye watching her. Her slim fingers rapidly opened the bag. Just as she was taking out a slice of mouldy cheese and hiding it between her breasts, she felt that a hand reached and touched her hip under her long skirt. Her pupils grew bigger and she stayed where she was. In truth, Saban acted as if he had been asleep at this secluded corner on purpose. He predicted that Kader would attempt to take the food and prepared the conditions for it. Then, he revealed his intention by slipping off her skirt. Kader attempted to run off immediately, but the man held the girl strongly, pulling her towards himself. In the past five months, he had slept with women only when they had a stopover. He was not satisfied with the men on the ship he slept with in return for money. Having been waiting for this moment for months with nothing in his mind other than his carnal love, Saban tried to restrain the girl with his big hands who was trying to run away:

"The baby in your mother's womb will die of hunger! Also bear in mind the fact that it might be heard that you were caught stealing...You know what would happen if I told your uncles that you came to my place... Come on and finish this thing," he said with saliva coming out of his mouth and slapped the young girl on the face, who was forbidden to raise her voice and shout, only sweating blood and struggling in silence to rid herself of the man's hands before she fainted. He gripped and squeezed the girl like a clamp and finished his job in two minutes afoot. When he was just about to pull up his trousers with a big grin, he came face to face with Cemil. Cemil looked at Kader lying unconscious on the ground first and later he saw the slice of mouldy cheese. He turned pale. With the punch he hit on Saban's face, the man was stupefied. Cemil held on Kader's shoulders and shook her. After being shaken a couple of times, the girl looked like coming to herself. The blurry face of Cemil became more and more clear. The fact that Cemil witnessed this did not double her pain as the pain she had could be no more than she already had. She wanted to die immediately. She stood back on her feet. She was trembling. She looked towards the deck. The desire of throwing herself into the water had sooner haunted her mind than she heard her mother scream. Cavidan's bitter scream echoed everywhere on the sinful ship. As she rushed to the chamber, a hoarse outcry passed through her lips. "Muuuummm!"

Cavidan had turned red in the face and doubled up with the repetitive severe pain. She looked for something stable to hold onto. Kader looked at her mother, who was in pain.

"Mum... Mum..." she murmured.

Cavidan had noticed the peculiarity of her daughter but it was not a good time to talk. She felt like everything inside her was breaking out with the water flowing between her legs.

"The baby is coming prematurely," she said, upon which Kader fell down unconscious where she was.

Mehmet and Haci came along from upstairs with the ship doctor near them. In the meantime, Cemil was beating Saban's brain out in a secluded corner. His upper lip was ripped and blood was flowing out of his nose in streams, despite which he did not seem to have learned his lesson as he was still after his sexual needs. He showed the dollars he took out of his pockets and leered:

"The girl did no good to me. Have a look at this money. Let me fuck you and you will have this money."

Cemil punched him on his face once again. It was harsher this time. He could not get enough of it and hit him over and over again. Each time he attempted to escape, he pushed him towards himself and kept punching him no matter where.

"Son of a bitch... No one will ever know about it, got it? No one will ever know what you have done to this girl!"

Despite being beaten so hard, Saban was still grinning with his face bruised and battered:

"What is it that bothers you so much? She volunteered for that. It is win-win," he said. Having got all steamed up, Cemil, with all his rage, held and lifted up the man just like a kitten:

"I'll kill you! You got it! I'll kill you! And I feed the fish in the ocean with your revolting carcass. No one would ever hear anything about it... I tell you to shut your mouth up or I'll throw you into the sea right now and no one could reach your body whatsoever."

Saban, who was as strong as a lion while raping a young girl, got scared silly to death and wetted himself. He was flailing about on his own pee leaking out of his shoes worn out on edges to the dark wooden floor under his never-wet trousers:

"OK! I promise. I won't tell anyone about it. I swear I won't," he said.

As Cemil was getting a promise out of the man he banged on the wall like a sack, Haydar, having heard the noise, walked to the secluded area of the ship on the tween deck. He saw that Cemil made the man drenched in blood. He looked at their faces carefully for a while to understand what was going on. He tried to get his friend Cemil off Saban, but he, himself, could not help giving him a kick while doing this:

"Good job Cemil! I have not liked this man since the first time I got on this ship... I was always looking for a reason to beat him. What did he do to make you so mad? Not being able to hear what Haydar was saying to him, Cemil furiously shouted at the man from behind who was running away from them limping:

"Fuck off! Get lost and go to your chamber. You'll stay there until we step on land. If I ever again see or hear that you are walking around, I will throw you into the sea. Don't forget that…" he shouted.

"Just tell me what's going on! What did this bastard do to you?" Haydar kept asking.

Cemil turned to Haydar:

"Never mind, I'll tell you about it later. How is Cavidan doing? I have just heard her scream."

"The baby is coming. Let me tell you something," he said and paused for a while:

"Cemil, do you think it would be inappropriate if I talked to Kader's father and asked for his permission to marry her before we get to England?" Cemil was shocked so much by Haydar's question that he felt he had turned pale. He quickly pulled himself together:

"Set up your business first. Earn money. Why should he marry his daughter to someone who does not have a proper job? Even if his father said 'yes', Cavidan would not give her consent," he said to evade him.

"Easy to say, but I cannot restrain my heart," Haydar insisted. Putting his hand on his friend's shoulder, Cemil continued to speak:

"Hang on there. Do not hurry. Kader would not want to get married now. She says she wants to go to school. See?"

"Going to school? No way! Don't put such a thing into her head. I don't want to wait."

"Let's wait till we get to England. You'll think about it then, OK?" Cemil said to drop the subject.

Haydar and Cemil crouched down in front of Cavidan's chamber and waited excitedly for the baby to be born. Some women brought the cradle to the chamber. They had sacrificed their eating space so that they would not feel stuck in the small chamber, into which they just brought the cradle which they thought they would first use in London where the baby was supposed to be delivered. Wooden toys were hung on the ceiling with ropes and a wooden music box ready to produce melodies for the baby was placed on a rusty, achromatic wardrobe looking more like a nightstand. Kader was thought to have fainted as she felt sorry for her mother. They splashed water on her face and made her smell an onion, upon which she opened her eyes but couldn't pull herself together for a while, remaining down at a corner. There was no one uttering a word and everyone was silent as dead, waiting for the good news of a baby. Cemil grew impatient and said:

"So that's how it is when one is tied up in knots, Haydar."

"Right Cemil! It feels a bit different to me. This baby. My sister in law. Or perhaps my brother in law."

Cemil looked at his friend's face to guess what he would do if he knew that the girl he loved had to offer herself to Saban for a piece of mouldy cheese.

As the passengers on the crime ship were praying for the baby, who, they believed, would bring luck to everyone there, the baby finally showed himself. It was a boy. Haci was very happy that he had a son after three daughters. He didn't mind the fact that he was not born in England, but in French waters instead. He finally had a son. Nevertheless, Haci's happiness did not last long. The baby would not cry. He looked lifeless. The doctor in a sweat spoke:

"It's probably oxygen deficiency which is common in premature deliveries." Everyone was shocked. As recently as two days ago, the doctor had said that his heart beats were normal and the baby would be born healthy. Haci burst out for his son who was born three weeks before his time:

"My son is gone. My baby is gone…" he cried.

There was not even a piece of land in which they could bury the baby. A couple of men, who could stand it, had a funeral prayer among themselves and dropped the lifeless, small body in the ocean. Cavidan's outcries "My little one!" was echoing everywhere on the ship. These outcries were not for the baby born dead, but for Kader as she must have understood her daughter's intention to commit suicide on the deck as well as the tragedy that had befallen to her. "Never leave your mum alone," she was only able to say. From that day on, Kader was always at her mother's feet whose blue eyes remained wet all the time.

It was the last straw for the illegal passengers that a baby had been born dead. Even those women who had been quiet till then went off the deep end.

"If this floating torture house has to turn into a floating coffin, it shall do so now," the passengers shouted. They all, as one man, attacked on the crew as well as the crime ring members, knowing that they would rather fight and die than be thrown into the sea wrapped in a piece of cloth before they could see a piece of land. They tied most of the crew to the poles...

Haci went for the captain's throat:

"If this journey hadn't lasted 5 months, my baby wouldn't have died," he shouted. The nerves of the crime ring members were also shot. The captain whose hands were tied to the pole behind him attempted to save his neck from Haci's hands and move him away from himself with a kick:

"We told you that the sick ones and pregnant women are not allowed on this journey. Why did you hide the truth? You must feel guilty as you were the ones who embarked on this journey with a pregnant woman. You deceived us," he said, but it was not possible to convince the passengers. Exploding with anger, the people announced that they would hold the captain hostage and they would throw the crew and crime ring members into the sea.

Nicknamed 'the chief', the head crew member found a way to get rid of these raving passengers. Laughing up his sleeve, he made an announcement in a jeering manner, supressing the revolt.

"Attention please!"

It is not a good time to cause trouble. The French coast is in our vision now. If we don't drop you off at the arranged place and leave immediately, they will send you along with us back to where we picked you up," he said and went on talking with his binoculars in his hand looking ahead:

"There you go... The French land is right in front of you!"

The passengers looked towards the direction the man was pointed at, but they could see neither a piece of land nor any lights. One among them:

"Are we seriously there?" Cemil grabbed the binoculars from the Chief in an angry manner and got down to pointing it to the surrounding area and scanning everywhere. In the dark night, all one could see the endless sea only with some dim lights from far away. He zoomed in on these lights. Although he was not sure, the place where these lights were lit could really be the French coast. He passed the binoculars to Haydar and turned to the passengers. The expression on his face was far from being relieved. Haydar shouted cheerfully:

"Yes... I have seen the coast." he was just about to pass the binoculars to Mehmet when the Chief interfered and got it back:

"Are we on a sightseeing tour? I said we arrived. We will be anchoring soon. You will all step on land. As we have agreed before, you will go to England by tractor-trailers."

They could hardly believe that this horrible journey was coming to an end. The executive officer was in an effort to make everyone believe that the French coast was in the vicinity in certainty. He pointed at somewhere ahead and spoke:

"Chop chop! Go and pack your stuff. Congratulations. We

are finally there." The fugitive took it seriously and believed that their journey came to an end, all together shouting and crying: "We are finally there!"

All the passengers came together and played music with their instruments and danced. There was only Saban who was not with them there. He was listening to the music being played outside in his dark, stuffy and small room. After he had been beaten by Cemil, he had no courage to stick his nose out of his chamber. He had not spoken to anybody, either. The only witness to the event was Haydar. He had asked Cemil what his reason was to beat him, but he did not say anything, just saying "I'll tell you about it later," to evade him. After that day, Kader was a bit unusual. She would not talk to anyone. She was too sorry to say a word. Thinking that this was due to the fact that she lost her baby brother, Haydar told the young girl many times that she should not feel sorry, but she avoided him each time. And Selcuk…Selcuk disappeared all of a sudden, too. In truth, no one cared about the absence of Saban or Selcuk. Apart from Cavidan, who had just lost her baby, Kader, who wanted to curl up and die and Cemil, who was the only witness to all that happened, everyone was cheering in joy, making jokes and telling each other how their revolt had worked.

* * *

Speedily manoeuvring in the moonlight of the dark night, the ship finally left the troublesome illegal passengers in dark waters behind, who had frequently revolted against them, and was moving away from them at full speed towards the port on the left hand side. In fact, they had told these people a little white lie while collecting money at the beginning... They hid the fact that they would drop off some goods in Singapore first and sail to France later, yet there was one truth and it was that the ship was followed for a short time. Moreover, they were going to keep their promise and hand them over to the truck gangs themselves. However, they became scared of these infuriated people after the baby's death and began to worry about their own safety, thinking that their lives were at risk. They looked for a way to get rid of them and dropped them off at a spot, off the coast, a bit far away from where they agreed to meet the French trucks. They had not even provided them with whaleboats. They were normally supposed to get Selcuk off the ship in Singapore, but they took him with them again in order not to attract the passenger's attention and did away with him at a later time. Stuart was giving orders in English to some guys on his walkie-talkie and the crew were going on laughing and chatting among each other. In truth, they hadn't been very unfair to the illegal passengers and they had given them an almost sufficient number of inflatable boats. It was natural that one or two of them could fail to survive in the water. If they could have shut their mouth and behaved themselves, none of these would have happened.

If the passengers could make it to the coast alive, the guys in France would meet and take them to England by truck without letting any trouble arise.

Shaking from one side to the other, the boats were about to capsize due to the fact that the people on them outnumbered the capacity. When they fought over the life buoys, the situation became even worse. Having understood that the ship crew had left them for dead, Cemil apprehensively shouted that anyone able to swim should jump into the water. Otherwise, they would all drown. Cemil took the lead and plunged into the deep ocean. When the boats fell on their sides and let water in, some others also jumped into the water with life buoys after those who could already swim.

The lights on the coast became more visible in the darkness. France was very close now. Cemil, Haydar and Mehmet were swimming close to each other. The light boats carrying only the women and children as well as those who could not swim were very close to the shore. Some other twenty people, most of whom were young draft-dodgers, were struggling to swim with the aid of life buoys. Those able to swim were swimming at intervals by taking some time to have a rest. Cemil looked around to check in on his friend for a moment. The moonlight shining on the sea surface was flickering as if dancing. He spotted Haydar once and lost him again. Swimming towards the shore, he noticed that Haydar was well ahead, lying on the water to rest, but Mehmet was missing. He looked around, right, left, back and front, but he was not there. His friend, who was worried about what reason to give to the police when in England even before he was about to jump into the water, was swimming behind him only a short time ago. He called out to him: "Mehmet!" He couldn't make himself heard to anybody. Near him, small pilot fish were swimming into the depth of the ocean. He turned his gaze to the coast. Everyone was busy with their own survival. "Mehmet!" he shouted even more loudly. There was no answer. Although terribly exhausted, Cemil went on swimming to the direction of the pilot fish which did not lead the way, but followed the ships and sharks around. After a while, he looked around again. He saw nothing but the reflections of the moonlight on the sea surface. The others... Some of them on the boats and the others struggling to swim in the still water with no more strength in their arms reached to the shore. Cemil was still looking for Mehmet like a headless chicken.

When the first light shone over the dark blue sea, Cemil was still looking for Mehmet, angrily punched the water and called out to his friend for the last time: "Mehmet!" Nevertheless, he could hear nothing except for his friend's imaginary voice echoing in his ear that remained from the times he used to sing his favourite song.

Running out of hope, Cemil saw no one, but the abandoned boats and life buoys when he got to the shore. None of these people noticed Mehmet's absence and waited, being worried about him. Having learned another lesson, though he was already familiar with that, from this journey during which they shared lives, he looked at the sun with a sad smile on his face. He rubbed his eyes which were dazzled by the sunlight as he hadn't seen it for months. Something caught his attention at the other side of the beach. There was a piece of cloth put up on a stick erected in the sand. It was flapping like a flag. As he came closer, he saw that it was Kader's cardigan, her only new piece of clothes, which was the same colour as her cheeks. Then, he noticed the message inscribed on the wet sand at the bottom of the pole:

"We are going with the truck gangs, Cemil. Your notebook is under the rock."

Cemil's laughters, mixed with tears of joy, echoed on the beach. The dark blue cover of the notebook was seen under one of the rocks there. The notebook which he wrote his longing for his love in and he had to leave on the boat when he jumped into the water was in his hands now. He looked at the glowing inscription on the beach once again. A message written in a hurry and a cardigan left behind as a sign became a sparkle of hope in his heart. He had never thought that it would fade away and disappear like a flower leaf flying in the wind after all that delicate girl, Kader, had been through. He was sure that she would make any branch bloom she touched. He grabbed the cardigan and ran along the beach flapping it like a flag and singing a song of freedom. It was obvious from the sweet smile on his face that he thought he had earned a true friend. While his song was echoing all along the beach, the pink cardigan in his hand was flying in the wind.

* * *

The illegal passengers had got on the truck without Cemil and Mehmet. They had destroyed their passports at the border.

Kader begged to convince them to wait for Cemil and Mehmet, but no one would listen to her. Cavidan yelled as loudly as she could, too: "Let's wait for the boys. Is it fair what you do? We have been patient for months. Can you not be patient for two hours more?" Haydar supported Cavidan's demand, but the others had already started grumbling. No one listened to the mother and daughter. As the truck was making for London, most of these poor people started to talk in joy about the fact that they had only a few hours left to reach a prosperous country.

* * *

When they were on their way to London, Cemil arrived in Picardie District of France by the English Channel by hitchhiking. Using his broken English, he spent his first night at a cafe as a dishwasher. The following day, he enthusiastically called his lover he had left behind in Istanbul. He was going to tell Melek to hop on the next plane and fly to London. Although he repeatedly called her, his calls were not answered again. He called his aunt Leman to ask her if she had ever heard from her or not:

"Forget her!" she said. Forgetting her? How could Cemil possibly forget the reason he embarked on this horrible journey? Leman, who had hidden the truth so as not to upset her nephew before, felt obliged to tell him about all that happened. Melek had given up on going to London and started to date another man already. She even announced that she was getting married soon. The receiver fell from Cemil's hand. He felt nauseous suddenly and rushed to the bathroom.

* * *

Almost piled up one on another, the fugitives were waiting for the hours to go by on an airless, narrow truck. They had no idea about which places they passed by. Judging from the expression on Haydar's face, it was not apparent if he was worried or upset about the possibility that his two best friends on the ship had gone missing in the water. He was smiling probably because Kader, the girl he loved was near him and he was turning his gaze and winking at her every now and then. Everyone looked exhausted and miserable. Except for Kader, no one minded the absence of Cemil and Mehmet any more. They had nothing in their mind apart from the fact that they wanted to arrive in London as soon as possible. The air inside the truck was too sweltry for them to breathe. Cavidan was napping with her head on her husband's shoulder and her children's heads on her chest. She stole a glance at Saban for a moment. She realised that he was constantly watching Kader and slyly smiling at her with his hand in his pants. She didn't know what to do. Her daughter, who had perched by the other side of Haci, was not aware of anything. Haci made nothing of the fact that his wife angrily asked him to change places with Kader. He just did what he was told. Cavidan got her daughter under her arm in the manner of an eagle protecting her offspring under her wing and she kept staring at Saban menacingly. She was sure that this man was responsible for what had happened to her daughter. Saban turned his gaze to somewhere else and took his hand off his trousers.

* * *

In the meantime, Cemil was also on the way with his friend Ahmet, who had picked him up from Picardie. He threw the diary out of the car which was full of love words. Some of the pages got stuck on the tree leaves and some others got stuck on the wet road. Cars were riding over them. Together with the notebook, he also threw Melek out of his life. They were riding through Dover, the border town between France and England. Whistling behind the steering wheel, Ahmet looked at Cemil. His friend, with whom he shared the half of his life, was sitting near him, but there was something troubling him. He spoke to his friend who seemed to be lost in thoughts:

"So we've made it. We are there. You should be smiling now," he said.

Cemil's pain was so severe! This damn journey caused deep wounds in his heart which were impossible to cure. The woman for whom he endeavoured to come to this country... Melek, for whom he could easily risk his life, was with another man. Kader, that young and tender girl, had sacrificed her virginity - the moment that was supposed to be the best moment of her life - with a rude, barbaric man, a monster in return for a piece of mouldy cheese. She, probably, would not be able to erase this rape from her memory throughout her life. And the baby who died after birth! And Mehmet! His kind-hearted, generous friend... Cemil could not help remembering his face and the beautiful songs he used to sing all the time. What salary or income could compare to all those things he had lost? What could England offer him? Could it be possible that this country, where the sun never sets, would make the sun shine for him, too?

* * *

Finally, the illegal passengers arrived in London, all being down and out. They had a big trouble at the police inquiry, resisting the officials altogether who attempted to send them back to their home country. These people, having had a close brush with death for months, had nothing else to lose any more. Either they were going to stay here or die altogether. Even the fact that this journey lasted seven months was itself a reason for their right to get an approval of their demands to apply as refuges. As they promised to each other before, they didn't forget about all the trouble they had to endure and resisted to death, which resulted in success in the end. They were put in cars and taken to camps.

At the door, the women and children were separated into a different car. Until a permanent camp was arranged, only men were going to stay at this camp and the others were temporarily going to stay at the church. The families did not want to separate from each other and another chaos broke out again until they fully understood what was going on. Fortunately, everyone calmed down soon. The women and children were put into cars and taken to the church.

After that horrible and dangerous journey, the food and

comfort at the camp was a shot in the arm for the men. Haci went out to the garden and lit a cigarette. Saban rushed after him. Being relieved of Cemil's absence, who had threatened to throw him into the water, Saban walked on the lawn and approached Haci:

"I have got a few words to say to you, Haci…"

"Spill it out."

Saban tried to figure out how he should bring up the topic and said it out of the blue:

"Your daughter is a grown-up now."

Haci was astonished. He looked at the man carefully and hoped that he wouldn't spill the beans and reveal his intention. As for Saban, he had no sign of feeling ashamed of what he had done and he went on shamelessly:

"What I am saying is … She has become a girl old enough to be wed."

"She is still a child. Don't be deceived by her tall body. And even if she were, it's none of your business." Meanwhile, Haci's brother and his nephew as well as some other relatives went through the entrance and came near them. Saban spoke boastfully:

"My uncle is coming from Harringay, Haci. He is very rich. He will rescue me from here."

Haci made him feel that he was trying his patience and answered him elusively:

"I wish you all the best, Saban." he said.

208

Saban went on with an annoying grin on his face:

"I just wanted to tell you before I leave. I am asking you for consent to marry Kader." Haci was shocked. He frantically gritted his teeth and said:

"Don't talk nonsense Saban! Mind your own business and don't get me into trouble out of the blue." Saban went on and insisted impertinently:

"Think twice, Haci. You may regret it later." Haci, who did not know what to do out of anger, looked around to find a hard object to hit Saban's head with. He went on speaking with half sentences:

"An already married man!.. How dare you have an eye on my daughter! Get the hell out of my sight before I have got your blood on my hands!.." he said.

"Why is this anger, Haci? Your daughter has already been mine. And she did this in return for a piece of cheese," Saban said obtrusively.

"What? What do you think you are saying?" Haci got hold of Saban and started to punch him. Meanwhile, the relatives came there to break them apart and heard what they were supposed to hear. Kader had an intercourse with a married man although she had a fiancé. If what Saban said were true, then what their traditional laws required would be done. Haci got his head between his two hands and cried:

"Oh no! Kader wouldn't do such a thing. No!"

Haci was crying and moaning. He was whispering prayers

209

to hope what he had heard would not turn out to be the truth. There was no one left around him and his brother got down to investigating the case. As for Haydar, he had his hair and beard shaved. He put on an orange shirt with the first and second buttons undone, a striped jacket over it and ironed clean trousers, going near the church with the hope of seeing Kader even if it had to be from far away. On the way, he heard the bad news as well. Kader… The girl who had always been in his dreams… Was it really the truth? Did she really offer herself to Saban in return for a piece of cheese? He didn't believe it at first. Tearing his hair out, he cried out "Kader wouldn't do such a thing!" He suddenly remembered the day Cemil beat Saban to death.

Haci went to the church and told his wife what he had heard. Kader desperately buckled under all those things being said near her. Cavidan roared like a lion all of a sudden:

"Hell with your traditional laws. I am not giving my daughter, no way!" She collared her husband:

"My daughter… She threw herself into fire so that our baby and her mother wouldn't die of hunger. It's nobody else's concern!"

Haci was desperate, too. It was obvious that he could not sacrifice her daughter, either.

"If I don't punish her myself, my brothers won't let go of her."

"Your brothers should go and kill the one who did this to our daughter. Not our daughter."

210

"He will be punished, too. Don't worry!"

"Go to hell! All of you. Get the hell out of here. It's me who breastfed and brought her up. If they ever happen to touch her, I'll kill your brothers myself!" Haci was desperately shaking his head and gave in to the idea of sacrificing his daughter. Cavidan collared her husband once again:

"Get the hell out of here. Whatever happened to us happened because of your desire to emigrate and traditional laws. I lost my son. But I won't..." Cavidan could not speak any longer. She fainted where she was... By the time one of the officials came near her, Haci had already left. One of the church officials wanted to pick her up from the floor. Her stiff body was shaken by her roaring that was filled with sorrow and despair: "My daughter! My angel-faced baby!"

There was growing fear that the traditional laws would be implemented at any time. Meanwhile, there were two Turkish women visiting the church from Oxfam and Cancer Research Charities. They had brought second hand clothes for the children and women there. It was impossible to say that these clothes were second. All of them smelled nice and were ironed. Cavidan talked to these ladies to ask for help and told them she needed an urgent place for her daughter to stay. But, she neither mentioned the rape nor the traditional laws. Kader's head was on her chest. She said: "I don't want to die, mum!" The poor mother was looking for a way to take her daughter out of here. Finally, she managed to get help from a Turkish newspaper. She had her daughter put on the clothes they had received. She would still look beautiful if she had worn a sack, though. She put up a dress reaching below her knees, a woollen panty under it and a nice, elegant cardigan. Kader was crying and her mother was trying to console her.

"Every cloud has a silver lining, my daughter. Remember how sorry we had felt when they said there was no vacancy at the refugee camp and your dad and we had to stay in different places."

"Yes, mum! Fortunately, we are not there."

"God saved you, my love. If we were there… your uncles would already… Whatever…"

Trying to pull herself together with her wet eyes, Cavidan took a piece of paper out of her pocket. She gave the phone number and address of the place she was going to go.

"Look! Aysegul and her husband will meet you. They have been recently married. Just like us, they came here a short time ago. Cem works at a big company. They said his contract is for a couple of years and then, they will go back to Istanbul. A couple of years later, we will think of the rest."

"Did they ask me to go there?"

"They have an old aunt. They said her name was Lizet, but I might have got it wrong. Whatever… You will look after her. "

"It's OK, but…"

"It's not a big deal. She sometimes wets her bed. You know we diaper babies. There are disposable diapers here. You'll use them. You won't wash them. You'll just throw them away when dirty. Can you do that?"

"Yes, but how…"

"Don't be afraid. I asked about everything. They will also give you a room."

They were still talking while walking to the main exit of the church.

"I got the address from the newspaper. Don't let them know the things that happened on the ship and that we came here illegally. Just tell them that we'll take refuge and it will suffice. Don't say why. Just in case. Alright, my girl? For now, we will hear about each other through the newspaper. Then, you will buy yourself a mobile phone. And if I can get one, too, we will call each other and talk. They will also pay you 250 pounds per week."

Cavidan was still making an effort to make her daughter smile as she was sending her off to the uncertainty:

"Your wage is equal to two and half billion liras in our currency. Isn't it great, ha? And there are also those British colleges. I have mentioned it. Aysegul will help you enrol as well."

Cavidan took out 150 pounds that Oxfam Charity had given to her and passed it to her daughter:

"This is your pocket money."

"They can't find me there, mummy, can they?"

"No, they can't, dear. The place is far from London. It is a place where no Turk lives. Look. The address is written here. It's a place called Weymouth. I'll forget the address soon. At the corner of the church, there is a taxi station. You'll call one there, but the taxi won't take you all the way to the address. Most of the drivers at this station are Turkish. If the driver is Turkish, don't talk so that they will think you are a foreigner. Give this paper to him. You will get off the taxi in Reading in case they should find this taxi driver. Then, you will take the train. Whatever… Look, everything is written here, my daughter. Come on and don't lose any more time."

Kader, who had just turned 18, was trembling.

Her mother could speak with difficulty:

"Run now! Go quickly."

"Mum… I can't do without you."

"I will find you. We'll meet secretly. Move now. Go before the murderers set out for you." Kader looked in the eyes of her mother, as blue as her own, who was the woman she had sacrificed herself for:

"Mum!…"

Cavidan's hands were detached from her daughter's palms. Kader turned her back sobbing. Her young body moved along the church wall while her mother's eyes wide open watched her behind. Under the pouring rain, she disappeared into London's dark and damp avenues.

Once she got to the taxi station, Kader paused for a breath and looked at the paper in her hand. She tried to restrain her fear. What was it that she should be afraid of? All she was supposed to do was to call "Taxi! To Reading." She hesitated for a moment. She looked behind. She remembered Gulcem and the fact that the traditional laws would be implemented. She reached with her head into the glass case and said:

"Taxi to Reading!" She didn't make out what the driver said, but she got into the car the driver pointed at and sat in the rear. Looking at the rear-view mirror, the driver asked:

"Where are you from?" Kader was surprised. Her mum said no one would ask anything. She repeated the only thing she was supposed to say:

"Taxi! Reading!"

The driver smiled:

"Are you Turkish?" he said. Kader was not sure if she should be glad or worried that she was travelling with some-one who spoke her language. She remembered her mother's warning. The driver kept asking and Kader remained silent. Finally, he gave up, too and didn't ask anything else. The taxi was on its way to Reading. Kader looked through the car's window and as they went away from Harringay, which resembled the suburbs of Istanbul, she couldn't help watching the changing view of the beautiful districts. While she was admiringly watching the swans playing in the creek, the houses with red roofs among green trees, the one-piece stone churches and the people playing music in the church yards, she was gradually going far from her mother, whom she loved so much and her sisters whom she had never left before.

Kader felt uneasy. The ugly grinning image of Saban, who was the main reason she had to hit the road to leave her family, fell into her mind. She nodded her head while she silently cursed him. Her emotions crossed. She turned her sorrowful gaze to the window in a resigned mood, believing that the strength to live honourably in this world had not been granted to her generously. The taxi was passing along beautiful streets, but Kader could not see anything beautiful any more. Would it be better if her uncles practised the law and killed her? She thought how painful it was going to be to move on with this shame. All of a sudden, she remembered the girl whom she shared the same destiny with at the Crying Rocks. She wished she could have told Cemil everything she had heard in Sile. After that horrible day, the day Saban did that horrible thing to her, Kader became dead silent. She didn't tell about the Crying Rocks anymore and Cemil didn't ask her to, either.

When the taxi got to the place she should get off, the driver asked her as if he understood she was Turkish:

"Is this the place where you want to go?"

"......."

"Look, my girl! Listen to me if you understand what I am saying. If you want to take another taxi, you should go this way. If you want to take the train, you should go through this big gate," he said and showed her the taxi station and the gate of the train station. Not knowing whom to trust and whom not to, Kader just paid the fare and got off the taxi, pretending to understand nothing the man had said to her. She secretly looked at the taxi from behind for a while. Then, she made for the taxi station the man had mentioned. What he had said was true. She took another taxi in Reading to Basingstoke train station and got off when she got there. Until now, she didn't have any difficulty because she travelled only by taxi. She took a look at the huge crow at the train station in fear. She thought that she would definitely get lost over here. She showed the address in her hand to a black official. Not having understood anything from what he said, he went to a corner and started to cry. She saw two young people coming towards her hand in hand most probably to offer her help. She immediately wiped her tears and turned her back, going away. After she pulled herself together in front of a café, she showed the address in her hand to another official, who, she thought, is British, considering his blond hair. In fact, all she had to do was to get on the train and take off in Weymouth, which was the final station. However, the young girl didn't understand anything from what this official explained to her, either. Kader had well recognised the currency of this country during the days she stayed at the church, which is why she knew that she had only 15 pounds left with her. Was it perhaps possible for her to go to the address by taxi with the money she had? If so, her mother would have written on this paper that she could take another taxi here. Pacing in despair, Kader couldn't figure out if she should take the red or brown line at the station. What if she took the wrong line and went to an even farther place? She looked at the paper in her hand once more. Suddenly, the idea flashed through her mind that she could call the number on the paper. They were a family speaking the same language after all. Perhaps, they could come and pick her up from here. There were a number of telephone boxes opposite the ticket counters.

She inserted one pound and dialled the number on the paper hurriedly. She heard a man's voice saying "Hello!" from the other end of the line. Putting the receiver back to its case right away, she started to cry in the telephone box once again. Given that the man who answered the call spoke English, there was a chance that the number she had might be wrong. Despite all the wisdom her mum had, was it possible that she gave her a wrong number? Perhaps, that man was Cem, but he answered the call this way just because the calls were supposed to be answered this way in this country. She wiped the tears in her eyes and inserted another coin in the telephone box, dialling the number on the paper once again. The same voice said "Hello!" again. This time, she answered back in hesitation: "Alo?" Then, the man went on speaking Turkish, for which Kader couldn't help but crow.

* * *

Aysegul and Cem Michel nicely welcomed the young girl. Kader had come to a huge house in a big garden resembling a forest. She was in a house, the style of which was like one of those she saw on TV. She was now with neat, clean, elegant, chic and smiling people. It was obvious from all their manners that they were rich and kind-hearted people. Cem Michel took her to Aunt Lizet's room and introduced them to each other. Having given her the look from head to toe, the old woman reached her hand for her to kiss. She spoke with a voice expressing her contentment:

"Welcome my beautiful girl," she said. Kader, feeling the affection in her voice, replied bashfully:

"Well met!" she said. Lizet remembered her past with an affectionate smile on her face. When she and her sister Rosa immigrated to Istanbul years ago, those were the first Turkish words they had learned. "*Hoş bulduk!*" "*Well met!*" Then, she remembered the first day they spent at Uncle Michon's house. The two sisters were as timid and bashful that day as Kader was now. She thought that having to live in a foreign land felt the same even if the time, setting and people were different.

"Come closer, please," she said. With her gaze fixed on the floor, she moved near her bedside. She reached for the young girl's hair and caressed it. She held her chin and asked her to look her in the eye:

"Look at me, sweety. What beautiful eyes do you have?" After Kader thanking shyly, she continued:

"Now, let Aysegul take you to your room. Have some rest first. Get used to your place. Then, we'll talk about how we'll spend our days together," she said.

As she followed Aysegul going upstairs and entering the room that would belong only to her, Kader couldn't conceal her astonishment. It was the most beautiful room she had seen in her whole life. Aysegul told her that she should have rest until dinner and that she could also have a bath and change her clothes if she desired. When she was left alone, she started to examine her room. There was an elegant bed, a four door wardrobe with brand new towels and nice smelling pink bed sheets in it, a television as well as a big worktable and even a computer on it. She slightly opened the door inside her room. She found herself in a bright small bathroom. There were colourful soaps and shampoos, packed toothbrushes and paste on the sink in front of the mirror. Thinking that this was even more beautiful than she could ever imagine, she returned to her room with a smile on her face. She opened the blinds of the small window with difficulty and looked at the green garden where birds were chirping altogether. The torches of the garden illuminated the whole garden. Next to the wall, there was another big house. When she saw a young man lying on a straw sofa and reading his book in the glass cased veranda, she got worried. She shut the window and pulled the strap of the blinds right away.

Even on the second day of her stay in the house, Kader and Lizet got used to each other as if they had been in the same house for years. The old woman looked at the young girl who was shy and bashful:

"If you miss your mum and dad, you may go and see them on the weekends," she said. Although Lizet tried to ease the young girl's mind, she seemed rather disturbed by these talks:

"No need. They are very far away. It's fine if I just stay here!" she said to avoid her. Kader met all the needs of the old woman even before she asked her to, changed her diaper a couple of times in a day without letting her make a request and tried to comfort her as she felt embarrassed. A Bulgarian girl, Maria came over to the house to do the chores like cooking, cleaning and ironing. As for Kader, she only took care of Aunt Lizet. Maria's job for today was to show Kader where she could find what. There were many rooms in this house. As they changed from one room to another, she put things in her mind not through what Maria said to her, but through how the room had been furnished. In fact, within two days she learned a couple of English words from Maria like "Good morning, good afternoon, good bye, excuse me, I am sorry, yes, no, what is your name?" In the first floor, there was the TV room, working room, saloon, kitchen and washing room that Maria called 'laundry'. In the middle floor, there was the big bedroom, next to it Aunt Lizet's bedroom, two bathrooms and two toilets. As for the third floor, there was her room and a guest room as well as a guest bathroom. Kader spent her first days getting to know the people in the house and the house itself.

In those times, when Lizet slept or wanted to be alone, Kader would go up to her own room. She couldn't believe that she had a room of her own and sometimes she thought she was in a dream. She had come to this house only with a small bag with second hand clothes in it. Aysegul brought new clothes to her, adding that they could still go shopping together if there was anything else she would like to have. Almost every night, she put the clothes Aysegul bought for her over her body and caressed them. These were the kind of clothes she could see only in the shop windows before. As for now, she did not have the heart to wear them. She did not know how to use the computer on the worktable yet, but it was OK. The time would also come for her to learn it. The small screened TV had only the

BBC broadcast. Although she did not understand the things being said, she still watched it excitedly by mixing the visuals with her imagination. Cem Michel had told her that they didn't have an antenna installed on purpose as she could learn English better in this way. She even had a lampshade on her nightstand sparkling light just like the ones she had seen in the films. Everything was perfect, but she still wished that her mother, sisters and father were with her.

The winter was gone and the weather started to get warmer. In those days when it didn't rain, Aunt Lizet and Kader would go to the park in the vicinity, wander around for a couple of hours and return home. That morning, they wanted to enjoy the good weather again and got down to preparations. As Kader wore the same clothes everyday like a school uniform, it was difficult for her to wash and dry them every two days. Her woollen cardigan was still wet. She opened the door of her wardrobe to put on one of the clothes Aysegul bought for her. She got one and put it on in a hurry. She looked at herself in front of the mirror. It suited her well, but she took it off, thinking that its cowl neck was too showy. She tried the others on. Although all of them were plain and casual clothes, she made a sour face as she had found some of them too short and the others too revealing. She had jeans, but they were too tight. Wearing these would reveal her shoulders, legs, breasts and hips, so although they were still wet, she put on her old clothes covering her beauty without ironing them. She rushed to the kitchen.

She placed a bag of stale bread for the swans and some cleaned fresh fruit for Lizet into her jogging bag. Then, she helped the old woman put on her shoes. As they went out of the garden gate, they encountered their neighbour Lawrence. They greeted each other quickly and the boy turned his gaze to the girl with a sweet smile on his face. What a beautiful young girl she was with all her innocent looks in her blue eyes, her thick curly hair outgrowing her hair clip and her captivating shy manners. He couldn't get his eyes off the young girl who looked like a character from fairy tales with her flower patterned dress, old woollen cardigan and dark coloured shoes. Lizet seemed happy to be chatting with Lawrence. She was speaking French with him. They would complain about the absence of neighbourly relationships in this country as they went for jogging every day. The young boy must have thought that he was taking them out of their way, judging from Kader's bored and shy manners. Pulling himself together, he politely wished them a pleasant day and left there in his gentleman fashion.

When Lizet and Kader arrived in the park, the families there, the majority of which were British, were mostly dads and kids playing games together. Two small, fat boys at the age of 3 or so playing games excitedly caught Kader's attention. It was true that the weather was warm, but not warm enough for the kids on the slide to be only with their diapers on. As for the boy under the slide, he was also running here and there completely naked except for his shoes. The shoes looked thicker and the shoes bigger on his naked body. Two boys seemed to be telling things to each other in different languages, but still communicating quite well. They were speaking so fast and excitedly… Both of their cheeks had blushed out of this excitement. The boy above was saying something through his dummy between his lips and the other was cleaning the sand stuck on his body with his hand and, as if understanding him, doing what his friend was asking him to do. As she watched them going around the slide and climbing on it, Kader was surprised at these boys understanding each other despite speaking different languages. She turned her gaze to Aunt Lizet in a way underestimating her courage when compared with children. Pointing at the children, she said:

"Even with this cardigan on me, I am cold… Aren't they cold as well?"

"Of course, they are. Don't you see? They've all got runny noses."

"But why?"

"They don't wrap their kids in warm clothes just as we do. When they see the sun shining above, they put them naked on the lawn."

"Don't they get ill?"

"They sneeze and cough for a while and get used to the cold temperature and don't get sick."

"Oh!"

"Even if they became sick, unlike us, they wouldn't take them to the doctor's right away just because they sneezed or coughed. Let's suppose they went to the doctor's; he wouldn't prescribe medicine or something. He would just recommend taking in vitamins and salty water. In short, they wouldn't return from the doctor's with a full bag of medicine when they were sick."

"Seriously?"

"Seriously!"

"Back in Istanbul, we used to go to the public hospital once a week. For my sisters."

All of a sudden, she remembered the beautiful, dark-coloured and thin sisters of hers. She sighed: "God knows where they are and what they are doing right now." Lizet went on speaking:

"There is no such thing here. You cannot keep the hospital busy here unless there is an emergency."

Kader couldn't be sure if it was better for a doctor to see you or not to see you when you've got the flu. Being puzzled, she turned her gaze to the families having a picnic and the lovers lying on the green lawn. How weird it was. More than mothers did, it seemed like fathers took care of the children. She envisaged her own childhood. She had never played games like this with her beloved father, who was looking for her to kill right now. She avoided this thought and looked around. It was nice that there were parks at every corner in this country. In order for people to have some rest, there were parks in almost every neighbourhood or near the shopping malls. She remembered her own plantless, grey neighbourhood. Unconsciously, she compared everywhere she saw here with her own neighbourhood, which was the only place she had seen in her country. She caught a glimpse of two artificial slides ahead over which water flew to form small waterfalls. Then, the Crying Rocks suddenly fell into her mind. She wondered if tears were still flowing through them. She looked at Lizet's face and asked her:

"Do rocks cry, Aunt Lizet?"

"I don't know if they cry, but I have seen smiling ones." Kader helped her sit on the bench after she said "Excuse me!" to the other person sitting there. She didn't know why, but in this country, everyone said this expression even when their eyes were accidentally met. Although she had learned this language well enough to be able to have short talks with people, she still wanted to fully acquire it very soon and be engaged in long conversations on any topic she desired. She gave Aunt Lizet the apple she sliced. The old woman started to tell her about the Smiling Rock as she was giving off strange noises with the apple she was gnawing with her false teeth:

"After the wedding of Cem and Aysegul, we went to visit Rosa's grave in Ortakoy. By the grave of my sister, there were pieces of rocks with their roots deep in the earth. We were never able to have them disrupted at all. They had become even more grey each year as if they were the ancient witnesses of history. Cemil Michel was talking to his mother as always while Aysegul was busy placing her wedding bouquet on the grave. I would never believe that if someone else told me about it. I saw a pair of smiling lips on the upper part of the old rock

226

there which had formed like a human face. It was like my sister was watching us as well as smiling at us sweetly." Her voice gradually got lower:

"From then on, I have neither mentioned the notebook with burned edges nor said anything bad to my niece in law," she murmured with a voice which was hardly audible. Kader took out a napkin to wipe the old woman's mouth and said:

"Then, it's true. If this rock could smile, those rocks must have been crying," she said to herself. Lizet curiously looked at the young girl:

"Who was crying?" she asked. The young girl didn't know what answer to give for a moment. She suddenly remembered her mother's warning. "Don't say anything to anybody!" she had said and by that, she must, for sure, have implied the fact that she had been raped on the ship. No harm would be given if she just told the story of the Crying Rocks. Even though there had been a great lapse of time since the girls in Sile told her the story, Kader would still cloud up whenever the thought of it fell into her mind:

"The rocks... I have seen the Crying Rocks. And I know why they are crying," she replied. Lizet becoming even more curious, Kader started to tell her about what she had heard from Binnaz and Nesligul from the beginning. They lost track of time. It was thanks to the rain drizzling and the wind blowing that they realised it had become dark. Considering that Cem and Aysegul might have been worried, they made their way home.

Upon seeing Cem and Aysegul were not home yet, they

had a sigh of relief. The couple returned home from work as the young girl was helping Lizet have her dinner. They came near and asked after her. Pleased that she was happy and healthy, they were just about to go to the living room when Cem Michel reached a card to Kader. Cem Michel:

"You can call your mum after you dial the numbers on this card. She called me at work today and gave me the number of the phone she had bought. I noted it down here. "

"Seriously?"

The young girl gleefully took the card and the paper she was given. She intended to ask questions about her mother, but she gave up soon. She had a phone and would be able to call her now after all. After she finished her meal, Kader changed Lizet's diaper and put her to her bed. She wanted to go and call her mother right away, but Lizet was touched by the story of the Crying Rocks very much. As Kader was laying her duvet on her, she was still talking sadly:

"Poor that little girl. She lost her mother. What was her name?"

When Kader was about to turn the light off, she paused and looked at the old lady:

"Doga…" she said.

"And her mother's name was Nefise."

* * *

A Turkish proverb says 'an ember burns where it falls' but

228

the truth is the sparks of this fire were burning others as well. Nesligul, who hadn't smiled once since her friend's mother died, came angrily and furiously back from school again. Throwing her school bag into the middle of the room, she started to cry, saying that Doga was still missing at school. Yasemin tried to console her, reminding that it hadn't been long enough after her mother's death and she would get over this death as the time went by, but all her efforts were in vain. She asked her mother: "Mum, is there any chance that they will place a bomb on my aunt's workplace as well?" Her mum didn't know how to answer her question for a moment. After that horrible day, Nesligul always had a fearful expression on her face caused by the fear of losing the people she loved most.

To relieve her daughter and drop the subject, she said:

"Don't keep your mind busy with this stuff. Go and get dressed. We'll go and see your aunt's new place."

On her aunt's lap, Nesligul was watching the spectacular view through the window of her new apartment. Meanwhile, her grandmother was giving instructions to the serving girl of the building waiting at the door:

"Don't forget to cook spinach, celery, cabbage stuffing once a week, will you?" The woman was about to take the money and leave when she called out to her again:

"And, make rice pudding every now and then. Gulcem likes it a lot." Nihal saw off the woman and went to the living room. Gulcem was looking once inside and twice outside of the apartment to make it obvious that she liked it very much.

Her father was ready to set out, waiting for her mother. Nihal was aware that it was high time they had gone as she was doing up the buttons of her jacket, but it was still difficult for her to say goodbye to her beloved daughter. Gulcem came closer to her mother:

"Mummy, can you please say my best wishes to Candas?.. Tell him that I am doing fine. And that I missed him a lot…" Candas was the name she had given to the freak in Sile. Nihal sulked at first… Then, she turned to her daughter, whom she always pampered and nodded to imply: "Ok, I will." Gulcem was aware that her family was not a fan of her relationship with a freak.

"He must be either on the beach or in the graveyard," Gulcem said and made it clear to her mother how much she wanted her to convey her best wishes to him.

The freak of Sile would go to the bathhouse once a month and rub his dirt blistering in the steam of boiling water. He would soap up his hair twice and rinse it. He would put on his underpants he dried up in the sand and wouldn't chill there for hours like others who wanted to stay for long and make the most of their money they paid by pouring water with copper dippers over their head a hundred times. He would be done in an hour and hit the main road leading to the cemetery with his dog waiting for him in the yard. The Freak didn't like this crowded street at all. Along the street, there were wooden bistro cafés built over the timbers standing upright and whitesmiths blanching copper potteries opposite them. On this way, kids would follow him from behind and pull his dog's tail.

The dog would not show his teeth to these kids. He would just go away from there just as his owner would do. Like his dog, the Freak wouldn't chase the kids. Instead, he would just hold them in esteem, greet them respectfully and enter the cemetery. Every time he had a bath, he would place his teapot on the fire and warm himself up over a glass of light tea.

Apart from the times he went to the bathhouse, the Freak knew well when exactly the beach was free of crowds so that he could wash his socks and undershirts. He would go down to the beach in the evening in spring and winter and after midnight in the summertime. His dog would also play in the waves of the sea, swim in the shallow parts and clean himself up. Then he would shake off the water on him and reach his neck towards him and the Freak would caress his head with his hands. Although he always had shabby clothes on him, he would still go and buy a couple of newspapers and read them every day.

That evening, he found a spot for himself again and started reading the news after he laid his wet clothes over the bushes to dry. His dog got out of water and while he was shaking off, it was like he tried to say something with his uneasy barking that sounded like growls. The Freak looked at the direction the barking came from and saw a group talking men in haste with dark blue suits in the spacious field on the hill overlooking the sea. He hurled himself like a father fox whose pups were in danger of being prey to a hawk and slyly approached there to be able to overhear the ongoing talks. One of the officials there was saying that there would be construction by pointing at the big area at the bottom of the steep slope where the beach ended. His panic turned into concern. He frowned his eyes with fear on his face, but later he tried to pull himself together. The mayor was speaking without minding the Freak who was standing almost under his nose and lending an ear to the conversation:

"Let the construction commence as soon as possible. The project must finish by the spring." The engineer pointed at the place ahead with his hand:

"We'll have the sand removed over there within one month," he said. The Freak looked at the place being shown in terror. He turned his back worriedly without hiding his feelings any more. He had heard what he was supposed to hear. Brooding on what he could do now, he angrily started to throw pebbles into the sea.

* * *

Kader's eyelids became so heavy and she felt sleepy. Aunt Lizet had rested her back on the pillows with her shawl she had wrapped on her nightgown. She was all ears, listening to the young girl. Kader stood up slowly. She uncovered Lizet's duvet. The old woman got her shy eyes off the young girl and fixed them on the bed. She watched her movements gratefully while Kader was changing her diaper uncomplainingly and helping her lie on the bed. Just as Kader was leaving the room after she turned the light off, she heard Lizet say:

"Dear God! I am grateful to you that you helped me wake up from a sound sleep and learn about life," she murmured.

In order not to see and disturb the newlyweds watching a film and drinking wine, probably in a close embrace in the saloon, she went down the stairs half way. As she always did, she called out to them "Good night!" from there. Usually, they would answer her back "Good night for you, too" and Kader would go back to her room.

This time, Aysegul asked her to come near them: "Kader! Could you please come down here for a minute?" Going down the stairs two by two, the young girl rushed to the saloon. Although Aysegul and Cem Michel had seen her like a member of their family, Kader always felt shy and regarded them as masters and herself as a slave. Cemil Michel wrapped his arm on her like a father and thanked her for all she did for his aunt. The young girl felt even shyer under this arm. Meanwhile, Aysegul reached out for a folder on the tea table.

"I almost forgot it. You are going to this college for two years."

"What? To college? She felt very happy and excited, but she immediately pulled herself together.

"Seriously?" Thank you so much, Aysegul!"

"4 hours on Friday evenings and 8 hours on Saturdays and Sundays."

"12 hours per week," Cem added.

"What about Aunt Lizet?" Kader asked thoughtfully.

"You know that we do not work on Friday evenings and on the weekend. And also, Maria will be here, you know."

"But it will be too much of a burden on you."

"No, it won't. If you need our help, we can also help you study on the weekdays. You will speak English in a much better way soon."

Thanking them respectfully, Kader went up to her room. She hid her own number and took out her 'Yes.' card. There were a lot of numbers on this card. Firstly, she dialled this number and did whatever the answer phone asked her to do. And Finally, she dialled her mother's number. The phone was ringing. She thought that they had all gone to sleep by this time of the day, but she kept waiting, knowing that her mother was expecting her call. Then, the phone was picked up. She was startled by her father's voice saying "Alo." She immediately pressed the button to hang up the phone. Kader couldn't sleep at all that night. Brooding about what her father might have thought after this anonymous call, she stayed up all night worriedly.

After she did her regular job for Aunt Lizet the following morning, she hid her number and took her card out to call her mother and find out what had happened last night. She dialled a lot of numbers again. This time, what her ears were filled with was her mother's warm voice. She immediately said that she had called the previous night and her father had answered the call. She asked if he had ever mentioned anything to her. Her father had not said anything about this call. She excitedly gave her mother the good news and told her that she would start the course. Later, she asked about her sisters and learned that they were all doing fine. She was pleased to hear that the government would give her family a temporary flat, but there was also the bad news. Her uncles were looking everywhere for her. Kader noticed that she was shivering for a moment. She pulled herself together quickly and didn't let her mother notice it. A part of her mind was with Cemil. She asked her mother about him. Cavidan told her that they hadn't heard from him at all. Perhaps, he had drowned in the sea in France. Kader didn't want to even bring the thought of such a thing to her mind. A gut feeling was telling her that he was still alive. Her mother went on making warnings to her with her warm voice.

"Don't put yourself in trouble. Don't mention what happened to you. They won't understand the true side of the story. You are very beautiful. She might be jealous of her husband because of you. Don't mention the bad days we had on the ship back then." Her mother was listing all her warnings. Kader started to speak to try to ease her mother's mind:

"Mum! Don't say such things. They are such different, such good people that they would support me if they knew it, but now that you don't want me to mention anything, then I won't," she said. After she hung up the phone, she went downstairs and thought that her mother was worried about the family she was working for just because she had talked to them only a few times and didn't know them well. Still, Kader's heart was filled with uneasiness. After what Saban had done to her... If they knew it... Would they all start seeing her differently? "What was my sin to deserve that horrible day?" She was filled with a sense of rebellion. She put these thoughts out of her mind right away and got down to unloading the cleaned milk bottles from the dishwasher. After Maria came back from dairy shopping every morning, Kader would put the empty bottles in the wicker basket in the garden, get the full ones and pay the milkman every week. When she went out to the garden to put the empty bottles that day again, she met Lawrence, who, as far as she heard, was the only son of their neighbours living next door. He was back from his morning running. With a sweet smile, he turned to Kader. He looked at her admiringly. He wondered where this outstandingly beautiful girl came from. She was going in and out of their garden, veranda and windows like a bird. How did she come and land on the house right next to theirs? Then, smiling sweetly again, he greeted her in English:

"Good morning!"

"Good morning!" Kader replied shyly. The boy intended to have a conversation with her for a while, but the young girl averted her eyes and went back in the house as if she had had an urgent thing to do. She poured the milk into the ceramic jar right away and rushed to the dining hall. It was obvious that Lizet, waiting for Kader at the breakfast table, was impatient. The mind of the old lady was busy with the Freak of the Crying Rocks and the reason why the construction to be made on the Sile beach mattered to him.

"Could it be that his gold was buried in this beach?" she asked curiously. Kader was spreading blackberry jam on Lizet's bread:

"His things which are more important than gold..." she said and started to tell the story again.

* * *

Being worried about his sister, Gulcem's brother was sitting with his psychologist friend Ferhan from high school and telling him everything that happened. He was expecting to hear the good news that could relieve him.

"Have you ever taken Gulcem to a psychologist before?" Ferhan asked.

"Yes, we have. It was nine years ago... she had an attack when our grandpa was lost. We took her to the psychologist those days. She didn't need to go there a second time as she had got over it."

"Are there any abnormalities with her behaviour?"

"No... In fact, she doesn't have a really big problem, but I am still worried about the fact that she has broken off an engagement for the third time or that she is running away from men. There might be a psychological reason for that."

"If you want me to diagnose, I need to speak to her herself."

"She is so absorbed in her job; she wouldn't come here to see a psychologist. Perhaps, we could go and see her together when you have time."

Ferhan visited Gulcem not long after this conversation was made. Two friends were seated on the wing chairs by the window and chatting. Gulcem went to the kitchen and came back to put something to eat on the tea table. Ferhan looked out of the big window and said:

"A marvellous view!"

The lights across the Bosporus were on. The moonlight had fallen on the sea. The lanterns in the Poet's Park were illuminating the bricks of the newly restored houses. Gulcem came with the wine bottle in her hand and sat across from them. She reproached her brother for not bringing his wife and kids along with him. Engin said that they just stopped by on their way. Ferhan, who turned his gaze to them from the boats cruising and leaving foamy traces behind as in fairy tales, envied how much these two siblings were fond of each other. He was in search of words to start speaking to Gulcem, who did not seem to have any psychological problems, but Gulcem spoke first:

"You are a psychologist as far as I heard, right?"

"Unfortunately yes! You know what they say. 'Cobbler's children have no shoes.' I am not very happy with my own mood," Ferhan said jokingly. Engin wanted to bring an explanation to the situation:

"Ferhan got divorced from his wife. His ex-wife doesn't let him see his son."

"Whatever... My lawyer is about to solve this issue," Ferhan said to drop the subject and pointed at a frame on the wall:

"If she didn't look old, I would say that this was Gulcem's picture," he said. "It's my grandma," Engin explained.

While she was pouring wine into the glasses, Gulcem told him that she was only 2 when she died and her brother had been sleeping with her until he was 11. She was using her cute gestures while speaking. As cheerfully as his sister did, Engin went on:

"I am lucky about grandma and you are lucky about grandpa, my dear." He turned to Ferhan and continued to speak:

"After my grandma died, my grandpa gave all his love and affection to Gulcem. He adored her." The mysterious expression on Gulcem's face after Engin said this did not escape from Ferhan's notice.

"Is your grandfather alive?" Gulcem remained silent and her brother answered the question:

"We don't know it, either. He went missing nine years ago."

"How?"

"According to the rumours in Sile, he took a boat out and told everyone that he was not going to return. We looked for his traces for years, but we haven't heard from him again."

"Sounds interesting."

"As a matter of fact, my grandpa used to take his boat to the South very often, but then he would always keep in contact with us and he would return home in a few months, wouldn't he, Gulcem?" In an effort to hide her discontentment with the subject, she took her violin in hand:

"Yes, would you like me to play the violin for you?"

How much the Freak of Sile was missing the melodies that came out of this violin... The melodies that the strings of Gulcem's violin produced sometimes made him cry and sometimes amused him just like a mirror reflecting the strings in his soul. Ever since the young girl left there, he had gone around their villa off-screen every Sunday and looked inside through dark windows. Just then, he felt like he was listening to the same melodies. As he was walking with his dog from the Crying Rocks to his daughter's grave, he would throw some food from his bundle to the green headed ducks with chunky bodies, large beaks and colourful feathers shining like silk swimming in the gradually decreasing water stretching from the left hand side of the pier to the hotels. It was apparent from the smile on his lips that he enjoyed doing this as he had undertaken Gulcem's job who used to carry full bags of bread from home to these animals. If only he could know that his wounded bird was happy wherever she had gone, then he would feel on the top of the world. As if he expected help from the blowing wind, he stretched his arms to the sky and wished for the happiness that could finally heal her wounds.

Gulcem was going to pick up her niece Nesligul from school and take her for shopping. Her hands on the steering wheel and her eyes on the road full of holes, she patiently looked at the pavements that were taken down and rebuilt continually as well as other drivers that were impatiently honking. There was so much traffic that she was able to move in the direction of her niece's school only by using the side roads. Some kids were running towards their school buses and some others were going home on foot through the school garden... Gulcem parked her car near Nesligul's school bus. She took out her ringing mobile out of her bag. While watching the kids in the car and smiling happily, she started talking to the mayor of Urfa. Gulcem was researching the villages of the girls who were exchanged with two sheep when they were still children, those not being sent to school, disappearing suddenly or committing suicide. She hung up the phone angrily because of the indifference of the mayor. She noticed at the last moment that Nesligul was out of school and taking the school bus. She was about to get off the car when she saw that the driver of the school bus was helping Nesligul get on the bus by holding her on her armpits with his two hands. She rushed out of the car with the worried expression on her face. While she was shouting at the bus driver, her face looked as if she had gone mad. "Leave her alone!" she shouted and pulled her niece towards herself quickly by holding her on her arm. The driver, who hadn't done anything wrong apart from helping a child, was shocked. Nesligul could make nothing of what her aunt did:

"Aunt! she called out. Gulcem came to herself and smiled at her after she pulled herself together. Nesligul fell into her aunt's arms happily. While they were getting in the car and going away from there, the driver was still looking at them from behind bewilderedly.

Going out of one store and entering another, they were

shopping at a shopping centre which was bigger and more luxurious than the one that had been bombed. Not being able to understand whether they were shopping or fighting in a war, they threw themselves into a café. After they had some rest, they headed to the escalators with the bags in their hands. Nesligul looked around for a while:

"Aunty! Do you think they have placed a bomb here as well?" she asked and put her worry into words. Gulcem looked at Nesligul's face carefully:

"I don't think so, but we can ask my friend if you want. Mr. Oguz Polat for example… He can tell you that there are not always bombs at every crowded place." Gulcem tried not to reveal that she was worried about her niece's fear.

Gulcem's mind was always busy with her niece's bomb phobia. As for Ferhan, he was trying to understand the psychological problem of his friend's sister. These two young people had met each other with totally different thoughts in their minds. The young man couldn't get enough of talking to or looking at the young lady, who was very elegant, well-educated and intellectual. They were sitting at a fish restaurant by the sea and drinking alcohol. While they were chatting, he felt that he was jealous of the moonlight that had fallen on Gulcem's face. At first, he thought that this might be the effect of the alcohol he drank. After a short moment of silence, he realised that he wanted to see her again as soon as possible:

"Let's have breakfast together tomorrow. What do you say?" he asked. Gulcem had no intention of seeing her brother's friend everyday who had popped out of nowhere. Yes, Ferhan was a good looking and witty man. She had noticed his Casanova manners tonight as well, but making these dates more frequent could lead to a dangerous love. The young man went on speaking half-jokingly in an attempt to read Gulcem's mind:

"You know breakfast is just the pretext for chatting. I'll give you a ride to work later," he said.

Gulcem did not even feel the need to give an answer to Ferhan's offer to meet again. Ferhan was watching each of her movements carefully. He was determined to find out why this young lady, being full of joy and love, was running away from men. He decided to play his physician card:

"A trauma in childhood may unfortunately leave a mark in one's heart which is difficult to treat in the future," he said all of a sudden. Gulcem frowned slightly:

"You are sensitive about these things as a result of your profession, I think."

"Believe it or not, I would still think likewise if I weren't a psychologist. I think that you had a happy childhood."

Gulcem nodded to imply 'yes', but it was apparent that she was disturbed by the question. The way to avoid this smarty psychologist's questions about her past was to draw his attention to another topic that was more important. Gulcem looked at her watch:

"In fact, there is something I'd like to talk to you about. But not tonight."

"Why not tonight?"

Reaching for her purse, Gulcem spoke half-jokingly:

"What I want to ask is a little sensitive matter. It may take some time. Whatever... I'll come and see you at your surgery." After she paused for a while, she went on speaking as if she suddenly remembered what to say:

"Actually, I had better make an appointment now."

Let me give you a privilege and tell you that you can come over whenever you want... You can be sure that I can treat you well," Ferhan said, upon which Gulcem laughed:

"No, no.., It's not me being sick. It's about Nesligul." Ferhan was very surprised:

"Nesligul?"

Gulcem mentioned that her niece had a fear of losing her loved ones, she was always alert in crowded places and that her brother and his wife were not aware of the problem although she herself was quite worried about it.

Nesligul's bomb phobia, which was considered unimportant at first, started to make the family worried as the situation got worse, upon which they began to get professional help on Gulcem's recommendation. The young lady, who met Ferhan because of her niece's situation very often, seemed to be pleased with these gatherings, but she couldn't rid herself of the distress that had been burning her heart, for which the cause was obvious. In these gatherings, which had become a cause for a new relationship to be born, Fehran watched Gulcem admiringly, spoke, remained silent and lost track of time with her. Gulcem, who had vowed not to fall in love again, brought the subject to her niece again:

"So, you're saying that there is nothing we should worry about Nesligul."

Ferhan was doing his best to help the little girl overcome her bomb phobia:

"Don't expect to see remarkable progress in a few sessions. She is having a happy childhood. She is enjoying life. She must keep away from violent films or news until we put a definite diagnosis," he said. Listening to the young man carefully, Gulcem considered all the things they should do as her family. As Ferhan was watching her graceful and cheerful manners, he didn't avoid revealing his true emotions. He asked the young lady private questions and put out the feelers. Gulcem, being a little tipsy, told him that she liked reading books and playing the violin in her free time in joking manners. Upon seeing the young man expecting her to continue talking about herself, she added that she enjoyed shopping and going to the hairdresser's half-jokingly... What's more, she also said that she drank five cups of coffee and ate a plate of salad every day.

"Do you have a boyfriend?" Ferhan asked by using his warm voice, giving an impish look to the young lady under his eyebrows. Gulcem:

"No, I don't. I don't want to," she said shyly and lowered her head over her plate to avoid eye contact with Ferhan. The modern young lady was gone and instead, a new introverted blushing girl wanting to hide under the table was there.

"Why?" he asked. The young lady, feeling off colour, refused to answer and played with her fork, implying that she was fed up with these questions. Ferhan put his hand over her hand in a friendly manner and took it back after a warm touching:

"Do you miss Sile?" he tried to broach the subject again.

"So much... I am longing for mum and dad. And a friend of mine as well. I call him Candas."

Ferhan looked at Gulcem as if he found an important clue.

"Hmm... Now I am curious about this friend," Ferhan said to dig deep and see her reaction, but Gulcem didn't want to make an already healed wound bleed again. With the intention of hiding the mystery in her past, she changed the subject to nature and the conflict between man and nature just as she did every time they met and when the subject of Sile was brought up.

On Sile Beach, the waves were beating the rocks even more angrily and the trees were fighting tooth and nail with each other. Even the regular fishermen drinking alcohol on their boats by the shore were not there that night. The Freak showed up all of a sudden on the beach which had become a creepy place with the furious cold of nature on this windy winter night. The digging tools in the wheelbarrow he pushed with his two hands could be hardly perceived in the dim light of the lighthouse. Although it was dark, he still checked if there was anyone around there and walked agitatedly with quick steps to the field where the mayor and engineers were talking a couple of days ago. He did not look like a mad man that night. He had even the decisive manners of those people who knew precisely what to do that night. What's more, he was even murmuring things and talking to himself. In fact, he was going to finish this thing before. Unfortunately, that bastard Selcuk had appeared again, but he himself was smarter than him. He was going to kill two birds with one stone. He was going to make him pay for committing a crime and getting away with it for years. Moreover, he had taken this time to send a petition to the organised crime control bureau this morning and reported that Selcuk would be involved in human trafficking of more than 100 people to France by the end of the following September. He went beyond the barricade the officials had built and put his digging tools on the ground. He looked around with his loyal dog. On the right hand side, he saw that there was no light other than the dim light of the fishing boats. He turned up the flashlight in his hand a bit more and bent over. He started to dig, saying to himself "Yes, it is the right place." The giant waves were beating one another in the sea and giving off scary noises before they were able to hit the shore. The Freak took the flashlight on the ground and pointed it at the pit he dug. He couldn't find what he had been looking for and felt troubled. He stood upright worriedly. It was obvious that he was thinking about Gulcem.

Gulcem left the pack of crisps in her hand on the side of the couch and turned off the TV. She looked out of the window in the saloon for a while. She seemed to be looking at not the blue islets the sea had formed, but the road that was covered with asphalt. She turned her frowned eyes to the inside of her apartment and her body followed her eyes. Then, she remembered why she had been pacing in her apartment for hours. Her mum was offended by the fact that she had not hung her grandpa's pictures anywhere in her home. She stood in front of the painting of her grandma who resembled her very much. For some time, she looked for the guilty fair-skinned person she intended to see. She couldn't see any. She watched her grandma who sat in the picture resting her white-skinned fat hand under her chin. In fact, both of her grandparents were from Konya. Once her grandpa was appointed to the district governor's office in Sile, they all moved to this small town. Her parents got married and Engin and Gulcem were born here. After her grandpa retired, they didn't go back to Konya and her grandma became sick and died in Sile. Her grandpa would always caress Gulcem's hair and cheeks, telling her that she had got her face and hair from her grandma. Gulcem loved her grandpa and her grandpa loved her so much. Gulcem asked him very often:

"Did you love grandma as much as you love me now?"

"Your grandma was a very beautiful, very kind-hearted person," he said and embraced his granddaughter. "I wish my grandma hadn't died and I could have a chance to see her," Gulcem always said to him. Gulcem's lips were swollen and her nose became red because of crying a lot. She was standing in front of the painting and looking at it with blank eyes. The tension in her flat was dispersed by the phone ringing. It was one of her mother's regular calls she made every night. She was calling to hear her daughter's voice and check in on her. While Nihal was repeatedly listing her warnings to her daughter, Gulcem told her that she was going to go to Sile as soon as she had set the things right. Then, she asked about the Freak:

"It's becoming cold. Have you sent the sleeping bag to him?" Having heard that she hadn't done it yet, she slightly reproached her mother.

As a matter of fact, the Freak didn't mind the cold at all. In the dim light of the flashlight enlightening the enclosed area on the beach, it was obvious that the three pits had been dug newly. He was digging the fourth one more slowly as he got tired. Just when he stood upright, he heard the banging of his pickaxe hitting a hard object deep in the ground. He had an expression on his face that showed he had found what he had been looking for. He took the flashlight again and pointed it to the deep pit he was digging. He bent over it and took out the old plastic boots that lay on the top. He put them in the wheelbarrow. He handled the flashlight and pointed it to the pit once again. The lid of a huge barrel stuck out like a sore thumb. Hitting it with the point of the pickaxe and struggling hard, he was able to slightly open the lid that had become inseparable from the barrel. After he had some rest to catch his breath, he took it out with a few movements and put it in the wheelbarrow. The main point was to take that big barrel out. He tried to move it by holding it on the edges. It was buried so deep inside that it was impossible for him to manage to do it alone. He grabbed the pickaxe immediately and started to dig around the barrel. Two drunk men were having a row at the end of the stairs leading to the beach and walking towards the seashore.

The drunk man attempted to throw himself to the sea, saying "Leave me alone, I want to go and swim," and playing the tough. The other man was trying to hold him back.

"Swimming in the middle of the night?"

"Our seven generations swim both in daylight and at night. Got it?"

"Yeah, I get it. Come on here. Let's sit and smoke a cigarette together."

"OK! Let's do it. You know my wife. My wife... Hah... She says she will put me out on the street. As if I am dropping by home..." As the drunk man was staggering and trying to keep walking, the dog was getting uneasy. The Freak hastily looked at the direction the dog's steps led to. Where on earth did these people come from just when he had found what he had been looking for? He looked at the barrel and turned his gaze to the direction of the noise once again. The drunk man:

"Let go of me!" he said and tried to free himself of the other man's hold. The Freak called his dog to come back and commanded him to be silent. He turned off the flashlight hurriedly. In the darkness, he stumbled on the pickaxe and fell into the last pit headlong. The dog was bustling for his owner and asking for help from the strangers to be able to take him out of there. The other man, who was less drunk, heard the noises:

"What was that? Who is there?" he said and looked around carefully. The drunk man was still preoccupied with his own trouble:

"It should be my wife. Let her search everywhere for me. I won't go back to her anyway."

"No bro... This is the Freak's dog. Look there. There is something over there."

"I don't care... You can go and check yourself."

The man lit his lighter and walked towards where the barking came from. He stumbled on the rope barricade he couldn't notice and fell down. He stood back with difficulty. He passed beyond the barricade under the rope and lit the Freak's flashlight. The dog was running between the man and the pit and making sounds begging for help. Meanwhile, the drunk man's voice was heard again:

"Hey! Where are you? I'll go swimming." The man was shocked when he saw the Freak having fallen into the pit in the dim light of the flashlight:

"Wait a minute bro... The poor man fell into the pit. Gosh!" The drunk man, staggering and standing upright, began to take his clothes off on that cold winter night. His friend was trying to get the Freak out of the pit:

"This man... Yes... It's that man. Remember... He used to wander around here. It's the Freak bro... His head is bleeding.

Is he dead? Damn it!" The drunk man was left with only his long calico underwear:

"You're kidding me! If only my wife fell into one of those pits as well."

The man, cursing his drunk friend, took the Freak out of the pit and laid him on the sand.

"Oh dear!" he said and checked his pulse. Then, he sat by the flashlight and dialled some numbers on his mobile phone. "Come on… Pick it up… Pick that damn phone up…" As he was trying to reach someone, the drunk man was doing what he felt like doing.

"Call my wife. She knows all the numbers of hospitals, police stations and coffee houses."

* * *

Nesligul's treatment was going on at a university hospital and her parents hoped that she would get over her bomb phobia soon. Professor Oguz, who helped Ferhan with the therapies, got out of the exam room and came to speak with the family. He told them that it contributed positively to Nesligul's treatment that she was growing up in a happy family environment, that her sickness was not at an alarming level and that she would be able to get over her bomb phobia very soon, upon which the family breathed a sigh of relief. When Prof. Oguz left them, Ferhan and Nesligul got out of the room and came near them. Ferhan slowly spoke in a joking manner:

"Let me tell you a secret. I think your daughter wants to have a sibling." Engin looked at his wife affectionately and said half-jokingly:

"So do I, but our mother has no intention of having one."

Yasemin thought for a moment:

"I'll consider this issue once more for the sake of my daughter's health," she said. Nesligul's eyes looked for her aunt. After she learned from her father that she could not come due to her job, she gave an impish look to Ferhan, implying that she was aware of some things like an old head on young shoulders:

"Uncle Ferhan must be sorry to hear that," she said. After a sweet laughter, Ferhan:

"Don't worry, young lady. I am with your aunt at dinner," he said and made Nesligul feel jealous jokingly.

Days chased days and Ferhan chased Gulcem. Early on, Ferhan saw the young lady through a psychologist's eyes, but when he met her that night, he declared his love, saying that his heart was beating for her. Nonetheless, Gulcem dropped the subject using her sleight of mouth and returned the focus to her niece's condition.

"She is henpecking her parents into making a sibling for her," she said and made Ferhan laugh. Though in a joking manner, Ferhan replied ironically:

"What else could this poor child do? She waited for her aunt to have a baby, but if she doesn't…"

"Well, blow me down!" Ferhan became serious and rested

his elbows on the table. He looked at Gulcem admiringly:

"When we first met, my psychologist identity was dominant." Gulcem started sulking and frowning. Ferhan went on speaking: "When I came to your place with your brother for the first time, - I don't know how to say it - the sad expression on your face when we talked about your grandpa made me really upset." The pupils of the young lady grew bigger. What was this man trying to mean? Was there something he knew?

"I didn't understand you!" she said angrily. Ferhan stood up and sat near her. He got her hands in her palms. He spoke in his voice full with affection:

"Later on… I mean I am so happy to get to know you!" Gulcem was relieved:

"Stop exaggerating…" she said while a warm feeling wrapped her whole body spreading from her hands in Ferhan's palms. What if the thing she feared most was happening to her again and she began to be burned with the fire of love she had sworn off… As Ferhan was addressing her in the depth of her eyes, she slowly took her hands off the happiness she was unable to control. If she could let herself go, she would hug the young man's neck. She restrained her feelings and told him that she wanted to leave. Ferhan, not changing his warm manners, held her hands and helped her stand up. He hung the young lady's purse on her shoulder with his own hands. As they were walking towards the exit with the young man's arm around her waist, Gulcem was happy, but filled with a strange uneasiness.

When she got home, Gulcem refilled her glass again and

again, and constantly drank water. She was sorrowful. As she was pacing in the living room lost in thoughts, her mobile started ringing. There was Ferhan's name on the screen. She didn't pick it up. She threw it on the couch. This time, she filled her glass with wine. She tossed it down as if she were drinking water. She refilled it. As she was drinking one glass after another, her phone kept ringing at certain intervals. Gulcem was in pain... She knew that the man she loved was in pain, too.

"My God! Please help me... I love Ferhan very much. Please let me be happy with him!" she murmured and cried. She looked at the painting of her grandma. She groped her neck as if looking for a necklace. The crazy look had fallen on her eyes that were fixed at the painting.

Meanwhile, someone was insistently calling the phone of the house in Sile. The chief of police invited Yalcin to the station kindly. His wife looking at him anxiously, he got dressed and left home quickly. The chief of police stood up and welcomed Yalcin respectfully.

"We have bothered you to come here. Our apologies..." he said. Yalcin was anxious. He sat on the chair the chief showed him.

"No problem, but my wife and I got really anxious. What is it?"

The chief took a heart shaped necklace out of his drawer. He opened its lid. There was a small photo of Yalcin and Nihal as well as Gulcem between them in it.

"I think this belongs to your daughter," he said, passing the necklace to Yalcin. He took the necklace. He was surprised. Unable to stop his hand trembling, he answered the chief:

"Yes, this is my daughter's necklace. It had been lost since the last trip she went on with her grandpa."

"Two days ago… Remember that freak man, whom your daughter loved very much…"

"Yes…"

"He was seriously injured and taken to hospital, but he lost his life last night."

Yalcin felt sorry.

"What a pity! May God rest him in peace."

"If he were alive, we would be able to find out a lot of things from him."

"Things like what?"

"A barrel was found in the pit he had dug before he died. And inside the barrel…"

The chief was having hard time speaking:

"Inside the barrel… How am I supposed to say… A dead body was taken out. This necklace was between the finger bones… And these plastic boots…" Yalcin was even more anxious.

"A body?"

"Yes, I am sorry, but we think that that is your father in-law, Nihat Tatlicioglu's body."

Yalcin was appalled. He leaned back with his shoulders sunken and remained so for a while.

"How is it possible?"

"In fact, we'll have the autopsy report tomorrow. We suspect that it was the Freak who buried the barrel in the beach nine years ago. But why? What might his problem have been with your father in-law? Considering his close friendship with your daughter, we'll carry out an extensive investigation. If you can remember anything you know, please do call me." Yalcin put the necklace in the pocket of his jacket and stood up. He asked the chief to be excused and left there.

When he got home, his wife was worried to death. Yalcin didn't know where to start answering her questions. He took the necklace out of his pocket and passed it to her. He told her what he had heard from the chief. Nihal, who started crying while listening, wiped her tears with the handkerchief in her hand. Her eyes were still on the necklace in her other hand:

"My poor father... He didn't have any enemies. Everyone in Sile loved and respected him. Why would the Freak want to kill him?" she said. Yalcin tried to console his wife, who was sitting near him:

"The Freak couldn't have killed him."

"Gulcem wanted me to send him the sleeping bag. I didn't want to help that guy for a reason I didn't know."

"Whatever... Don't upset yourself. Let's wait for this autopsy report..." Nihal was still looking at the necklace that she couldn't drop:

"Do you remember? This necklace was not on Gulcem's neck when she had gone to the beach with her dad and come back alone. Nihal envisioned the day her father disappeared. She remembered that day like yesterday.

Gulcem was at the age of 16. She was down on the beach with her grandpa. Her parents wouldn't be worried about her as long as her grandpa was with her. They had barely sat for dinner when Gulcem came in. Her grandpa was not with her. Her white dress from Sile cloth was covered in fig stains.

"It seems that you climbed up the fig tree again." she said, but her daughter didn't answer. She noticed that there was something wrong with the behaviour of her daughter who had started to drink like crazy. After a moment of silence, she asked: "Where is your grandpa?" Gulcem dropped her eyes and kept drinking water:

"I don't know. I think he took his boat out to sea, mum!" she said.

"I am worried that he will be caught by a storm one day," Yalcin said to express his concern, upon which Nihal calmed her husband down, being comfortable when it was about his father's marine skills:

"Don't worry, my love. My father has gotten over so many storms before."

"But he has become old now. And you know he's been drinking a lot recently." Gulcem was turning a deaf ear to this conversation and drinking as much water as to draw attention. Seeing her daughter drinking so much water, Nihal looked at her and realised that the necklace that she never took off from her neck was missing.

"You never take off your necklace." Gulcem suddenly groped her neck with her hand.

"My necklace! My necklace is gone…" she cried out. Yalcin smiled, looking at his daughter's stained dress.

"Don't be sad, my girl. It might have been stuck on the tree when you were picking figs. We'll go and buy a new one," he said.

Gulcem went out to the terrace with a glass of water in her hand. Nihal went after her daughter and heard her speak to herself with an angry, trembling voice after drinking up the whole glass at once:

"If only this water were as bitter as poison. If only it could suppress the pain inside me." Nihal immediately took her to the doctor, but she healed soon and didn't want to go to the doctor again.

* * *

When Kader was back from the course, Aysegul was texting with her friend on the computer and Cem Michel was taking the films he had just bought out of their covers. The young lady rarely saw the couple. When she was asleep, they were at work. When they were back, she rushed to the course. And when she was back, she could hardly see them around. After she helped Lizet go to bed right away and put the fruit plate she had prepared in the kitchen onto the big tea table in the living room, Aysegul got her head off her computer:

"I could have prepared it, Kader. You are already tired," she said. Being content with her condition, she smiled cutely:

"I am not getting tired at all, Aysegul."

"Do you do your homework?"

"Yes…"

"If there is anything you can't understand, please don't hesitate to ask me. OK?"

Kader nodded approvingly. Aysegul passed the book in her hand to her:

"You should study this book as well when you have time for it. Your English is good enough for you to read it now."

"What is it, Aysegul?"

"It's a study book for citizenship."

"Is there a book for that?"

"Of course, there is. You have to know the history, geography, social and political conditions of this country if you want to become a citizen. Kader took the book despite being worried that she wouldn't be able to memorise all these things.

"I have to be a citizen of this country, don't I?"

"Yes. Your mum mentioned that you would apply for asylum. Your lawsuit should be opened soon."

"That's right."

"I'll tell our lawyer to follow your cases. And he'll apply for citizenship on your behalf."

"Thank you, Aysegul. Good night for you," she said.

By the time Cem Michel and Aysegul wished shy Kader a good night, she had already made for the stairs. She went to her room and called her mum right away. She told her that she was given a book to become a citizen. Her mum told her not to worry and added that she would call Aysegul and speak to her. She was going to say that Kader would apply for citizenship on her own as she was over 18. Kader thought that she became worried for no reason and sat at the computer table. It had no internet connection, but she was allowed to use the one in the living room if needed. In fact, she had no idea what the internet was, let alone how to use it. She didn't feel the need to learn it by now. Even if she had needed it, she wouldn't have used something that didn't belong to her. It was enough for her to keep a record of her course materials on her own computer. She was so comfortable with this family that she could ask, read, learn and do research about anything she was interested in. As she did every night, she took a look at the newspapers of the previous days like The Guardian, The Daily Mirror, which Aysegul and Michel had bought and read… Looking at the pictures and using the dictionary in her hand, she tried to read and understand what happened in the world. Then, she skimmed over the TV programmes in it and tried to translate the theme of the film she wanted to watch. A film called 'The English Patient' was on BBC tonight. As far as she could translate, the film was set in the Second World War. It featured Almasy who had severe burns on his body as a result of a plane crash. The only part of his body he could move was his eyes.

The film was about this man being in deathbed. A nurse called Hanna looked after him in an Italian monastery. The wounded man began to remember his mysterious past. Kader thought that the film might be a good one as far as she understood from what she had read. She checked the time it would start immediately. There were still two hours ahead. In this case, she could watch one of the films Aysegul gave her in this gap. She set apart the ones with subtitles. She learned a lot of new words while watching these movies, thus improving her English as well as having fun. In fact, those without subtitles could help her learn faster, but she found it easier to watch them with subtitles especially when she had time to amuse herself. What the young lady enjoyed doing most was to watch films. Although she had never gone to the cinema and watched all the films on DVD, the cinema always had a special place in her life. Suddenly, she noticed the DVD called 'Sophie's Choice'. She remembered that Aunt Lizet mentioned the name of this film... It was the story of a mother who was obliged to make a choice between her two kids in a Nazi camp. Whichever child she chose, the other was to be put to death. She chose one of them, but both were killed in the end. The first time Kader heard this story from the old woman, she hoped to find and see this movie of the mother who managed to escape from the holocaust, but ended up committing a suicide after living a life full of mysteries. She looked at the picture on its cover... An actress called Meryl Streep played the mother. She put on her flower patterned pyjamas and put a glass of water on the night-

262

stand by her bed. She also placed the chocolate box that she had bought with her own wage. She took the film out and put it in the DVD player, making herself comfortable by leaning on her pillow to enjoy the movie.

Aysegul was cheerful, texting with her friends on the computer. The moonlight enlightened the spacious shady glass cased living room overlooking the veranda and the flowers of the fruit trees filled inside with beautiful scents heralding the arrival of spring. Cem Michel offered his wife to go and drink something outside, but she was too lazy to accept the offer as she had already changed her clothes. Both their marriage and professional lives were on track. What's more, Aunt Lizet, who had been the biggest obstacle for this marriage for years, turned out not to allow anyone to speak ill of Aysegul. Everything was fine, but still not perfect. It was obvious that there was a matter which everyone in the family was aware of, but unable to speak out. They didn't say anything to Aysegul in order not to make her upset, but she couldn't get pregnant although they had been using no contraception at all. Nonetheless, it was still apparent that they were longing for a baby. Aysegul suddenly saw on the screen that Ahmet was online. Then, she received an instant notification. After a few messages asking about each other, Ahmet gave her the good news… Focusing on the message on the screen, Aysegul read the sentence letter by letter: "Cemil is with me!"

"What!" she wrote and rushed to let her husband know: "Cemil is here." Breathing a sigh of relief, Cem Michel looked at his wife. Aysegul wrote and listed her questions one after another: "When did he come? Where is he now? How is he doing?" Then, she couldn't stop herself any longer and jumped on her mobile phone: "I am calling you in a second."

It had been long since Cemil came to London, but he didn't want to call and upset Aysegul as he was in trouble with the British Police at first. Fortunately, the problems were solved one day ago. "We can surprise Cemil when you are available someday. He is having a rest at Macit's place tonight." Ahmet said… Being available? No matter how tied up she was, Aysegul would always have time for Cemil who was the person teaching her what friendship, solidarity and fellowship meant:

"As soon as possible… No later than tomorrow… I want to come and see him immediately," she replied.

The following morning, the husband and wife let Kader know that they would be late tonight while they were having a quick breakfast in their usual smart and elegant clothes:

"A friend of mine came from Istanbul. We are going to have dinner together."

"OK! Aysegul. Don't worry about Aunt Lizet," said Kader, who wouldn't wait for a moment to go with them if she knew that this friend was Cemil.

Although spring was getting ready to give its place to summer, it rained so much in this country that they could seldom see the sun these days even in this city where there was usually more sunlight in comparison with the others. Kader took the old lady out to the garden and turned the straw chair towards the sun. She helped Lizet sit across from the sun which continually appeared and then disappeared as if playing hide and seek. She was about to rush inside to get Lizet's cardigan when she saw Lawrence mowing the grass with the grass mower in his hand at the house next door... The air was wrapped with a fresh scent of grass and soil. She thought that Lawrence enjoyed playing with the soil and doing this on his own as everyone else there had it done by other men from private companies. Kader greeted the young man in a rush and went inside. She knew English well enough to be able to communicate with him... In addition to doing things at such places as post offices and banks by herself, she could also have quick talks with Lawrence in short sentences after greeting him. However, she still avoided engaging in long conversations and kept her eyes fixed on the ground probably because she didn't think she had the right to look him in the eye.

Upon coming back with Lizet's cardigan in her hand, she saw Lawrence leaning on the garden wall and saying something to Lizet in French. Lizet must have realised how affectionately the young man had been watching Kader as she offered him to come over for a coffee. Lawrence must have been waiting for this offer for a long time because he jumped over the wall at once after he thanked her politely. Kader, believing that her English was still not good enough, just asked him if he wanted milk for his coffee in English. He replied in English with his usual polite manners and his eyes overflowing with affection:

"A little milk, please!" Kader was already on her way to the kitchen though Lizet called out to her from behind:

"Maria can bring it. Sit down please," Kader didn't even hear her and got down to preparing the coffee with milk. When she came back with the coffee tray in her hands, Lizet was talking to the young man in French by looking at Kader:

"Kader is no different than our own daughter," she said. The young lady didn't understand what they were saying, but hearing her name being told in a sweetly articulated sentence made her pleased and she got her own cup and sat down. The old lady would usually talk to the young man asking about each other without getting into private topics when she met him some mornings. But this morning, she talked about herself and her country quite a lot. And Lawrence told her in his sympathetic manner that he studied media at Kingston University and his family was not happy at the beginning that he had chosen this department. Once they realised his talent at the cinema, they also supported him for choosing it. His dad was a plastic surgeon and his mum was an academician at Greenwich University. Both his parents were British. Lizet politely complained about the fact that the concept of neighbour visiting was a bit different in this country as she could meet them only when they coincidentally saw each other in the garden. Neighbour visiting! The young man was alien to this concept, which suddenly warmed his heart. He tightly embraced these two words.

Lawrence, sitting as if he had no intention of leaving, was looking and smiling sweetly at Kader, trying to extend the conversation as long as possible. Kader was lowering head and giving short answers. Meanwhile, Lizet kept talking about the skills of the young girl half-jokingly. Knowing that the boy studied cinematography, she said:

"Kader loves watching movies a lot. You know?" The young man turned to Kader, considering that they had a common interest:

"Is that right? I have a big film archive. If there is anything you particularly see…"

"Thanks a lot," she said and nodded. As Maria was picking the empty cups, Lawrence thanked for the coffe and headed for the garden of their own house. Kader felt the experienced eyes of Lizet on her and she lowered her head as if she did something bad.

"So, was the killer really the Freak? Tell me about it briefly, please. I will burst with curiosity," the old woman said, upon which the young lady raised her head. The story of the Crying Rocks was being told once again by Kader, whose voice filled the garden.

* * *

Coming to her office in the TV channel she worked at, Gulcem looked sleepy and tired the following morning of the night Ferhan proposed to her. After she sat at her table, she took out a pill from her purse and swallowed it. A little beyond, the reporters were feverishly discussing the day's agenda. Rich countries allegedly took a common decision to release the debts of poor countries for once only... And these countries could use the money they no longer had to pay back for self-development. Gulcem, who was already depressed, didn't know if she should laugh over this news or take it seriously by considering the possibility of its being real. The reporters were just about to make phone calls to investigate further when Gulcem implied that they were just wasting their time: "They first colonised these countries and made them poor and now they are deleting their debts... Drop it... The large-heartedness of our people will be enough for us," she said and pulled the daily newspapers towards herself. Meanwhile, a boy came inside with a bouquet of wildflowers in her arms. As she could guess, Ferhan sent these flowers. She gently placed the flowers on her table and picked up the phone that was ringing. She smiled when she understood that it was her mother who was calling. Gulcem was happy to hear that they were coming to visit her on the weekend. Nihal had neither given her the bad news nor let her notice anything with her voice. In the meantime, she checked the screen of her other mobile which was also ringing insistently. She saw that Ferhan was calling, but didn't care at all. Shaking angrily and sadly on her chair and drinking water quickly again, she got down to reading the news that had caught her eye. She felt even worse to have read the story of a 15-year-old girl who hanged herself in the stable of their house in Sanliurfa. There was no way for her to keep working that day. She decided to go to her sister in-law's place to see her. She stood up. Seeing Nesligul could perhaps do good to her. In the meantime, Ferhan was parking his car at the car park of Gulcem's workplace and talking to his ex-wife on the phone, accepting her demands which he could not deal with for the time being. Telling her that he would pay her credit card bills that she couldn't pay by herself, he hung up the phone. Just then, he saw Gulcem approaching her own car hastily. She seemed sad and bothered.

"Gulcem!" he called out and walked towards her. Although the young lady was feeling bad enough to faint there, she tried to look indifferent. "I didn't know that you would leave work early today. I wanted to surprise you," Ferhan said with a sweet smile on his face. Gulcem neither replied to him nor looked at his face, looking for the car key in her purse. Ferhan could not find out the reason for her weird behaviour:

"I want to talk to you if you have a slot for me in your calendar."

"I am sorry, Ferhan. I am on my way to my brother's place," she said and ignored his request with a cold look. Ferhan's cheer was also gone.

"Is that so?" he asked slowly.

Gulcem realised that Ferhan was offended by her rudeness, but she had no intention of having a sincere apology talk:

"Nesligul hasn't recovered yet. I should go and see her," she said and bent over her car. While she was inserting the key to open the door, Ferhan spoke in a decisive and serious manner.

"You are not answering my calls. Can I think that this is all about Nesligul and breathe a sigh of relief?" Gulcem didn't know how to answer. She averted her eyes from him and got into her car. Ferhan went on talking, holding her door open:

"Alright! I'll call you again. If you don't pick it up this time, I will think that I am disturbing you... And I won't call you ever again."

He bent and kissed her on the cheek in a friendly manner. He shut the door of her car. Gulcem started her car without saying a word. Ferhan looked from behind until her car went out of sight.

When Gulcem went to her sister in-law's place, Nesligul had just returned from school. The little girl felt really sorry about the fact that Doga left the school and was taken to her aunt's place in Izmit. "An aunt is the second mum to every child," Gulcem said to console her, but Nesligul told her that her friend needed her first mum and not the second. What was the bombers' problem with her mother, Nefise? It was not possible to console Nesligul.

"I used to be proud of having raised a girl who is very sensible, honest and compassionate... Now, I can't stop questioning myself whether we have made a mistake after all she has been through. I am even angry at myself." With her sister in-law's sentences, Gulcem remembered the girl in Sanliurfa about whom she read in the newspaper:

"Life out there is so cruel... Kids hesitating to hurt even an ant are offering everyone flowers. How are they supposed to cope in a world which is full of people that shoot bullets on flowers? How are we going to manage to overcome all these?"

After they chatted for a bit more, they decided to take Nesligul's old clothes to the child welfare charity. Gulcem joyfully packed each piece of clothes into the suitcase along with their stories. They were very excited to bring the clothes, each evoking a happy childhood, to the children whose pasts were full of both sweet and bitter memories. After spending a happy day together and giving her niece and sister in-law a lift to their house, Gulcem felt the burden of her own problems on her shoulders again on her way home.

When she was in the car, Ferhan called her once more, but she didn't answer it or didn't want to answer it again. This must have been the last time the man she loved called her. He had said so in the morning. She realised that she was troubled by the likelihood of such a thing. She could be neither with nor without him. As she was pacing in her living room, she fixed her eyes at her mobile that remained silent. She didn't remember how many hours it had been since. All the ashtrays in the living room were full to the gunwales and the wine glasses were empty. She turned the TV on. The channel was mentioning her own project. Her mood was not good enough to watch even the first broadcast of the campaign 'all girls should be sent to school', into which she had put so much effort. She shut down the TV. She lit another cigarette. She started to undress herself after she plugged her mobile phone on the charger, which hadn't still rung. She left each of her clothes wherever she took them off. She walked on them and went under the running water in the bathroom. She splashed the water all over her body long enough to expect everything that troubled her to be gone away with the water. In the meantime, she thought that she did something good by not calling Ferhan. She could, for sure, overcome the pain of love by biting her hand one day and by biting her arm the next day. She was going to arrange a different programme for each day, travel a lot, thus not having time to think about him. Just then, her phone rang. As if it was not her who made all these decisions a minute ago, she rushed out of the bathroom with her hair shampoo foam on her. She had to catch this call. She had barely grabbed it when the phone got silent. She looked at the screen. It was Ferhan. She called him back right away. How could she do such a thing? She heard the heart-warming voice of the man she loved without having much time to think if she should hang up:

"Thanks for calling me back, honey. How is Nesligul doing?"

"She feels sorry about Doga, but she is OK now."

"I wish you could know how much I wanted to be with you right now."

Gulcem remained out of breath for a while. She couldn't speak. Her tears were running down her cheeks. Ferhan's voice was in her ear.

"Gulcem! Are you there, my love?" She wiped her tears with the back of her hand and replied with a crying voice:

"I love you, but I am also very scared of it."

"Never be scared of love, sweetheart. I love you so much, too."

272

"I hope I will never wake up from this dream."

"But you are not dreaming! Wait. I am almostgetting to your home."

Ferhan came. They talked and talked. They promised not to break up from each other. Gulcem started to feel great. She got angry about torturing herself until today. Upon her lover's repeating the marriage proposal, she hugged his neck happily.

"If you let me have five kids, then yes, I will!"

"Are you serious?" They hugged each other in a big love.

"Yes..."

"This weekend, my parents are coming here from Sile. They will be very surprised at my decision to get married."

The following day, they had both lunch and dinner together, making plans for their future. They spent their days talking about which flat they would live in, whether they needed any more furniture and where and how the wedding would be. Gulcem was looking forward to giving her family the good news. Finally, the weekend arrived.

She prepared their parents' favourite dishes by herself. It was obvious from her cheerfulness - running here and there- that she was extremely excited.

"I am very happy that you came here. I have good news for you after dinner." she said without knowing that her family had actually come to give her very bad news. Her parents talked to each other and decided not to give her the bad news on such a happy day. They were not going to tell her that the

Freak was dead and her grandpa's body was found. They could talk about it at a more convenient time. Nesligul was very curious about the news her aunt would tell them.

"Come on, aunty. Tell us the surprise news," she kept saying and pulling her cardigan impatiently.

"Let's serve the dessert first and then I will," Gulcem said and walked to the kitchen with her niece.

Yasemin followed them for help as well. Yalcin seemed to be relieved to see his daughter so happy. He looked at his wife with a light heart:

"I hadn't seen my daughter so happy for years," he said. Nihal looked at her husband and her son:

"But let's be very careful and not let anything about Sile slip out," she said and warned them over and over again.

While Gulcem was putting the desserts on plates in the kitchen, she touched Yasemin's belly jokingly:

"You can start going on a diet. You wanted to look slim at my wedding. Remember?"

Yasemin dropped the plate in her hand out of astonishment. She knew that Gulcem was dating Ferhan, but she had never thought that they would get married. Gulcem showed her how serious she was by saying that nothing could make her change her mind. Nesligul:

"Aunty is getting married! Aunty is getting married!" she cheerfully shouted and ran to the living room.

When Gulcem and Yasemin came into the living room

with the dessert plates, Nihal was waiting standing for them as she had jumped to her feet out of astonishment:

"Is it true what she's just said?" The young lady placed the plates on the table and announced the great news in high spirits that made her happiness apparent:

"Yes!.. Ferhan and I decided to get married." The family forgot all about what had happened in Sile and became wholly absorbed in the lure of their one and only daughter's marriage decision. As they were eating their desserts joyfully, Gulcem dropped a kiss on her mother's cheek and asked:

"So... Is everything alright in Sile?" After a moment of silence, her mother smiled and spoke:

"Everything is the same. Exactly how they used to be…"

"I missed him a lot. I mean Candas. How is he doing?" Nihal and Yalcin looked at each other in a meaningful silence while Engin and Yasemin averted their eyes from her. Gulcem repeated:

"Mummy!"

"……….."

"Are you asking about the Freak, aunty?"

They all became worried in fear that Nesligul might blurt something out. Yasemin tried to warn her by squeezing her leg under the table, but Nesligul let the cat out of the bag:

"Candas is dead." Gulcem dropped the fork in her hand. As Nihal was telling off her granddaughter, Gulcem was looking at the others. She expected one of them to say that it was a joke.

"I am telling the truth, aunty. He fell into a pit." Yalcin went on, thinking that there was no way of hiding the truth:

"We didn't really want you to be upset on your happy day, but ...." As Yasemin was trying to console Nihal, Gulcem, who was rocked, asked with a voice hard to hear:

"What pit? How did he fall in there?" She started drinking water quickly. His elder brother: "What happened happened, honey. Let's talk about everything now if you want and not bring up this topic ever again." Nihal came near her daughter and caressed her hair:

"We felt really sorry, too, when we first heard about it... The Freak... They said that he dug a pit on the beach nine years ago... Those days when my father disappeared..." She tried to tell her about the event, but couldn't continue as she saw the expression on Gulcem's face was getting worse and worse. She began to cry. She went into a deep silence. All she did was to refill her glass and drink up water again and again. Engin sat near her sister and said:

"Calm down, my dear. He was already very old. They did everything they could at the hospital but he couldn't make it..." Engin wanted to hug Gulcem and put his head on her shoulder, but the moment he touched her shoulder, she pulled back and jumped to her feet as if a fireball had touched her body. She fixed her eyes at a certain point and two words escaped through her lips, behind which her teeth interlocked out of fear:

"A pit?" Everyone in there stood up, not knowing what to do except for looking on.

"They took out my grandpa's body as well as your necklace from the pit," Engin said.

Gulcem was shaken forward and backward with a complicated expression on her face and fainted where she was.

* * *

Although Kader was only in charge of Lizet's care, she got up early in the morning and finished the chores which were not her responsibility. As Lizet was having her breakfast, she did the shopping list. She was going to send Maria to the supermarket, who was supposed to come for cleaning soon. Both Aysegul and Cem trusted her for any issue. She was happy in this family, yet she still missed her own family, in particular her mother. If she could see them every now and then, she would be the happiest person in the world. She remembered her uncles. They must be looking everywhere to kill her.

While Kader was clearing the table, Maria called her to say that she was sick and not able to work today, so Lizet and Kader decided to do the shopping together and went to Tesco in the vicinity. Lizet sat at the café of the supermarket and Kader did the shopping. She dropped the things she had bought near Lizet and asked for her permission to go and get some local Turkish newspapers given away for free in front of a small grocery shop near the market. She couldn't still understand why newspapers were offered free of charge on the undergrounds, trains and at some stores.

When they arrived in the garden of their house, they met

and greeted Lawrence, who got off the car that approached the garden gate at that time. From the way the young man rushed out of the car and looked at them smiling, Kader felt that he was going to come near them. She averted her blue eyes from him and took Lizet's arm, yet the young man still stood before them with two cinema tickets in his hand. He said both in English and French:

"I wanted to come and see you," he said.

"Come on in," Lizet replied.

Lawrence turned to the young lady in a warm manner that resembled that of a father, a friend or a lover:

"Would you like to go to the cinema with me tonight? Shakespeare in Love..." he said.

Kader felt stuck between her emotions of being sad or happy for a while. The newspapers and journals were all advertising this film. It was a love film nominated for an Oscar. As she always watched her films on the small screen of TV, she was in fact desirous of seeing this film at the cinema, but going to the cinema with Lawrence that was in the middle of London seemed impossible. In accordance with the traditional laws, the death penalty was decreed, which is why it was dangerous for Kader, who was being researched by her uncles, to go to Reading, let alone the city centre. However, Lizet was unaware of these worries of hers.

"Of course, she would like to... Why wouldn't she?" she said. The young lady who blushed with the thought of going to the cinema, pulled herself together and spoke in a decisive manner:

"Thank you… But I can't," she said.

Upon Kader's refusal, who was a cinema lover as keen as Lawrence himself, he didn't insist, but he was just surprised. He stood up and left there with his usual smile without showing offence. Hiding her beauty under her clothes as if being beautiful were a sin, Kader wanted to go inside and read the newspaper right away. Almost every step Turkish people took was written in these papers. Perhaps, there might even be something about Cemil in them.

She cleared the table quickly after Lizet finished her meal. Once the old woman got to her place to read her holy book, the young lady got down to reading the local news. Her eyes caught the events of the Turkish Education Association. If Cemil was alive, he must be attending these events. He had mentioned the names of these organisations very often. He had also mentioned that paying a visit to these places on certain days of the week could be useful. "Thanks to the friendships made through these organisations, no one becomes homeless or unemployed," he had once said. The newspaper in her hand had enabled her to find a shelter in Aysegul's house. She looked at the job advertisements in it once again. She considered where she could take shelter when Cem Michel's job was done here. There were so many advertisements… She felt relieved… What's more, she hadn't had to spend much money in this house except for buying chocolates and snacks for only a few pounds and was able to save money. She read that there were many workers needed for jobs that were suitable for her. These jobs were mostly posted by foreign families looking for employees to stay overnight. The responsibilities were generally to take kids to school and back or do household chores. There were also some Greek and Italian restaurants looking for dishwashers or waitresses. After she unwillingly underlined those which provided accommodation, she went down to the kitchen to cook dinner. Generally, Maria cooked dinner or they ate out, but when Lizet slept longer than she normally did or read her holy book, Kader wouldn't idle about, but would use this time to try the various recipes from world cuisines that she had learnt recently.

After Lizet woke up from her nap in the afternoon, she wanted to go for a walk to the park. Normally, they would go on their daily walk in the mornings, but they had spent their time doing the shopping that morning. Although walking with the old lady restricted her freedom, it was the time of the day Kader loved the most. It made her feel relaxed to think about her village, her sisters and her beloved mother while feeding the swans with bread by the creek and above all to tell Lizet about Gulcem's story, who shared the same fate as her.

Once Lizet sat on the bench and took the stale toast bread out of the bag in her hand, she asked with her trembling voice:

"So… Did Gulcem recover after all?"

In the hope of enjoying the comments Lizet would make, Kader resumed telling Gulcem's story without skipping any detail with the illusion of the Crying Rocks before her eyes and the voice of the young lady in her ears.

* * *

The first lights of the morning were falling on Gulcem's face. With the crazy expression that had become fixed on her face, she was looking motionlessly at a certain point under the influence of the medications. Ferhan was sitting by her side, caressing her face and hair:

"Don't be sad, sweetheart. It's all gone and you are perfectly fine," he said to bring her back to reality. However, Gulcem seemed not to hear the things being said to her. Once Ferhan left the room to speak to the young lady's doctor, her parents sat by her side.

Engin was pacing on the aisles of the hospital where doctors, nurses and other medical staff were in their routine hustle and bustle, and trying to forget about his sadness and despair. He went to Ferhan when he saw him:

"How is she doing?"

"I think she is going through a serious depression."

"She had never been like this before. She looks as if she were in another world..."

Ferhan put his hand on his friend's shoulder:

"She is now under the influence of medication, Engin... These are strong medications... Let's give her some time for the treatment... She'll come to herself step by step and be back

281

with us," Ferhan said to give strength to both Engin and himself. They went to speak to Gulcem's doctor together. It seemed that Ferhan already knew his colleague:

"Please, tell me something!" he said before they sat.

"I wish I could, but I haven't been able to make a diagnosis yet. However, I have good news. No harm was seen in her MRI and blood tests." Feeling relieved a bit, Ferhan sat on the armchair and got his head between his two hands. He was in great pain. The doctor turned to Engin:

"I think this is not her first attack."

"In fact, she hasn't had such a severe attack before. Except for that day, of course."

"Which day?" the doctor asked.

"The day our grandpa disappeared... She was as crazy that day as she is today. She drank water one glass after another when she came home. She didn't talk to any of us for days. We took her to the doctor's that day, of course. She recovered soon after she underwent a short therapy."

"When did your grandfather disappear?"

"Nine years ago... As we explained before, she became like this when she heard that our grandfather's body was found."

"If you could tell me all the details about how your grandfather disappeared, this might be helpful in the course of the treatment."

Engin started telling them everything he could remember while the doctor as well as Ferhan were listening to him with great interest.

"Gulcem was 16 years old. She went down to the beach with my grandpa as usual. Gulcem came back from the beach alone. We were told that my grandpa had taken his boat out to sea. We didn't mind it at first. There had been many times before that he did so without letting us know, but he came back after a while. We waited for him to return and looked everywhere for him for a long time." Having taken note of what Engin had to say, doctor looked at the young man thoughtfully:

"What was the reason for Gulcem's intimacy with this man and such a big sympathy as to give him the name 'Candas'[10]?" He asked and turned to Ferhan to keep talking:

"If we can find the answers to these questions, we may figure out the reason for the trauma Gulcem is going through."

Being confused by what he had heard, there was only one thing Ferhan was sure about: His love for Gulcem! No matter how long it should take, he was going to wait for her recovery and marry her. As these thoughts were flushing through his mind, Engin was saying that the police would also be involved and carry out an investigation to find the answers to many questions. The most important information that could help the doctor was the answer of the question why Gulcem had a strong liking for a man who was nicknamed 'the Freak' and mocked by the people in Sile. Engin thought that his compassionate sister felt pity and sorry for him and that's why she showed him intimacy, but the doctor went on by saying that he didn't agree:

"I don't think it's so simple. Besides, there is the necklace

10 Candas refers to the Turkish word for 'soulmate' or 'life mate'

issue, which was found within your grandpa's bones."

After a short moment of silence, the doctor asked a new question:

"Did your grandpa drink alcohol?"

"Yes... Especially in his last times, he used to drink a lot. He was very drunk that day as far as we know."

Ferhan, struggling to be able to help with his beloved patient's, his love's treatment, turned to his colleague:

"And she came back from the threshold of marriage three times." The doctor looked at Ferhan carefully:

"This is more important than the rest of what you said. Why was she so afraid of marriage?"

When Engin came home to take clean clothes to his sister, he heard the phone ringing. When he picked it up, he was told by the chief of police that a man called Selcuk Gur was caught as the suspect of their grandfather's murder and his first questioning had been done, upon which Engin breathed a sigh of relief. Then, the chief of police went on explaining the details, assuming that Gulcem's family already knew what had happened to her:

"He admits for now having raped Gulcem, but not having killed your grandfather..." Engin remained silent for a moment:

"What? Gulcem was raped?" he could say and looked for something to hold on.

"You didn't know about it? Yes... Selcuk Gur admitted

284

committing this crime but..." The receiver in his hand fell off. It can't be true what he just heard. His one and only sister was raped when she was only 16. It seemed impossible to believe that. Why didn't Gulcem let him know about it? How was she able to endure such suffering at that age? How could they not think of the possibility that this might have happened? He kneeled down where he was as if he had felt, in ten minutes, all the suffering his sister had had for so many years. On the couch he had fallen onto, the moment his sister was raped flashed before his eyes. He rushed off from his seat like a madman. Yasemin, who went down upon hearing the noises, found her husband crazed. He was hurling everything he grabbed around and punching the walls.

After a while, Engin rushed to the hospital. He told everything he heard from the chief of police to his family, Ferhan and the doctors of his sister. The family could hardly believe that such a tragedy might have occurred. Ferhan did not get devastated by what he had heard as the others did. Quite the contrary, he seemed to be relieved. He had already guessed and thought about the possibility that Gulcem might have been raped at the age of 16 when she went down to the beach with her grandpa. He had been considering the possibility of domestic abuse until then and thus he felt relieved upon hearing the news. From now on, the treatment for the woman he loved would be easier.

Days went by, but Gulcem's condition showed no progress. Meanwhile, Nesligul overcame her bomb phobia and she could get into crowds easily without being in fear. In fact, Yasemin had been through the same event and had the same bomb and death phobia both for herself and her loved ones although she never confessed it to anyone before. Along with her daughter, she treated herself and admitted that her fears were groundless. There were many people dying every day in accidents, hospital rooms, or through honour killings and celebration bullets in weddings. It was a fact that fearing would not make one's destiny any better. Nesligul, who was missing her aunt so much, insisted that her father take her to the hospital as well.

"Dad! Please take me with you to the hospital. It's been 46 days since I last saw my aunt." She spoke so profoundly and sincerely that her mother caressed her hair affectionately.

"Look at her! She is counting the days," her mother said. In fact, Engin did not think that it was a good idea that Gulcem would see her aunt in this condition. He looked at her face carefully. All that happened had made his delicate daughter so mature. What's more, this visit might do good to his sister as well:

"Alright, we're going," he said.

In the hospital room, Nesligul and Gulcem hugged each other tightly.

"I miss you so much," Nesligul said, kissing and smelling her aunt. Gulcem's face shined for a short moment, which seemed to fade away soon. She didn't talk, but at least she was affectionately looking at Nesligul. She was tightly holding her niece's hand.

"Let's not make your aunt tired," Yasemin said. Nesligul spoke in her childish manner:

"I will get very sick if you don't come back home soon. For your information!" she said half-jokingly and half threateningly. However, her aunty wouldn't say a word. Nor would she smile or get any better. The only improvement was that her glassy eyes glowed a bit when they met her niece's eyes.

On their way back home, Nesligul and her mother met Ferhan in the hospital garden.

"When will my aunt be fine?" she asked, holding his hands. She looked at him hopefully, implying that he could treat her aunt just as he had treated herself. Ferhan smiled and caressed Nesligul's hair and said: "Don't worry! Your aunt will be fine soon."

Days followed days, but there was no improvement in Gulcem's condition. Nihal, who was in her daughter's arm in the garden of the hospital in Erenkoy, had been discharged from another hospital two days ago. She kept telling Gulcem that her tired heart would not be able to endure sadness any more. She was looking at other mental patients passing by. She thought that Gulcem's condition was better than theirs and couldn't imagine her daughter to be as ill as they were. Gulcem revealed her fear of losing her mother using her facial expressions and she got worried. Ferhan was approaching them with a sweet smile. Being encouraged by the expression of the woman he loved, he decided to talk to her about everything. He asked Nihal to go and have some rest, saying that she looked tired. He wanted to be alone with the woman he loved so that he could try to free her memory of that horrible event.

As Nihal was going away with her mind still on her daughter, Ferhan took Gulcem to the arbour in the hospital garden by wrapping his arms around her. They sat at a table and he got her hand between his palms:

"You're getting better and better day by day, honey," he said and pulled her towards himself to rest her head on his chest:

"I know all that happened to you, Gulcem. The police told us everything."

Hearing this, Gulcem was moon eyed. The young man went on speaking:

"Tell me about it, my love. It's just your body and soul being so tired. I mean, if you really want it, you can heal and get out of here right away. And as soon as you get out of here, remember what you said… Five kids…" Being told that everybody knew all that happened to her, Gulcem shook her head in despair. Why did she hide from her family that horrible tragedy she had been through for so long?

"My mother would die if she heard about it," she whispered with a voice that was hard to hear. Ferhan raised his hopes for the recovery of the woman he loved as she was finally able to say these:

"Your mum already knows everything," he said calmly. The words flew around the hospital garden and resonated in Gulcem's ears again and again. Her mother can't have known everything. If she had, she wouldn't be alive now. She turned her pupils that grew bigger to Ferhan. She started to carefully listen to every word coming out of his mouth:

"Your mum is getting worse as long as you don't get better. They trust you. Believe me, my love. Your family already knows everything. What matters the most to them is your health and wellbeing. I will always be with you. No one can harm you anymore. Come on, my love. Just forget or tell me about everything that happened when you and your grandpa got to the Crying Rocks. Free your mind of everything that gives you nothing but pain. You have got your family, who loves you so much. You have got me, who will always be with you."

When Ferhan smelled her with a deep breath, Gulcem attempted to free herself of his arms and run away at first. Ferhan caught and embraced her tightly. He calmed his lover and kissed her face, hand and eye. Gulcem began to cry quietly. This was a good sign. She had to laugh or cry if she could not speak. As tears ran down her cheeks, she raised her head and whispered:

"So, my mum knows everything, right?" It was apparent that she was eager to speak. Now that her mum knew it, she had to get the strength to find the happiness that God had begrudged her in this world. She wasn't supposed to turn her back on the love that life was offering her now. She sniffled and wiped her tears with the back of her hand.

Meanwhile at the police station in Sile, the police inspector was talking to the man called Selcuk Gur, who was said to have raped Gulcem. Selcuk admitted having raped Gulcem, but not having killed her grandfather. He contradicted himself when it came to details he gave each time and his testimony didn't sound credible to the police. The inspector said "Keep talking!" by yelling to Selcuk who was seated before him with his head lowered and eyes fixed on the ground.

"I loved her. They were rich and I was poor. It was an impossible love as you see," he said, upon which the inspector became even more angry and raised his voice:

"Don't tell us the same things over and over again. Why and how did you kill her grandfather? Tell us about it!" he said and let him know that he was still suspicious of something hidden between lines in his testimony. It was difficult for Selcuk to talk as he knew well what exactly the inspector wanted to hear:

"I'll tell you everything, sir," he faltered and began to cry all of a sudden.

The inspector came to the understanding that the course of the investigation had changed. He commanded the two standing policemen:

"Take him!" he said.

While the man was being taken out of the room in company with the policemen, the inspector, pacing angrily, said to the policeman near him that they were running out of time to refer the suspect, whose testimony had been left incomplete, to the courthouse and they should keep on investigating for more evidence in no time.

* * *

Lizet, who seemed cheerless at dinner, had only eaten the vegetables on her plate, and had not even touched the meat although they were both cooked by boiling. She had been feeling weak lately. While the rest of the family kept on eating, she withdrew to her corner by the window and lowered her head with her holy book in her hand. As Cem Michel was enjoying the fig dessert that Kader had made, he raised his head and looked at the young lady who was busy covering his aunt's shoulders with her scarf:

"We've got a surprise for you," he said. Kader turned to them in curiosity.

"A surprise?"

"Guess who I am bringing here tomorrow." Kader thought for a while. Her mum came to her mind.

"Are you bringing my mum?"

"Yes, along with your sisters…"

Kader jumped to her feet with her mimics mixed with crying and laughing as well as her cheeks having gone hot all over. Out of excitement, she hugged Cem Michel, to whom she had always kept her distance till then. After him, she hugged Aysegul this time. She hadn't seen her mum and sisters in months. Cem Michel, while smirking, offered a glass of wine to calm down Kader, who was easy to make happy even with small things. As he was passing the wine glass he filled for her, he said:

"We are not at home tomorrow. We are going to the hospital for my aunt's regular check-up. You can take your time to catch up as you wish."

"Thank you so much, Cem."

"We'll pick your mum up from London centre at around nine o'clock. We should be home sometime between twelve thirteen. We have our appointment at fourteen at the hospital."

"Alright."

"We'll eat out. If you'd like to prepare dinner for your family, you can call Maria to help you."

"I don't need her. I can cook something," she said and hesitated for a moment. She considered which ingredients she was allowed to use and whether she should ask them or not. Aysegul must have understood the young lady's concern because she hugged her and said:

"Something won't be enough, Kader... You should prepare exactly in the same way we prepare for our guests visiting us at our place for the first time. Please don't hesitate to do as you wish. Set a table full with dessert and fruit, having no missing part." Kader's eyes got filled with tears upon all the words Aysegul had uttered sincerely:

"Thank you, Aysegul." she said and hugged her again. Aysegul held her with her two arms and took her in front of her. She gave her a warm smile and looked at her faded dress, her cardigan, probably bought here, which she never took off and her thick socks, which were obviously second hand.

"So tell me! Why don't you wear the clothes I bought you? You didn't like them?"

"I will, but I spared them for special days…"

"What special days? I bought them for you to wear casually."

"But, if you don't like them, let's go and buy new ones," Cem Michel added.

"No, no! Thank you, I'll wear them. Let me wear them out first. We shall buy new ones later."

The following morning, Kader had her eyes on the clock while preparing various dishes for her mum and sisters. "They must be in Basingstoke now!" she sighed and went on cooking the most expensive and nutritious foods, some in the pot and some others in the oven. She took out and washed the best fruit that were imported and not found in Turkey. They didn't even know their names. She checked the time once more:

"They must be in Southampton now," she said and placed the milk, eggs and flour to make pancakes. She took out various jam kinds and chocolate cream to spread on the pancakes and checked the time again. She decided to spread these on the pancakes later and went upstairs in a rush. She took a quick shower and wrapped her long black hair in the towel. She opened her wardrobe and picked one of the closed-necked dresses that Aysegul had bought and she had spared for special occasions. Even the spring was behind them. It was cold outside, but warm inside the house. Her cheeks got pink because of the heat and excitement. Her blue eyes were glowing. The doorbell rang when she took the drying machine in her hand. It could not have been her mother. She thought that they must be in Hamworthy now at the nearest and they should be here no less than half an hour. She went down the stairs. Once she opened the door, she saw their neighbour Lawrence smiling at her. Kader's hair was still wrapped in the towel. First, she felt embarrassed and later talked in English to the young man, thinking that she had no time to kill.

"There is no one at home and I am busy at the moment," she said. She was just about to think that she was being rude, but she soon dropped the idea. The people in this country were quite straightforward already.

When Lawrence said 'Merhaba!' and greeted her in Turkish, Kader was surprised that he was speaking her language. She pulled herself together and smiled at him sweetly. As Lawrence was passing the English book in his hand to the young lady, he couldn't get his eyes off her. She looked gorgeous with her innocent eyes like those of a baby, trembling lips in the middle of her cheeks like a heart and her black hair curls falling out of the towel onto her white shoulders. He did not know why, but he had no sooner felt he finally built the love attachment with her than he lost it again. There was no cardigan over her brownish needle cord dress to hide her beautiful breasts. She was just standing there on her bare feet with her awesome legs stretching down from under her skirt. Although the young man was just looking at her eyes, Kader still bent her knees to hide her legs and hunched her shoulders to hide her breasts. As she got smaller and smaller out of her embarrassment, she was growing bigger and bigger in the eyes of the young man. She reached out for the book with a shy smile and accepted it thankfully. She looked at the cover of the book and showed her contentment. It was the book titled 'A Tale of Two Cities' by Charles Dickens. With one of his legs on the door sill and the other on the first stair step, the boy was watching the girl as if glued where he was and pleased with this situation even if he had to stay like this till the end of his life:

"If there is something in it you cannot understand, we can read it together," he said in English. Kader must have thought that she had wasted too much time, so she replied quickly:

"Alright! Thank you..." she said. Seeing the rush in Kader's manners with her hair wrapped in the towel as well as the new clothes on her he saw for the first time, the young man realised after a while that he had come at an inappropriate time. Pulling himself together, he apologised to the young lady and walked towards their own garden.

After she went inside quickly, Kader was thinking about Lawrence as she was drying her hair. The loud noise of the drying machine drowned out her heart beats. From the fact that she thought about him in her bed, in the lesson, on the tube, in short everywhere possible, she understood that she also had a crush on him. Up to now, her heart had not beaten like this before. Lawrence was four years older than her. He was a typical Englishman. He was handsome. The way he looked was great. Perhaps, he was not handsome, but it was only Kader who found him handsome. He had thin hair and greenish eyes. He was tall and slim. On the upper part of his cheeks and the sides of his nose, he had freckles that were hardly visible. Kader liked these freckles so much that she not only thought that these freckles suited him very well, but also she remembered that she used to make freckles with colour pens on her cheeks as well as her sister's when she was younger. Lawrence was going to graduate from his university in a couple of months. Kader found it strange early on that he lived with his family although he had his own house. It was because the young people did not generally live with their parents. Who knows? Perhaps he did so as he was the only son of a prosperous family. Was it possible that he also thought about her and missed her? She sighed and thought that he also had a crush on her as she felt his warmth and affection in his eyes and he came to visit her every day for some reason. Yes, but what could happen at most even if he loved her? Would he still keep loving her if he knew that she had been raped? What's more, she was a poor girl from a poor country. As for Lawrence... She dropped the idea of him immediately and focused on her preparations for her mother and sisters.

* * *

Kader did not know what to do when she saw her mother... She almost couldn't recognise her. Her collapsed cheeks were filled again and her fair skinned face became attractive with her hair tied behind her neck. With a pair of cream linen trousers and a chic blouse with folded sleeves on her, she stood before Kader more like her friend than her mother. Her mother gave birth to her at the age of 20, so now she must be 38, which was women's most beautiful age. It was normal for the woman - already beautiful with her slim and tall body and blond thick hair - to look gorgeous. Kader's astonishment was due to the fact that she was used to seeing her mother sad and tired doing chores at home in old dresses with faded colours all the time, especially in the past one year when she was pregnant on the ship and in the church, where she did not even want to comb her hair after all that happened to them. Her sisters also looked better than she last saw them. They also got rid of their old clothes that evoked poverty and began to speak a little English and adapt to this country with their clean hair and sport clothes, which were a sign for neither poverty nor richness. They hugged each other tightly and got down to catching up. Cavidan looked at the house for once and later looked at her daughter. She breathed a sigh of relief and began to smile. She was sure that her daughter was in good hands, but she hadn't thought that her condition would be so good. She was at someone's place after all. Kader and her family had been talking and crying together for half an hour. As Kader's sisters were listening to her right beside her, they were also examining the house, where she lived and which they found magnificent.

"What else could I want from God after I saw you and my sisters so well, mum..." Kader said and hugged her mother again half crying.

"We prepared extra carefully just because we were coming

to see you. We are all fine. Thank God. What's missing is only you my love."

Kader brought up the subject of her father finally.

"How is my father? Is he OK?"

"He is OK. He tries not to let us know, but he also misses you. He is checking me out if I know anything about how you're doing, if you're dead or alive, but I think he assumes that you're fine as he sees how light-heartedly I behave when it's about you."

"I miss my dad, too."

"Look… I brought you his photo." Kader looked at the photo that she could handle with her trembling fingers. Her father was giving bread to the swans by the creek in a park.

"Did he lose some weight?"

"No, no! He is fine." Her sister put her finger on the photo and pointed at something excitedly:

"Look sister! This is Golders Green Park. We went there by train. It's so big and there is everything in it. We have become friends with Pakistani girls. Look…" Her sisters were telling her something. As she was looking at the photo of his father swinging her sisters, Kader, who just the other day envied the girls she saw playing games with their dad in the park, thought that not his father, but the uncivilised mentality of her country should be put the blame on as it was this mentality which banned fathers to show affection to their children and deprived her neighbourhood of such a playground. As the little girls went on talking enthusiastically, Kader was very pleased to see how happy they were. Again and again, she hugged and smelled her sisters whose hair she herself used to comb from the day they were born till the day they fell apart. The sofa was covered with the gifts she had bought for them. Although they were trying to hide it, the girls couldn't get their eyes off the glowing packets. The youngest one couldn't resist any more and grabbed one of them:

"Are these for us, sister?"

"Yes honey… Let's open and see if you'll like them."

As her sisters were unwrapping the gifts with a crunching sound and unbinding the ribbons on them, Kader asked her mother silently:

"How about them… my uncles?"

"May God damn them! They are still after you, my daughter. They will never give up and let go of you for the sake of their traditional laws, but don't fret. They cannot think of searching Reading for you, let alone here."

"Mum, I am getting my residence permit soon. The lawyer Aysegul hired for me said that."

"I think everything is getting back on the rails, my daughter. Our trial will be concluded soon as well. They say the government will give us permanent housing."

"Is that for real?"

"Yes, it is."

"You know we'll apply for citizenship after we get our residence permit…"

"Yes, hopefully, my daughter"

"Do you think my uncles can find where I am then? I mean through the registrations..."

"I don't know... Let me ask it to our lawyer as if it was not your but someone else's question."

"Please don't! I'm just asking you as I thought you perhaps knew it already. If we should ask it to a lawyer, I can ask mine as well. My uncles might find your lawyer and threaten him."

"You are right. It's better if we do it this way. Thank God you are fine and comfortable here."

"The only problem is that I'm missing you so badly, mum."

"Be alive and the rest doesn't matter. We can find each other anywhere."

"How about you, mum? Are you comfortable there?"

"Pretty fine... We are getting unemployment pay from the government as we don't have any job, but your father found a job at a kebab restaurant. He's working illegally. If it should be known, they would cut off the employment fee. In short, we are getting two salaries. My intention is to save some money and buy a house in Istanbul."

"What if the authorities catch my father... I mean catch him working illegally?"

"I was also against it, but he wouldn't listen. He says this is what most of the foreigners here do and there is no way for the government to catch him. Don't worry about this stuff. Just don't mention it to anyone. My main concern is actually..."

"What is that mum?"

"Aysegul and Cem will leave soon... What are you going to do then?"

"Don't worry mum. There are so many similar jobs here. Of course none of them will provide me with the same comfort as here, but I won't be unemployed for long."

"Is that so... I talked to her on the way here and she said that she wouldn't leave without making sure that you're in good hands, but I am still worried... So tell me more. What else do you do here?"

Kader and her mother went on talking in turns. The young lady once wanted to confide herself in her mother and asked her what she would think if she loved a rich and foreign boy and whether they had a chance together, but she gave up right away. Her mother would think of thousands of things then and perhaps she would even think that she had a boyfriend and would want to learn everything about the boy. Then she would probably start worrying about her even when there was not something serious in question. Instead, she preferred to eat, drink, and talk to her mother and sisters to catch up.

The owners of the house brought Aunt Lizet home, which meant that it was the time for them to leave. Cem tried to console Kader, saying that he would bring them again at the earliest convenience. Cavidan thanked them again and again for taking good care of Kader and held her little daughters' hands to walk to the sports car waiting in the garden.

Cem Michel set out to take Kader's mother and sisters to

the train station where the train to London Centre was to depart. Aunt Lizet was glad that she didn't have a major health issue apart from a little high blood pressure. Kader was the one who had a busy agenda… She asked the young lady how her day was and how her family was doing. She learned that they had a really nice time together, but she also felt from her manners that Kader was not very eager to talk about her family. The old lady remembered her days in Kuzguncuk where their Turkish neighbours came to visit them. They used to tell their own life stories, yet Lizet's mother would never tell their own. She guessed that this delicate, introverted girl who reminded her of her own days they spent hiding from everyone else, had been through something that hurt and made her feel ashamed, but she was not also very curious to find it out. What she was curious to find out was the Crying Rocks and who Gulcem had been raped by. However, she thought that the young girl had had a very tiring day and hesitated to ask her to keep telling the story. Kader must have understood what the old lady desired:

"Aunt Lizet, you know what… Actually something you would never guess happened to Gulcem."

"What… What happened to her… Come on… Please keep telling me!"

* * *

As Gulcem was sitting on a bench in the hospital yard away from watching eyes, Ferhan sat near her and started caressing

302

her hair slowly with his arm on her shoulder. He was looking at her affectionately:

"Ok… I am listening to you, my love," he said to encourage her, upon which she began telling what befell to her in the ominous afternoon of that August.

"I had just turned 16…

A summer day with plenty of sunlight was about to come to an end. I was on the swing by the pool in the garden. My dad and grandpa were chatting at the table. My mother had waited for the boiling sun to go away to water the roses in the garden. Our serving girl Binnaz was collecting the towels on the sunbeds. I had a smocked yoke dress out of Sile fabric with embroidered necks on me. I was not as slim those days as I am now, but I was a bit plump. While I was on the swing, I was singing a Rock'n Roll song that was quite popular those days. As she was watering the flowers, my mother would come and push the swing at intervals. Everyone in the family, especially my grandpa used to pamper me like a baby those days. He was becoming more and more fond of me, probably because he thought I looked like my grandma. He drank up a full glass of Raki at once that day and said that he was going down to the beach near the boat.

"Wait for the weather to cool down a bit, father. You can go there later," said my mother. However, he was determined. Neither did I want him to go down to the beach when drunk.

"No, the sun is about to set," he said and stood up. I called out to him from the swing.

"Grandpa! Let's go there together tomorrow morning…"

"We can go there tomorrow morning again. This time, together OK?" he insisted, upon which I jumped off the swing:

"I am coming, too," I said. As he left through the garden gate, he answered without turning his back.

"OK! Hurry up."

Gulcem gulped in pain… Ferhan feared that once she paused to speak, she would never be able to continue telling. He understood that the pain that Gulcem suffered, who was too lost in memories to be able to wipe the tears running down her cheeks, was bigger than he had thought. Fearing that she would give up telling and withdraw into herself again, he hesitated to move or even to breathe normally. After she had a deep sigh, Gulcem went on telling, looking far away.

"Hopping and jumping, I ran towards my grandpa and took his arm. I loved him so much. Even the idea of my grandpa's passing away one day just as grandma did was enough to scare me to death. We were walking on the main road in the city centre of Sile. I admiringly looked at the blouses and nightgowns from Sile fabric that were displayed in the stores at both sides of the road as if I had seen them for the first time. We greeted our acquaintances sitting at the cafés and patisseries that we passed by. We reached the steep stairs with fig and mulberry trees on both sides that connected the road to the beach. I joyfully went down the stair steps three by three. My grandpa was joking with the people going down the stairs behind me. We were going to the beach while everyone else was going back home. At the end of the stairs, I climbed up a fig tree. My grandpa called out to me from behind: "Watch out! Otherwise, you'll fall down."

"Don't worry about me, grandpa!" I said and went on picking up figs and eating them. I could see him reach the beach.

It became dark. The last remaining few people got their towels and baskets and headed for the stairs to leave. My grandpa drank two men's Raki who seemed to be his peers and who were also getting ready to leave. My face, hands and dress had become sticky because of the figs and I got the shovel and bucket of our neighbour's son to fill it with sand. The boy was stomping his feet to get his bucket back. I always enjoyed annoying him. I gave his shovel and bucket back and went near my grandpa. Frowning angrily, I grabbed the Raki glass in his hand.

"You have already drunk a lot, grandpa," I said and put the glass away. Having drunk so much, he was having a hard time standing. I washed my hands and face with the sea water to get rid of the dirt from the figs. My grandpa was only able to take a few steps and then fell down on the beach. He stood up and tried to walk again. While he kept falling and walking again and again by splashing sea water on his face, I was having fun both in the water and on the beach and I was keeping an eye on him from far away as well. The skirt of my dress became wet and touched my body to make me feel cold. I squeezed it quite well. Stepping on the sand which was still warm and walking in his direction a couple of metres away from the sea, I went near him. I was not comfortable as the soaked parts of my skirt were stuck on my hip. I wanted him to put an end to his walk on the beach in no time. We had come to the Crying Rocks.

"Are you up for a race to the rocks?" my grandpa asked.

"No, I am not because you are so drunk. You will fall again," I said.

"You're scared that I will beat you even when I am like this, aren't you?" he insisted. I felt that I shouldn't turn down the offer of my beloved grandpa. I was going to be near him after all if something happened. We joyfully went up to the Crying Rocks in water splashes. The light of the Moon that appeared in the sky had fallen on the sea surface. My grandpa stumbled while lighting up his cigarette. "Grandpa... You'll fall down," I said in panic and ran towards him.

"Nothing happens to me. Don't worry!" he said. I held his arm and helped him sit. He hugged me while sitting:

"You smell just like your grandma. And your skin is just like hers," he said. He used to use every opportunity to tell me that I resembled my grandma. I loved my grandpa so much, but I had a strange feeling. I told him that I was cold and I wanted to go home. Meanwhile, he was yawning and struggling to be able to stay awake.

"OK! We shall go, but let me have a quick nap first," he mumbled.

"OK! Have your nap. But only for 15 minutes... OK? If you don't wake up in 15 minutes, I'll push you into the water,"

I said. I was making splashes with my feet and having fun on the sea waves which rose up to half of the rocks. When I started singing, the cigarette had fallen off his hand and he had already fallen asleep. I was amusing myself with the song;

"All alone before the eyes of everyone, how I believed you..."

At the same time in Sile, Selcuk was being questioned at the police station.

"You were saying that you had an eye on Gulcem and you were following her." The young man started talking as if he had been living that moment again:

"Yes... That evening, I saw the girl singing on the Crying Rocks with her bare feet hanging down. Her grandpa was asleep. Looking at her legs playing with water, I swam towards the rocks fast and silently. I approached slowly."

The inspector was running out of patience. He collared the man in a desire to beat him:

"Tell us about those bloody boots first!" he shouted and Selcuk gulped.

"Eeeee, I approached the rocks with the boots in my hand. Gulcem had stopped singing. Out of excitement, I hit the back of her head with the sole of the boot. She fainted. I don't think she saw my face. This time, her grandpa woke up. He tried to hold onto Gulcem, who was lying there unconsciously. He was able to get a hold of the necklace on her neck. He pulled it off and the necklace remained between his fingers. I didn't push him down... he fell off the rocks on his own and he was shouting while falling: "You bastaaard... Noooo!" He fell over the rocks below and hit his head so badly. The necklace he was holding tightly was still in his hand. And I raped the girl who was still unconscious."

* * *

The leaves of the trees in the garden of the hospital in Erenkoy were swishing sweetly and making sounds as if they were talking to each other. Gulcem, sitting at the bottom of an old plane tree, had wrapped her arms around her crossed legs tightly and kept talking tremblingly. In the meantime, Ferhan was listening in despair and thinking if it would be appropriate to get up from the bench he was sitting on and go near his lover, who was looking at him with her eyes that did not see him.

My grandpa was sleeping so sweetly that I didn't have the heart to wake him up. After a while, my eyelids also felt heavy. I rested my head on a rock and lay down. I also fell asleep. Suddenly, I jumped out of my place with severe pain. My head hurt badly as if I had hit it somewhere. I thought that I hit my head on the rock while sleeping, but I soon realised that it was not actually my head that hurt, but it was the heavy person on me, whom I was struggling to get rid of. I pushed my grandpa back with all my strength. "Grandpa!.. Noooo!" I cried. In order to fall off, he tried to hold the necklace on my neck. While he was rolling down the rocks, I still remember that my necklace was still in his palm. My underpants were on my legs. There was utter darkness. I could see there was a boat sailing away. There was a dog barking in the vicinity. I wanted to throw myself off the rocks after my grandpa. The tear like flowing water at the Crying Rocks was roaring. A man along with his dog by his side was coming towards me from the bottom of the rocks with a flashlight. That moment was the first time I met Candas. The dog was running back and forth between us. I was about to let myself fall off the rocks when Candas caught me from my back at the last moment and splashed water over my face with his palms. He was the only one who saw everything. He examined my head to see the swelling. My head was not bleeding, but it began to hurt. My teeth were interlocked and all my body was shaking just like a pony in the death agony. Candas was looking at me affectionately. He took off my underpants and threw them into the dark waters of the sea. He washed my legs with the water he got in his hands. He tried to pull my dress together and made it look neat again. After he wrapped my trembling body with his old jacket he took off, he looked at my face carefully:

"I think your grandpa slipped and fell. His leg was slightly wounded," he said. That night, when my eyes were fixed only on the ground, I was carefully listening to the man whom I later named Candas. He continued talking slowly:

"Your grandfather's nose was bleeding slightly. He sailed away by his boat a few minutes ago. You know he does this all the time." There was really an engine sound off the shore and I noticed a boat sailing away far-off in the moonlight. I was not conscious enough to question how soon he sailed so far away at that moment. When I remembered that moment later on, I always thought that the person I saw on the boat that night was my grandfather. However, two or three years later, when my grandpa came to mind, I was sure that he was not my grandfather. Whatever… To put my mind at rest, Candas said that my grandfather told him before leaving that he would not come to Sile again and that we shouldn't worry about him. I was glad that my grandfather would not come back to Sile ever again. As he was affectionately caressing my hair and took me to the front of our garden wall and slowly got his jacket that he wrapped my back with. I just looked at him from behind. He walked fast and diverted to the road leading to the beach instead of the one leading to the cemetery for some reason. I couldn't enter the house for some time. I thought that my mother would die if she happened to know what my grandfather did to me. I was so ashamed that…"

Gulcem rested her head on legs and stayed in this position for some time… She felt tired and weak because of telling all these. Ferhan slowly approached and sat near his fiancée. Fearing to hurt or scare her, he wrapped her with his arm and pulled her towards himself. Seeing that she didn't pull herself back, he felt encouraged to caress her hair. The young lady lifted her head from her legs and looked at Ferhan's face. There was so much pain and despair in this looking that Ferhan felt that his heart was bleeding for her. Gulcem's nose and eyes had turned red and her lips were swollen. He rested her head on his chest and spoke affectionately:

"My love… You were unconscious at that time when you think you were sleeping. Who raped you was not your grand-

pa, but some other guy. They caught him. His name is Selcuk."
Gulcem rid herself of Ferhan's arms quickly. All her body was
shaking:

"I might be sick, but I am conscious enough to remember
what happened that day. It was my grandfather... Everything
was so real! As if it all happened just today:

After a moment of silence:

"They kept looking everywhere in the country for my
grandpa. And one year later, they gave up hope as they saw
they would not be able to find him.

After a while, I found out that that man whom I named
Candas was actually known to be the Freak of Sile. In fact, he
was very clever. From that day on, he didn't speak to anyone
until the day I decided to break off my last engagement and
settle in Istanbul. He was talking to a young man that day. It
was the first time I saw that man he was talking to. "If you
try to destroy the evidence ever again, I will report your other
crime to the police and turn you in," he said to the man with
a stained boot in his hand. I was very surprised. He kept quiet
when he saw me. The young man near him sneaked off quickly. I wanted him to talk to me as well, but he didn't say a word.
He insistently didn't break his silence. I didn' know anything
about his family life apart from the fact that he lived by the
grave of his daughter who had died at the age of 13. Now, I understand how his daughter died. To protect me and my family
from the same disgrace, Candas buried my grandfather's body
in the pit and told me that he had sailed to the South by his

boat. In this way, what my grandfather had done to me was going to be a secret between him and me and no one else was going to know that I pushed my grandfather off the rocks and killed him, either."

"You're wrong, honey. It was this man called Selcuk Gur who did this horrible thing to you. I am also suspicious whether this Freak whom you called Candas was perhaps his accomplice."

"Don't talk like this about Candas." Ferhan kept quiet for a moment upon this confident voice of the woman he loved. And later:

"OK! It's your choice. The man confessed his crime. Why would he take the blame and say that he raped you? What's more, the inspector will let you face that monster called Selcuk if you ever want to."

In company with her doctor, Gulcem went to Sile to meet the arrested man. He was undoubtedly that man she had seen talking to Candas. Her mind was bombarded with loads of ideas. She first thought that Candas might have used this man to hide this event. But why would this man take such a blame? Her thoughts in her mind not allowing anyone to speak ill of her Candas were clouded by what that man told her. Selcuk told Gulcem everything he had told the inspector. Gulcem believed him. She might have been unconscious during the time she thinks she was asleep. She considered that day over and over again. So, he had hit her on the head and caused her to faint, right? But, how didn't she feel anything when she was hit when she was awake? She had felt the pain on her head not before she fell asleep, but after she woke up and thought that she had hit her head on the rock. In fact, she had pain all over her body that night. But… But… When she woke up with the pain she felt, that body lying on her?.. Perhaps, her mind played a trick on her. Can't it be possible? Here he was… The man confessed everything he had done. With all the details…

Gulcem gained all her cheer back in one month. She was being discharged from hospital. She took Ferhan's arm which was reaching for the small bag:

"So, it seems that I will become your private patient," she jokingly said.

"You are not my patient. You are the world to me."

* * *

Kader was still going to her language course at Weymouth English Centre and she wanted to enrol in a ceramics course after she finished this one. The fact that there were almost no Turkish people in Weymouth, a fishing town with a beautiful marina in the southern part of London, helped Kader improve her English faster out of necessity. During the time they stayed at the church in Harringay, she was a bit daunted by the fact that even those people living in England for 20 years still spoke broken English. However, she was determined not to be like them and she went to the course enthusiastically to speak English like her mother tongue at all costs. There was not a single person from Turkey at this course where she met lots of people with various nationalities. The majority of them were from Poland, Bulgaria and Brazil. Although she communicated with them in English, she still wanted to have a friend with whom she could speak her own language. According to what she had learned from Aunt Lizet, Turkish people lived in the North of London where they formed a community.

Kader went out of the college garden taking fast steps. She greeted a few familiar faces she saw all the time. Even in those days when she did not speak the language, she had a warm feeling for strangers and a magical love with sincere feelings arose between them out of the discrepancies they had. On her way to the train station to go home by using the Wessex Line, her phone, which rang very rarely, started vibrating. It was her mother calling her. Her voice sounded happy and excited. They had settled in the house the government allocated to them. It was a two storey house in a garden with three rooms. Her sisters had their own rooms now. Everything was so good and so nice, but Cavidan was already missing home. The concept of neighbour visiting was very different here. The natives of this country had a certain time for work. They used the rest of their time either in bars or on journeys. However, the case for foreigners was quite different. All family members had to work day and night. What's more, most of the Turkish restaurants and markets had no doors at all. Their doors would never close as they worked all day long. They made the most money after other restaurants and markets closed and the owners of these places went home to sleep. The natives were still very understanding. They would never complain about foreigners settling in their houses and taking over their jobs. It was probably because they needed neither these houses nor these jobs. However, the economy was getting worse. Even the Turkish newspapers wrote that young English people started complaining that they could not find a job with their desired salary. The workplaces were inspected very often and those working illegally were detected. When Kader expressed her worries for her father, her mother said that he had no fear or hesitation. In case inspectors came and asked him what he had been doing there, his answer was ready. He was going to tell them that he was visiting his uncle there or he was just helping them out since there was a big meeting that night. There were lots of things that she should tell, but it was not the right time. Cavidan excitedly told her daughter that she had a surprise for her. Kader, who thought that her mother's excitement and trembling voice were due to their new house, was quite wrong. Her mother said that she would give the phone to someone else and reminded her that she should not mention the place where she was or the family she worked for. Thinking what her mother might have implied, she heard a familiar man's voice: "How are you?" As she was trying to guess who this voice might belong to, she heard the same voice speaking both English and Turkish: "If you ask me, I am well." She recognized the owner of this voice and she was astonished. When this person said who he was, Kader almost rolled down the stairs of the train station. "Cemil!" she crowed. She was still talking to Cemil as she was getting on the tram. Due to security reasons, Cemil refused to find out where Kader lived. Nor did he ask where she worked or how she survived. It was a small world. The flat he shared with Ahmet was very close to Kader's uncles, who had been looking everywhere for her. They might follow him. In order not to upset her, he didn't tell her that they had hung up her photographs saying 'WANTED' on the walls of a couple of mosques where the Turkish community members were the common visitors. Yet, he did not forget to remind her that she should still keep being cautious.

As Kader used the same train at the same time on school days, she would greet most of the commuters in English and write the new words she learned at the course ten times in her notebook until she arrived at the station she would get off. Seeing the young lady holding her phone tightly on her ear and speaking Turkish, those familiar faces understandingly looked at the girl and thought that it was a different day today. It was the first time they had seen this innocent looking shy girl talk in her own language, her cheeks had blushed and her face had smiled so sweetly. They understood that she was talking to someone she had been missing for a long time and thus turned their gaze to the view outside the window to leave her alone with whoever she was talking to at the other end of the line. She did not have enough attention to see her surroundings after all. She was only focused on what Cemil was telling her:

"You know, Kader, I am returning to Turkey."

"What!"

"My case lapsed. What's more, An amnesty was granted

316

in Turkey during the first days I was on the ship. When I told the police that I was wanted, I went into trouble as I was not wanted anymore. But we figured it out later. Let's get back to you… How are you doing?"

All the cheer the young lady had was gone after she heard that Cemil was going back. She could hardly stop her tears:

"But Cemil, why are you going back?" She tried to say something."

"We'll talk about all this stuff when we meet. Shall we meet somewhere not close to where you live before I leave?" Cemil said, upon which she was a bit relieved.

"Of course, Cemil. We can meet any time you want," she said, but she couldn't help repeating her question with a sad voice:

"Why are you leaving?" Cemil was determined to go back. He couldn't get used to living in this place. Kader was young. It was easy for her to adapt to changes, but it was not the case for Cemil. He missed eating fish in Yenikapı, drinking Raki with his friends and talking to them. Her aunt Leman had already started the paperwork for his return.

Kader was pacing on the veranda of the house with her hands on her chest and thinking how she could say to the family that she wanted to meet Cemil. What if they misinterpret the situation? It would be such a shame. Perhaps she could just tell them that she would go shopping.

"I think it's best that I tell them I would go shopping with the Polish girl I met at the course. Nevertheless, having to tell a lie also disturbed her. As Kader was pacing in the house out of excitement, Aunt Lizet raised her head from the armchair on which she was napping and said to Kader:

"I think you'll kill me out of curiosity. Don't keep it long and tell the end of the story. Did Gulcem and Ferhan get married?

* * *

All the family was together in the living room of Gulcem's house. Some of them were sitting and the others were standing, snacking on the food at the buffet station set on the table by the window overlooking the Bosphorus. Gulcem was making her niece eat the cheese meatball on her plate.

"Aren't you going to play us something with your violin, aunty?" Nesligul said.

"You know that there is no way for me to reject it if you want me to do something. So, tell me! Which song do you want?" Gulcem said and grabbed her violin. Not being able to reject her niece's request, Gulcem started a rhythmic melody she liked. The house was filled with the melody that the strings produced. As the serving girl was serving the food, Engin popped up a champagne bottle. Yasemin gave champagne to her daughter and Ferhan's son Cem, who was at the same age as Nesligul.

"Let's raise our glasses to your aunt's marriage decision.

They tossed their glasses.

"So, when is the wedding?"

"Soon." Nesligul clapped her hands.

"Mum, you should start going on a diet right away."

"Your mum looks beautiful as a full-figured woman as well."

"I know… but it was her who kept saying that she would be very slim at my aunt's wedding. On the contrary, she gained too much weight."

They began to joke with each other. Engin:

"It was when she had no more hopes for your aunt to get married." Yasemin dropped a kiss on Gulcem's cheek.

"And I have seen that things are getting serious, so I decided to have a baby rather than go on a diet."

"What? A baby…?"

"You are pregnant?"

"I am."

"Whaaat!"

It was obvious that Engin already knew it. He could not give anyone the good news because his sister was sick.

After Gulcem and Ferhan's wedding, Yalcin, Nihal, Yasemin and Engin were welcoming the guests coming to the ceremony that was being held by the pool at a hotel in Sile. The team organising the ceremony was working quite hard and the DJ was exhilarating everyone. In short, everything seemed to be perfect in this party that was shaking Sile. Gulcem's friends were filming this happy night. Finally, it was the time for the bride and groom to walk down the stairs as it happens in every wedding ceremony. They both looked very elegant. Gulcem looked adorable in her pearl white wedding dress. The young lady was very cheerful, greeting all the guests with her smile full of love. She finally caught the love and happiness she deserved after all those things she had been through. Her brother had also organised a firework show for this small but elaborate party, for which it was apparent that he prepared everything with great care. There was no one who did not share the happiness of this newlywed couple who were doing their first dance under these fireworks.

In the meantime, there was also another party going on in the prison. Selcuk, who had been arrested for rape, thought for self-consolation that he had got away with his actual crime without joining the people having fun there. Perhaps, he wouldn't be alive now if the Freak hadn't helped him survive by doing an artificial respiration when his boat sank while trafficking humans and guns to Greece and his unconscious body came ashore. Moreover, he was able to get rid of the Freak easily who witnessed the sinking ship off the shore and knew that he caused 58 people on board to die. He did not care about the guns which disappeared from the pit and wherever the Freak hid them. He had no intention of staying here for long after all. He was going to settle in Singapore soon. In fact, he could have also gotten away with this crime easily, but the cunning man had buried his bloody boots along with the corpse in the pit. He tried his chance to deny that these boots did not belong to him, but the blood samples and fingerprints gave him away. While these thoughts were flashing in his mind, one of the prisoners gave him the Turkish instrument 'baglama' to play. In the small and narrow space, a group of young people began to dance by letting out a yell and clapping their hands. Trafficking, raping and murder... As if he were not convicted of all these crimes, he grabbed the musical instrument he learnt to play in the prison where he had been a common resident since he was a child. They started singing all together. It must have been so loud that everyone kept quiet and returned to their own corners once the ward bully came in. Unable to bring himself to being in the same ward with Selcuk, he seemed to be quite annoyed:

"You're singing a song? What a shameless person you are! Is it possible for a rapist to stay in the same ward with me?" he roared. Selcuk, who knew quite well what such a bully was able to do, dropped the instrument in his hand quickly, but the bully was very angry. His smirking sidekick buttered him up:

"You're right, bro. Just give us the command to kill him and consider it done." Then, he started to wait for the command to stab him. When the ward bully bent his neck to one side instantly, the expected sign was given. Selcuk, who was sent a message by his friends two days ago that they would find a way to rescue him from prison, had not considered that there were men in prisons who had no tolerance for those raping little girls and did not keep them alive for long.

* * *

The moonlight illuminated everywhere. The number of dark blue sea sparkles off the shore had increased. While they were cheerfully running to their hotel, Gulcem, who was kissed by Ferhan every other second, threw her shoes in her hand to one corner and raised her hands up to the sky:

"I am very happy, God! Thank you so much," she shouted. In the meantime, Selcuk, being stabbed and lying on a stretcher at a hospital, was talking half consciously while he was being taken to the operating room:

"I did not do anything to Gulcem. It was the Freak's will. The Freak's wil…"

Having returned home at the end of this happy night, Gulcem's family had no sooner fallen into a peaceful sleep than her father's phone started ringing to give him the bad news. Without saying anything to his family and his daughter, who was spending the night at a hotel in the vicinity, the father met the police inspector in the hospital garden. The inspector told him that Selcuk Gur might be sentenced to a long imprisonment. Gulcem's father was about to have sigh of relief when the inspector added the missing information:

"But, not for raping your daughter… I had always been suspicious of the possibility that he might not have been the one who raped your daughter. He seemed to have taken the blame because he was involved in a bigger crime and wanted to cover it up in this way. As a matter of fact, it was understood that this was the case. The man who was known to be the Freak put the blame on this man who was already a criminal. We have to take Gulcem's testimony about her grandfather's death even if it is a mere formality. I would like to ask you first as it is her first happy night with her husband." Yalcin's mind was on his beloved daughter, who had been raped by her grandfather. Ferhan carried Gulcem up the stairs of the hotel. After watching the nice view in a close embrace for a while, the husband and wife went to their room. The moment Gulcem felt the lips of the man she loved on her own lips, the idea of Selcuk haunted her mind. Then, she remembered seeing the Freak take a pair of boots from when she saw him speak for the first time. She wanted to erase this horrible image from her mind. What was the point of thinking about all this stuff at that moment? What she was supposed to do was to let herself relax in the arms of the man she loved. Ferhan felt the tonelessness of Gulcem's lips and he smiled:

"What about having a glass of drink, my love?" he said.

Gulcem took Ferhan's arm and smiled with an impish look:

"No… First baby."

Joking with each other, they walked to the bed arm in arm. Ferhan took all her clothes off except her panties with his gentle touch. He was careful enough not to startle Gulcem, who had become his wife only a few hours ago. While he was taking off his jacket and shirt, he thought that he no longer had to resist the desire he had for Gulcem, who was lying naked on her back with all her beauty doubled by the moonlight that had fallen onto her body through the window.

"You're so beautiful!" he smiled and bent over her to drop

a kiss on her lips. His wife not pulling him towards herself, he gently lay near her. He dropped another kiss while his hand reached for the zipper puller of his trousers. At that very moment, the hand on the zipper turned into her grandfather's hand and the cream trousers turned into her grandfather's brown shorts. The same thing had happened in her previous attempts. Before Ferhan was able to understand what was going on, she screamed "Nooooo!" and got up from the bed. She rushed out of the room crying.

Gulcem was running barefoot on the beach. After her naked body, on which the moonlight was shining, went out of sight for a while, she appeared on the top of the rocks again. With the thunderstorms being heard from far away, she let herself down the rocks into the red waters like a flying bird without having a second thought. The dark bottom of the rocks under dark clouds was flashed by the lightning and an unclear whiteness was disappearing among the waves. As Gulcem submerged in the sea and went completely out of sight, Ferhan's voice, as if it had been in a race with the sand storm to reach the rocks first, echoed over the Crying Rocks:

"Gulceeeeem!"

This story was the reason why these Rocks were called the Crying Rocks.

* * *

Kader left home on Saturday evening to go to the course as

soon as Aysegul came home. She got on the train. She greeted the familiar faces. Some of the passengers had already begun to read their books, some to read the free newspapers left on the train, some to eat sandwiches, drink coffee, and some to freshen up their make-up. At first, the young girl found it strange that in public transport these people behaved as if they were at home. It was because in her tradition, it was a sin to eat something in front of someone, and it was a shame to put on make-up in the presence of adults. Later, she was convinced that it was not a sin or a shameful thing to use the time wisely that would otherwise be wasted on the train or in the car. Everyone was so full that it was for sure that no one would have an eye on the food while someone ate something. It was the case even for animals. One day she got scared of the big foxes that frequented her gardens. Aysegull: "Do not be afraid, they are very full. They won't hurt anyone," she said. And what she said happened exactly. Foxes would visit their gardens almost every night and return to the forest without harming anyone. And Kader gave up going to the course and writing the new words she learned ten times for to-day when she got on the train. She was over the moon as she was going to meet with Cemil, to whom she had sent a love message with a cardigan she hung on a piece of twig. She took out her phone. As instructed, she hid her number and called Cemil. She said they could meet earlier. She wanted to spend more time with him. Cemil had stopped by a friend while he was in the district, but he said he could come right away. He would wait in a pub near where the college was located. Would he ever come from so far away if he didn't care about her!

Kader, who always walked by watching the people doing water sports off the marina, walked this time quickly towards the pub without even looking at the people doing sailing. It was a beautiful place. It was dim inside. She wasn't used to places like this. In fact, she had been to the pub once or twice with her classmates. However, since she drank coffee herself, she was a little embarrassed among her friends who drank beer one after another. However, some of her manners gave the young girl a magical privilege. She was loved and respected among her friends, and they envied Kader's strong will, who was always unwilling to smoke cannabis and cigarettes. Kader sat at a wooden table and looked left and right. Cemil was not in sight. She was just about to call him when she felt a hand touch her shoulder. She turned her back. She came face to face with Cemil. Their intimacy caught the attention of even strangers, who wouldn't normally care about what was going on around them or wouldn't turn to look at the people making love right next to them.

There was so much to talk about. Kader first asked about Mehmet. Cemil told how his friend got lost in those dark blue waters in front of his eyes. There was a brief silence between them. The words seemed to be stuck in their throats. They drank a glass of wine without speaking. Cemil was the first to pull himself together:

"I meet your mother from time to time... I see that they are doing fine. Your father is happy, too."

"Yes... They are doing great. They've got a house to live in and everything else they need."

"The majority of those who came by the ship are happy with what they have, yet some of them regret that they have come. I have once seen Haydar."

Kader remembered the day she begged Haydar to wait for Mehmet and Cemil before they went to get on the truck. She had taken a dislike to him that day. It was obvious that she was not curious about Haydar at all and her mind was on something else, but she still listened to Cemil because it seemed clear that he was not going to go into much detail about him, either.

"They say that he is going to go to another country and he doesn't like this place. He once participated in a protest here to support the hunger strike in prisons in Turkey. Some other things also happened. I won't tell you long. He went into prison and stayed there for a few days. They put it in a cell that was even worse than the ones in our country. You see, he keeps saying that he is treated like a third-class person here. He's actually right, but…"

As Cemil saw that Kader was not interested at all, he changed the subject:

"And what about you? What have you been up to?"

In fact, there was something that Kader was very curious about. Something about their adventure on the ship.

"Cemil, don't get me wrong. I will ask because I am very curious. What happened to Selcuk on the ship?"

"We first asked if he had a cut mark on the right side of his abdomen. He was stabbed as you described. Shortly after he recovered and returned to prison, he was beaten so badly that he was hospitalised again. He was kidnapped and brought to the ship by human traffickers. Then he was killed during a fight among themselves."

"So, that Selcuk was that Selcuk. And he is dead, right?"

Cemil talked about the fact that the crew of the ship would most likely flee by leaving them in Singapore, the precautions they took, the benefit of knowing what they had done in the past, and the young girl's contribution to this.

"What I still can't understand is the relationship between Selcuk and this freak man."

"The man they called the Freak was actually a very smart man, Cemil. He thought that if Gulcem believed that the person who raped her was not her grandfather but a stranger and also if she knew that she didn't push her grandfather off the rocks and kill him, but he still lived and thus she was not the murderer of her grandfather, she would be able to overcome this pain more easily."

Cemil, who hadn't listened to this part of the events before, said while lighting a cigarette, "So you were ashamed of sharing Gulcem's destiny and you couldn't explain it." he muttered, passing the pack of cigarettes to the girl whose head fell forward.

"Do you smoke?"

"No."

"It's good...Oh, don't you ever try. I wish I hadn't gotten

328

used to it either, but I'll quit when I go to Istanbul. All right, but how did the Freak and Selcuk know each other? One is the madman of Sile and the other is a human trafficker who spends his life in the seas."

"The crime network was doing the smuggling from Sile in those years as well. Selcuk was unaware that someone was living in the cemetery, but the Freak suspected that someone was smuggling people to Greece by boat, and weapons were brought from there. That night, when the storm suddenly broke out, the old boat, which could not stand it anymore, broke apart and sank. Dozens of people drowned and died. When Selcuk washed ashore, half unconscious, covered in blood, the Freak was there. He didn't know yet that he was a human and weapons smuggler. He thought he was one of those poor passengers and immediately gave the man an artificial respiration and brought him back to life with great difficulty, but he then realised one or two chests that washed ashore. When Selcuk regained his senses and the Freak pressed him a little, he understood who he was. Every time the man committed this crime, he either went into prison for a few months or was let escape by the help of his men without going to prison. The Freak said he would not turn him to the police, but on one condition. if what happened to Gulcem is heard one day, you will take the blame for the rape, and no one will ever know what her grandfather did. I will hand over the weapons and clothes to someone I trust very much."

Cemil tossed his beer onto the table:

"Woow! Well done for the Freak. What a brain!..."

"Yeah! Tell me about it… After making sure that he blamed the rape on him with the evidence, he also informed the authorities that this man was going to smuggle people to France."

"So, if we were followed, we were followed because of the Freak."

"How could he know?"

"How well he did and reported it to the authorities, but the bastards were able to cover it up. Or perhaps Selcuk lied to the Freak on purpose and told him they were going to France to mislead the police. Can't it be? Indeed, the police may have followed us for a while. They may have given up when they saw that the ship was heading towards Asia. But when I got to the upper deck that night we got caught in the storm, I realised we weren't being followed. I even did a little research after the storm. The ship was a regular cargo ship. Of course, if you had told everything you knew, it would have been revealed earlier that our Selcuk was that Selcuk."

"You know; I was always asking you on the ship if this man would ever throw us into the sea?"

"Well, you didn't tell me the end of the story... How could I know?"

"I was going to tell you, but my father was a little angry... Just because we talked too often in private." Cemil realised that the young lady was having difficulty saying all of these and he understood what she implied:

"Oh my god... It also occurred to me. But anyway! So, were the rocks shedding the tears of those people having drowned?"

"Now, I will come to that point, Cemil."

"If you explain everything in such detail... We are not on the ship anymore... This place will close in three hours."

Kader looked at her watch:

"Yes, it's really late. Cemil, how are you going to go all the way back to London at this time?"

Cemil smiled:

"Don't worry. Remember I told you I stopped by my friend who lives just two stations away. When you phoned and offered to meet early, the conversation was cut short. They insisted a lot. I will stay with them tonight. I will also tell them about you. In fact, they will return to Istanbul, but I still want to introduce you."

"Really? Okay, I'll call Aysegul and let her know that I will be late."

"Aysegul'?"

"Yes... I'm looking after Aunt Lizet, her aunt-in-law. They are very kind people." Suddenly, her mother's advice came to her mind, but she did not mind telling Cemil, whom she trusted very much.

"Let me finish telling you about the Crying Rocks, and I'll talk about the family I work for and what I've been doing."

Being very surprised, Cemil took the young girl by the hand and lifted her up.

* * *

That night, until the first rays of the morning sun began to illuminate the living room, Kader told; Cemil, Aysegul and Cem Michel listened to why the rocks were crying. "So, Aunt Lizet has been listening to this for months. We were wondering what you were talking about," the husband and wife jokingly said.

Kader did not go to the course the next day, even though it was the weekend. It was also Maria's day off. Together with Cem Michel, they rushed between the dining table and the kitchen to prepare a sumptuous breakfast on the veranda. The veranda was centred in the garden of the palatial house, resembling a corner of heaven. In this country, the never-fading red geraniums, the lush green grass that covered the ground like a soft carpet and the colourful roses emitted fragrant scents. Unable to bear the weight of their branches, which were adorned with more flowers than leaves, the fuchsias were grown as large as a tree and oscillated in the light breeze as if they were accompanying the rhythm of a magical melody to make the fragrant flowers jealous. Aysegul, giving Cemil a tour of the garden, said:

"Why wouldn't these grasses be so green in our country?" she sighed.

"Well, that's because God waters them every day here," said Cemil.

"There has not been a drop of rain in Istanbul this spring again," he complained. Aysegull took her friend's arm and said:

"Yeah, that's also what I heard. I don't know about you, but I'm very hungry," she continued, and they made for the veranda. Aunt Lizet had taken her place at the breakfast table. Aysegul and Cemil, followed by Cem Michel, sat at the table with hungry looks. While they were happily having breakfast on the veranda shaded by the trees without being disturbed by the rare sun although it was noon, a squirrel running after the pinecone he had dropped caught Cemil's attention. While the other squirrels were playing with the snails on the bark of the tree branches, the squirrel snatched his pinecone and buried it in the ground. As he passed by their table, the squirrel reached his head and looked at them as if saying 'bon appetite'. Then he started jumping up the tree. Cemil couldn't help laughing:

"He ate his own food, and he went and buried what he couldn't eat, so cunning."

"Sometimes these idiots forget what they buried. And then that's how it becomes a tree," she said, pointing to the forest-like garden. Cemil was surprised:

"Ah! Really?"

"Of course."

Neither the gardens of his home in his beloved country, nor the trees with cones in his garden, nor the squirrels that buried their buds in the ground were left. While the two friends were talking about the weather, Kader approached them with the plate in her hand:

"Look, I did them for you, Cemil. They call them pancakes here."

"Thank you, Kader. Mmm, they smell really good."

"Enjoy your meal. I'll bring the drinks."

As Kader rushed into the kitchen, Lawrence entered the garden. His loving expression, his gaze shining with the gleam of love, found Kader. Cemil looked at the two young people for a long time. There was a smile on their lips and happiness in their eyes.

- THE END-

Ingram Content Group UK Ltd.
Milton Keynes UK
UKHW041901240723
425711UK00005B/221